In this fine novel, Colby Grayson learns that coming-of-age is sorely more than a passing formality in his rural eastern Kentucky community. On his 13-year-old shoulders rests the near impossible task of helping his family survive after the untimely death of his father, Vernon. The circumstances are daunting, even for the strongest of mature adults. He knows there is a tobacco crop to raise and a household of hungry mouths to feed; and then, there's the matter of Mama's singing, which is consequential to a family secret.

Steeped in the sense of place and traditions of the past, where "hardship was more than tolerated, where it was expected and accepted," the community reaches out to heroic Colby and the Graysons—both overtly and stealthily. But what beckons, the good folk find, is eerily more than their assistance in the fields and help with financial resources; it's their help in confronting the harsh reality of Mama's need to sing.

—Steve Flairty, author of the *Kentucky's Everyday Heroes* series

BOTTOM DOG PRESS

# Mama's Song

## A Novel

## P. Shaun Neal

Appalachian Writing Series
Bottom Dog Press
Huron, Ohio

Bottom Dog Press, Inc.
PO Box 425, Huron, OH 44839
Lsmithdog@aol.com
http://smithdocs.net

**CREDITS:**
General Editor: Larry Smith
Cover & Layout Design: Susanna Sharp-Schwacke
Front Cover Art: Vincent R. Tentora
Back Cover Art: "Lancaster Tobacco Barn" photo by David Speace

**ACKNOWLEDGEMENTS:**

I would like to thank the following people for their help and support: David Miller, my primary editor/agent whose assistance has been incalculable. My friends in Atlanta, especially Dave Devitt, Todd Valentine and Will Atkins for giving me feedback and encouragement when I needed it most, and to Steve Flairty, who helped me get the ball rolling.

And finally, thanks to my wife Lisa Neal, who never let me give up the dream, even when I wanted to.

## DEDICATION

To the two women in my life: my mother, Martha Ann Neal,
and mostly to my little yellow haired girl, my wife Lisa Wilson Neal.

"Look homeward, my angel, and see me standing there."

May 17, 1949

This then: this clear and seamless world; this land, brown and rich; this blue sky smeared with perfectly white clouds; this green enclosure, grass, trees, crops and cool mold in the root cellars and algae in the watering ponds. White clover blossom and goldenrod, yellow spring dandelions and purple round thistle blossoms; thorny blackberry bushes growing along fence rows, where the last of the swaying fields of bluegrass, top heavy and lazy-looking with gray-blue seed heads, give up at last to the scraggly, thorny, tough growths of the mountains. Cedars and redbuds growing out of the limestone hillsides and wild dogwood trees blooming white and pink all spring.

This place of callused, poorly dressed men, silent men, strong and guileless, of people who were shrewd but unlearned. This place of fear and distrust of strangers and complete, needy, unquestioned trust of family. This place of crusty, jagged faith in the Lord, of quiet thankfulness and bitter want. This place where life was celebrated with conspicuous abandon yet harbored in deep, secret places the fierce shame of the Baptists. This place of respectful, crew-cut children, dirty but able, keepers of the legacy, the steep and costly legacy, the lonesome legacy, the blind, brutal legacy that tumbled through the generations like a malformed bullet. These children who never asked why, who knew nothing of other paths, other ways, who knew only to follow the path of their fathers.

This place where they nurtured life in their crops and cattle, then slew each year, the accepted slaying of the self-sufficient, the guiltless killing of survival. This place where life was close, immediate, and death, too, was a neighbor, familiar and not astonishing—where life was a gift and death a silent demand. This beautiful and perfect place in Kentucky, where hardship was more than tolerated, where it was expected and accepted, a summons. Where even the young acknowledged the hushed dominion of death and the inevitable cascade of life.

And above all, more than all, greater than any of their ideals or dreams, warm but uncaring: the land, the hills and mountains, the valleys and ridges, the farms and the forests, the creeks and stones. The land, first and last.

This then.

# SPRING

# Chapter 1

Colburn Grayson woke up sometime before the sun. His first thought today, as it had been every morning since Vernon's quiet and shocking death, was, "Daddy's gone now." He wouldn't have even noticed his father was gone if not for the silence. Every day for the last two years, he had awakened to the sound of Vernon putting coffee on the stove. Every day, even on Sundays, Colby had silently dressed, gone into the kitchen, poured himself a glass of fresh milk and sat at the table where his father sat smoking. Colby would drink his milk in silence until the coffee was ready. Then Vernon would get up, pour himself a cup and say, "Cup of coffee, Colby?" He would grin and Colby would grin back and say, "Think I'll pass this morning." Then his father would say, "Suit yourself." They were sharing a joke about the one time Colby had tried coffee. The hot bitter sip caused Colby to screw his face into a look that made Vernon laugh out loud, one of only a few times that Colby had witnessed that.

Colby had to do the milking; then, he supposed, it would be up to him to get his family up, up and moving, dressed and to the church.

Visitation took place at the Rowan County Baptist Church. The eulogy and funeral would begin here tomorrow morning at ten.

On the dais at the front of the church a casket held the body of Vernon Grayson. The sacrament that usually sat on the dais had been moved off to one side. The only flowers were spring bloomers—tiger-lilies and purple and white irises.

The church, like the mourners within, possessed a gloamy air of weary solemnity. It was one room only, this hall of worship, no more than fifty feet long and thirty wide. The coal soot stains on the ceiling were fifteen feet from the unfinished wooden floor.

Two large doors in the back were topped with an oval glass mosaic stained blue, red and gold. The doors were equidistant from each other and from each led an aisle, thus dividing the church lengthwise into thirds. The left door and aisle, as well as the pews along the left wall, were used by the men. The right door, aisle and pews were used by the women and older children.

The middle pews, between the aisles, were mostly used by families with small children but still they sat with the men on the left and the women on the right.

There were two coal burning stoves along either wall, situated exactly halfway between front and back. The warmer seats around them were politely saved for the older members of the congregation during the winter months. They were the only concessions to comfort in the church.

The Reverend Lucas Tannehill sat with the widow in her time of grief. He sat beside her in the front center pew, one hand atop hers, the other clutching a worn, leather-bound Bible to his chest. He offered her soft, confident words of comfort and assurance as people leaned over in front of her and formally expressed their condolences.

"She's doing fine, Mrs. Fitch," Reverend Tannehill said to the sturdy lady before them. He turned his head slowly toward the widow. "Mrs. Grayson knows that, with the faith of our Lord God and his son Jesus Christ, all the pain of this world is but a small and temporary thing and that a greater reward is awaiting the true believers in the Realm of our Father."

Reverend Tannehill spoke slowly, with a sense of grave and burdened knowledge. His voice today was stretched and threadbare, papery and insubstantial. In this voice he conversed, conducted business and even preached—most of the time. About once a month, the Reverend worked himself up while preaching and then his voice changed right along with his message. On these occasions he preached of hellfire and repentance, and his voice pealed and thundered off the walls, through the church and out the doors into the green lands beyond.

Today his voice was strained, small, and his message one of quiet hope. He was not a large man, just a bit taller than most of the women of his flock. He had thin, oily hair that he kept combed back from a tall, wide forehead. The Reverend's nose was small, sharp and perfectly straight between high, pronounced cheekbones and over a thin, unremarkable mouth. Only his large blue eyes, watery and thick-lidded, attracted attention. He appeared to keep them half closed almost all the time, as if he dared not open them all the way and drink in too quickly the burning beauty of the world that his Lord had provided.

"Amen, Brother Tannehill," Mrs. Fitch said to the Reverend with a nod. She leaned closer to the widow and put a hand on her forearm. "Anne, I'll come by tomorrow after the funeral with a nice casserole. Don't you worry too much. Everything's gonna be okay." Mrs. Fitch stood there a moment, awaiting a response and, receiving none, turned back to the Reverend.

"Thank you, Mrs. Fitch," he said. She nodded and moved on to pay her respects at the casket.

Next, up in front of the widow were Mr. and Mrs. Russell Traylor. They owned the farm that backed up to the Grayson property. Mrs. Traylor nodded at the Reverend and put her hand on Anne Grayson's shoulder.

"How are you feeling, Anne?" she asked.

Anne Grayson looked up at Mrs. Traylor, as if seeing her for the first time. "My back is much better," she said.

"Is that so?" Mrs. Traylor asked.

"Yes, it is. My back always starts to feel better when the weather turns warm."

Mrs. Traylor glanced quickly at the Reverend, then back at Anne. "I'm glad to hear that, Anne," she said.

"Yes."

Mrs. Traylor waited a moment longer, then straightened and looked at the children seated to Anne's right. Colburn, the oldest at thirteen, sat at his mother's shoulder. Beside him was David, eleven. Next to him were the twins, ten-year-old Timothy and Annetta. The twins were involved in a quiet game of their own making, but David was beginning to fidget. They had been here for well over an hour.

Colburn looked at the tall, serious Mr. Traylor and wondered if he would be addressed; however, Russ Traylor merely nodded at Colby, waited, then put an inoffensive hand on Anne's shoulder and nodded grimly at the Reverend. He gently took his wife's elbow and they walked together to the casket.

After the Traylors paid their respects, the Reverend looked heavily toward the back of his church. Seeing no one else waiting to speak to the bereaved, he slowly stood up, and then leaned down to speak softly in Anne's ear.

"Mrs. Grayson? That's everybody. Shall we visit now the casket?"

The widow rose without responding and started toward the casket. The Reverend walked with her, holding her elbow with his fingers only and motioned the children to join them.

Anne stood before the casket, resting her hands on the unpolished wood. She looked down at the body before her with a look somewhere between anger and surprise. Though she was different from most people, her reaction to Vernon's death had been nearly the same. She was shocked, simply shocked.

Even in death, the long body before her looked stronger and hardier than many of the men grieving over it. The left side of Vernon's wrinkled, dead face drooped. His hair, turning gray but still thick and curling, was combed more thoroughly than anyone there had ever seen it before.

He was thirty-nine years old.

Reverend Tannehill, still holding Anne's elbow, leaned slightly backward to speak to the eldest son. "Colby, it would be proper for you to stand on your mother's other side and hold her arm."

"Yes, sir, Reverend. Where should the others stand?"

"Children, you stand beside your brother."

13

Colby lightly held his mother's arm just above the elbow and the other children lined up as told. The Reverend leaned in front of the widow and looked down the line. Seeing that everyone was properly solemn, he nodded.

"Shall we pray?" he said. Anne remained motionless, while the children all bowed their heads.

"Our gracious heavenly Father: we stand before you today in this, your house, humbled and hungering for your blessings, hungering for the light of your undying mercy and your infinite wisdom. We ask not for knowledge but merely for solace and comfort. Worthy though we may not be to know the reason you have chosen to call home one of your own, we pray for your mercy and that you may provide healing and comfort to the family of Vernon Grayson. We ask that you watch over the eternal soul of Vernon Grayson, until such time as he is reunited with his family and with your family in your kingdom, the kingdom of Heaven. We ask these things in the name of your Son, Jesus Christ, Amen."

## Chapter 2

By 11:45 the next morning, Colby's father was in the ground. The funeral was over, and the mourners were gathered at the Grayson house. David and the twins, along with most of the other children, were outside playing and enjoying the weather, the death of an adult as easily accepted among them as the death of a pet.

Colby sat beside his mother on the couch in the front room where people stood around with plates in their hands, as well as in the kitchen, plates piled high with food, food in more abundance than they had ever experienced, except perhaps at weddings.

Old Man Tom had brought a ham, and Elijah Settles had killed two chickens that his old wife had fried. There were dozens of deviled eggs, pickled green beans and fresh hot biscuits drowning in salty, sweet butter. Spencer Kirk had brought some of his recently deceased wife's pickled peaches and there were home-canned beets and turnips and corn pudding made with last year's sweet corn.

Colby watched the people, all neighborly and decent, as they ate and talked. They seemed to be trying to act cheerful but not overly so. Most of the women doted on his mother, fussing over her and trying to get her to eat something. Most of the men, as they made their dutiful way by, looked at his mother, then at him, nodding. None of the men spoke to him, though, unsure of Colby's current status. Russ Traylor was the first to speak. He nodded, as had all the others, then walked over.

"Mrs. Grayson," he said. "Colby."

"Mr. Traylor," Colby replied.

Russ looked hard at Anne for a moment, thinking that she was about to speak to him. Her lips were moving, slowly, calmly. Her eyes were looking not at Russ, but somewhere else, across the room, through the room.

Somewhere else.

He watched her lips moving and almost leaned down to hear what she was saying, thinking that maybe she was about to break down in a fit of weeping, then he realized that she was singing, softly singing, softly singing a song to herself.

He looked back at Colby.

"You think I might could talk to you a minute, Colby?" he said.

"Yessir," Colby answered. Russ took a step back from the couch and Colby scooted up to the edge. He turned and faced his mother.

"Mama, I'm gonna go on out and talk to Mr. Traylor now, okay?"

Anne nodded without focusing her eyes, and Colby rose and followed Russ outside.

Russ walked out the front door and around to the side of the house, opposite to where the children played. He stopped beneath the Graysons' huge and ancient walnut tree and leaned against its trunk. Colby stopped a few feet from him. Russ pulled a cigarette from the breast pocket of his dress shirt and ignited a wooden kitchen match with his thumbnail. He lit the cigarette, took a drag and spit out some stray bits of tobacco before looking down at the boy. Colby silently met his gaze.

"That's a tough break, Colby. Your daddy was a good man."

"Yessir."

"I knew him when he wasn't no older than you are now."

"Yessir," Colby said.

Russ nodded. "Uh-huh, a good man."

Russ knelt down and picked up one of last year's walnuts; the hull was black; soft and mushy, wet and rotten.

"Colby, I wanted to ask you if your daddy said anything to you before he passed on."

"He couldn't talk too good, Mr. Traylor. It was like one whole side of his face wasn't working. The left side."

"Yes. One of my daddy's uncles went that way. A stroke, they call it."

"Yessir. That's what Doctor Cardiff said, a stroke."

"Uh-huh," Russ said. He dropped the dark, soft walnut and stood back up. One of his knees popped loudly.

Mr. Traylor was clearly waiting for Colby to say more, but Colby knew he couldn't. He would not attempt to describe to Mr. Traylor the last days of his father's life and the awful, horrible sight of Vernon, tall, strong, hard Vernon, lying motionless in his bed, his mouth frozen open in a silent scream of outrage and humiliation, and the room, smelling of his sweaty, sick body and his body's functions and the sounds—the whispered, sad knowledge of certain death and the pathetic, nearly unbearable whimperings of his suffering father.

"So then…" Russ said.

"No, Mr. Traylor. He didn't say anything, nothing at all."

Russ nodded, getting the answer he expected.

"Well then, Colby, I must say that I am wondering about what you're planning on doing. It ain't none of my business I know, but Vernon was a man that I would have to say was my friend. Again, it ain't my business, but your mama might not be up to decision-making right now, so I reckon it's going to fall on you to make the decisions."

"Decisions about what?" Colby asked.

Russ took one final, deep drag on his cigarette, threw it down and crushed out the ember with his heel.

"Well, about this crop, this farm, and so forth."

"I aim to keep right on doing what we've always done."

"So, you're planning on bringing in this tobacco crop, are you?" Russ asked.

"Well, yessir, I am. I reckon I know how to use a hoe and how to top it and cut it. I been helping him two years now," Colby replied and stood up straighter, suddenly aware of how much taller Russ was than himself. He stared directly into the older man's eyes and Russ stared back.

"I ain't saying that you can't, Colby. I reckon that if anyone could do it, it would be Vernon Grayson's son. He was the hardest working man I ever saw, and I know he raised you the same."

"Ain't a problem in the world that can't be solved through hard work," Colby said, echoing his father's favorite saying, his only saying.

"I'll say yes to that, Colby. I heard Vernon say that myself and I kind of figured that you'd be planning on bringing this crop in, so I wanted to offer you some help."

"We don't need no charity," Colby said simply.

Russ knew that Colby would say this, knew even the words he would use. Russ had known Vernon Grayson very well, better by far than Vernon had known Russ.

"I know you don't need no charity, Colby, and it ain't charity I'm offering. Truth is I ain't got any charity to offer you, anyway. Things is real tough around here about now, tough for everybody. But let me tell you what, I'm a pretty good farmer myself. If you were to maybe have any questions about your tobacco here, well-sir, the truth is you could do a durn sight worse than to ask me for advice."

Colby looked at Russ with a measuring steadiness that unnerved Russ.

"We don't need no charity," the boy repeated.

"I know that Colby," Russ said.

Colby nodded, as if this signaled the end of their talk. He started to walk away.

"Colby?" Russ called after him.

"Yessir?"

"Colby, you gotta start being a man now," Russ said, then turned and walked back to the house.

Colby could hear the children playing on the other side of the house. He stood still a moment, confused. He thought that being a man was exactly what he had been doing.

## CHAPTER 3

The next morning, Colby awoke, listening to the crickets. They were unaware of how the world had changed. They chirred their ceaseless, harmless song, waiting for the old rooster to take over at dawn. Colby sat up on one elbow and looked at his brothers, David and Tim-Bug, still asleep in the double bed. Annetta's little bed in the corner was empty and Colby remembered that Baby-Anne had crawled in with Mama last night and had slept there. It seemed right to Colby and he wondered if the arrangement would be permanent. He would be sorry if it was. Most mornings, Baby-Anne was lying silently awake when Colby first looked over at her and she would share a wordless, somehow knowing smile before rolling silently over to go back to sleep, often before Colby was even out of the room. Her ability to shuttle effortlessly between sleep and wakefulness amazed Colby, and if last night's arrangement was permanent, Colby would miss their conspiratorial morning ritual, the most intimate part of their relationship.

He finished dressing and walked out to the kitchen, mind wavering as he expected to smell coffee. Snapping back to the present, he walked to the ice box and poured himself a glass of milk. He would have liked to put some coffee on to boil just so he could smell it, but he didn't know how.

Colby sat down, stuck his right index finger in the glass and stirred. Mama never could get all cream out and what was left had floated to the top. Colby didn't mind. He liked his milk good and rich, except in the summertime, when Doris ate the wild onions in the barnyard, making her milk taste like onions. The cream only made it worse.

He tried to sip his milk but it all felt wrong. Unless he could start drinking coffee, he knew that this morning ritual had died along with his father. Gulping the milk down with three long swallows, he put the glass in the sink and went out to milk Doris.

Just outside the front door, he reached up and took the lantern off the nail where it hung. While the house had been wired for electricity for five years, the barn was not. He started down the dark path, paved with coal slag left over from their furnace and it crunched dully beneath his feet in the foggy Kentucky morning.

The barn itself, two hundred feet behind the house, was a monstrous affair, far too large for the humble needs of their meager farm. Colby's paternal grandfather, Vernon's father Denton, had built the barn twenty-four years earlier with the help of hired carpenters out of Morehead. An abnormally large tobacco crop had coincided with a one-time leap in tobacco prices. In the spring, after selling the last pound of his crop, Denton had found himself with an unexpected and unprecedented monetary windfall, and simply did not know what to do with the money. Russ Traylor's father, Ward Traylor, suggested that Denton replace his old, decrepit barn with a bigger one.

It was a fair consensus in later years that Denton had not only taken Ward's advice, but had taken it far too deeply to heart, and lost his mind in the process. Early the next spring, Denton tore down his rickety barn and, for reasons that would remain forever unclear, had built the most ridiculously huge structure within thirty miles of their community. It was far larger than the Grayson farm would ever require; even if they tripled the size of their usable farmland, they wouldn't fill its rails with hanging tobacco.

Some said Denton was so accustomed to spending whatever money he made in a year that the idea of saving his windfall never even occurred to him. His failure to spend some money on the barn and some on something else, perhaps the house, surprised no one. Denton, like his father before him and his son after him, was abundantly blessed with singularity of purpose. There was not a man among them with the inclination, nor indeed the nerve, to point out to Denton the absurdity of his undertaking. Instead, the neighboring farmers began speaking in quiet tones of Denton's Folly.

A quarter of a century later, it remained the largest barn in the community.

To Vernon, it had been a source of simultaneous shame and pride. Pride that his impoverished family could own something so grand and extravagant, and shame over its silly wastefulness. To Colby, it was merely a part of what made this place their home. It was simply "the barn that Grandaddy built," always with plenty of room for things.

He entered the big barn and set the lantern on the work bench. As he lit the lantern, Doris lowed. Her udder was full and she was ready to have it emptied. "I'm coming. I'm coming," he called. Colby pulled the milk bucket off of its nail in the wall and hung the lantern in its place. He set the bucket beneath Doris's udder, pulled the stool over with his right foot, sat down and started milking.

This was one chore that Colby never minded. It was the first job his father had given him and now, with two years experience, Colby was proud of filling a milk bucket as fast as anyone in the county. In just over fifteen minutes, he stepped out of the stall, lantern in one hand and the bucket of fresh, foamy milk in the other, both warm against his legs.

He started to walk back to the house but stopped. Something was wrong, something other than his father's absence. He couldn't quite pinpoint the problem, only that something was a little off in his morning ritual. He furrowed his brow and looked out the huge barn door at the horizon. It was something about the sky. When the old cock crowed, Colby realized what was wrong. As a rule, the cock crowed as he was milking. No matter what time of year it was, his father had him out here milking as the sun started up. Every morning, Colby carried the milk to the house preceded by his forty-foot-long shadow across the slag path.

Although he had missed the time only by a couple of minutes, his ability to not think about Vernon's death was taken from him. Alone, here in the morning dark, nobody expected bravery from him. He didn't even know what time to get up in the morning without Vernon, and this felt like an unforgivable breach of the silent contract between his father and himself. The undeniable knowledge that he was a fatherless boy slapped him cruelly. This morning, with Vernon buried, Colby was wholly and terribly on his own, the full weight and immediacy of his loss no longer a concept, but a hard fact.

For the first time, Colby cried over his loss. The lump came up into his throat as tears came into his eyes. He hated himself for it, even as he knew it was unstoppable. Setting the milk bucket down, he carefully blew out the lantern and sat on the scrap lumber pile just inside the barn door. Trying one last time to swallow the tears, he knew he would fail.

He put his face down in his hands and his shoulders shook, as he wept freely, but as quietly as he could.

He wept out of simple grief, for the fact that his life was now and forever different.

He wept over the loss of his father but also the hard lesson that God would take someone so unimaginably strong, so unbearably hard, someone who was not yet forty years old.

But most of all, Colby wept out of fear. Knowing this shamed him and made him cry all the harder. His nose ran freely as his tears plinked down and soaked into the well-seasoned lumber at his feet.

His weeping finally settled from panicked, chopping sobs into a smoother, cleansing type of tears. He began to take deep, shuddering breaths in an attempt to control himself.

"I'm sorry, Daddy," he mumbled into his slick hands. "I'll wake up on time from now on. I will. I promise." He took a couple more deep breaths and dried his face on his shirt. He blew his nose, one nostril at a time, into the barn dirt, wiped his nose with his hand and dried his hand on his pants. He sniffed once and picked up the bucket and the lantern.

"And I promise I won't cry no more."

Colburn Grayson kept this promise longer than most men could have.

## CHAPTER 4

One hour later, after a breakfast of scrambled eggs and biscuits with butter and blackberry preserves, Colby stepped out the front door and surveyed his crop. He had been working the crop since Vernon fell ill, but up until his death, it had still been Vernon's crop and Colby had only been minding it. But now, it was indeed his own crop.

He walked back down to the barn, wondering exactly where to begin. The tobacco plants hadn't been in the ground long enough to need weeding. All the tools were repaired, sharpened and oiled. Except for some leaks in the roof, the barn was in good enough shape, maybe. The vegetable garden had no weeds and it was still much too early to sucker the tomato plants. Colby stood in the barn and looked around…what to do?

Work. That was the answer. "Ain't a problem in the world that can't be solved through hard work.," an answer was so clear it seemed as if someone had spoken it aloud. He grabbed a hoe off the wall and walked toward the front field. He'd get a jump on the weeds for now.

The sun completely up, he started back up the path, hoe over his right shoulder. David and the twins were running up the driveway, on their way to school, books in hand. They reached the road at the same time Colby reached the front field. He smiled, remembering the two-mile walk to school. Suddenly, David turned and looked back at Colby.

Colby watched his younger brother stand perfectly still, then Colby raised his hand and waved. David hesitated, then returned the wave and ran to catch up to the twins. Colby watched them run down the side of the road until they were out of sight, then Colby bent to his work.

The sun was warm on his back and the breeze that blew gently across his face and whispered quietly in his ears was spring cool. It would be a comfortable day to work. Starting at the edge of the field, Colby looked at the dirt between the first two rows. As he already knew, there weren't many weeds and the few that had sprouted were less than two inches high. He was sure he'd be done by lunchtime. Easy.

Hoeing was mindless work, untaxing both mentally and—since the weeds were so small—physically and so Colby slid easily and gratefully into the quiet rhythms of the labor. After a few minutes, his pace was set and his mind began to wander.

He thought that it would be a good idea to figure out exactly where he and his family stood, so he began putting together a rough inventory.

First, he was pretty sure that they would eat. They had Doris for milk and butter (and the buttermilk, which Colby would not touch). They had fifteen chickens that kept the eggs coming with a fair amount of regularity. They had the old rooster who did nothing but crow at dawn and strut around. Colby thought they might eat him at Thanksgiving.

They still had plenty of last year's canned goods in the hand-dug root cellar: Mason jars full of green beans, turnips, beets, tomatoes and pickles.

He had buried about three dozen apples in the cellar's dirt last fall, his own personal and secret treasure to enjoy throughout the winter yet forgotten about until just now. He knew they would be wrinkled but still sound and sweet and he decided that he'd dig them up that afternoon.

They had a huge sack of cornmeal and a fifty-pound sack of brown beans, the only things besides flour, sugar and salt that they store bought regularly.

With care, this year's vegetable garden would feed them all summer long with peas, cucumbers, onions, lima beans, half-runner green beans, tomatoes, corn and cabbage.

He was sure that food wouldn't be a problem.

They had the tobacco crop—this seven-acre front field and the twelve-acre back field with row after row of golden burley tobacco. He wasn't clear how it worked, but was fairly sure that he would raise the crop, some men would come and buy it, and then they would make cigarettes and chewing tobacco out of it.

They had the house and the big barn.

They had the old wagon and the old mule, Leviticus, to pull it around. There was some debate as to which was older, the mule or the wagon. Both were stored in the barn and used only for hauling tobacco, trips to town on Saturdays and riding to church on Sundays.

They all had clothes to wear and beds to sleep in and chairs to sit on.

They also had one last thing, the one thing that Colby prized above all others. They had the radio.

The radio brought them news and music and some funny shows and that was fine for his mother and the kids; they seemed to enjoy it. For Colby, however, the radio had but one purpose. One use only. One single reason for being and, for Colby, it was more than enough. The radio brought him the Cincinnati Reds, live from Crosley Field.

The Reds were the only passion that Colby had ever known, the only thing that had kept him awake at night long after everyone else had gone to sleep. On those summer nights, the moon would appear in the lower left side of the window in the kids' bedroom and rise slowly to the upper right and Colby would watch it and replay in his head the game he had just heard. His father let him stay up until the end of the night games and, if there was a day game, Colby hurried through his chores so that he could be seated in front of the radio for "the home-half of the first inning."

When he had first started listening to the Reds two years ago, it had been nothing more than a novelty. He could still clearly remember that first time. He had woken up sweaty on a hot July night after having been in bed only a short while, needing urgently to relieve his bladder. He had quickly pulled on his pants and, without buttoning them, walked straight through the kitchen and front room and out the door. He had barely noticed his father sitting in the rocking chair, smoking and drinking creamy sweet coffee, listening to the radio.

After relieving himself on the far side of the walnut tree, he walked back inside much more slowly than he had walked out. He heard the sounds of the game and, deciding that it was too hot to go right back to sleep, stopped and listened. He heard the announcer say that there was a man called "Big Klu" up to bat. He looked at his father, who didn't look back.

Colby knew what baseball was, even had a good idea of the rules but he had never had an urge to listen to a game. He figured that he probably never would have developed an urge if not for one thing, and that one thing was the crack of the bat.

Big Klu had lined a two-two pitch over the right field fence to tie the game at four in the eighth inning. It wasn't that Big Klu had tied the game, or the frenzied cheers of the crowd that had so completely captured Colby. No, it was definitely the crack of that bat.

Colby had been stunned, utterly amazed, that way down in Kentucky he could hear the ball hitting the wood from all the way up in Cincinnati. He had looked again at his father, wanting to ask him if he knew what that sound was and if so, why wasn't he as amazed as Colby? Why wasn't he excited about this? Why hadn't he told Colby before?

Colby was slapped with the jaw-dropping knowledge that he was listening to this game at the exact same time that it was happening. All the way from Cincinnati! And not just the announcer's voice, but the actual sound of the ball hitting the bat!

He had sat down in the floor right then, in front of the radio and tried to make himself as unnoticeable as possible, sure that Vernon would tell him to go back to bed. But he hadn't and Colby sat there listening for other obscure sounds. He could hear the crowd easily at all times but every so often he could hear a single heckler's voice rise above the others. If the crowd had been lulled by inaction into temporary silence, Colby could hear a pitched ball smack into the catcher's mitt. Every time a batter connected, he could hear the crack, even foul tips. Much to his delight, the game went into extra innings and, in the bottom of the twelfth, he heard a vendor yelling, "Peanuts! Get yer peanuts here! Peanuts! Get yer peanuts here!"

Colby couldn't remember who had won that game, but it didn't matter. He was hooked.

"They play again tomorrow night, Daddy?" he had asked.

"Reckon so," Vernon had answered.

"You think I could listen to them?"

"Reckon so." And so Colby's passion was born.

At first, he had been only mildly interested in whether or not the Reds won. It was enough just to listen to the game. Although they never once had a conversation, it made Colby proud to sit in the front room, just he and his father.

Over the course of that summer, though, he started hoping that the Reds would win. Vernon had never cheered or clapped or demonstrated in any way that he was even listening to an athletic contest, so Colby had learned to keep his own growing emotions silent. Still, there had been a few occasions when the Reds came back to win in the ninth that Colby's excitement had been too great for his young body to contain and it had spilled out in a whoop or a yell. When this happened, Colby would grin with goofy guilt at Vernon, who would look at his son a moment, then turn his attention back to his cigarettes and coffee.

Colby began worrying about whether or not the Reds won. He started hoping that the teams ahead of the Reds in the league standings would lose so that his Reds could move up. The only place Colby could get news of the standings was during the game. Between innings the announcer gave the previous night's results along with ongoing scores and, during the seventh inning stretch, would list the league standings.

At some point during that fall Colby graduated to the next level of fanaticism. He started hating another team: the Brooklyn Dodgers.

His loathing of the Dodgers grew in pure inverse proportion to his love for the Reds. He hated everything about them. He hated their name. He hated their players. He hated their manager. He hated the whole city of Brooklyn. But he hated them mostly because, this particular season, they were beating his Reds with outrageous regularity.

It was from this combination of love and hate that Colby's fantasy life came to be. It was this one fantasy that ran through his mind as he hoed his newly inherited crop of burley.

The premise was simple. The Cincinnati Reds were playing the Brooklyn Dodgers in the 1949 World Series. Colby knew that the Reds and the Dodgers were both in the National League and therefore couldn't meet in the World Series but this was merely an inconvenient fact, a meaningless bit of static that barely interfered with the smooth running of his fantasy.

The fantasy was rich and detailed and, to Colby, meaningful and important. It always started with the player introductions before Game One.

The visiting Dodgers were introduced first and the crowd booed so loudly throughout that it was impossible to even hear the announcer. The fans in Colby's mind loathed the Dodgers with the same well-oiled hatred that lived in Colby.

After minutes of solid booing, the announcer would then say, "And now, for your Cincinnati Reds!!!!" and the crowd would cheer wildly.

Then, just as the crowd began to quiet, "Batting first and playing shortstop…Colburn Graaaaaayyyyyssssooooonnnnn!" The roaring adulation of the crowd as Colby trotted out to the first base line, acknowledging his fans with a careless tip of his hat, was so loud that he couldn't hear who batted second.

The fantasy always started this same way—no embellishments, no variations—but from there, it was always different. Sometimes the Reds swept the Dodgers in four easy games. Sometimes it went seven games, every one a barn-burner. Sometimes the Reds fell behind three games to none and staged the most miraculous, impossible comeback in the history of baseball.

In each one of these scenarios and many, many others, there was one player who, with his quick glove and even quicker bat, almost single-handedly carried the Reds to victory: World Series MVP, Colburn Grayson.

On this day, as Colby chopped at the weeds in the cool May sunshine, he envisioned a seven-game Series. He had fantasized his way up to the ninth inning of the seventh game. The Reds were behind 5-2. The bases were loaded. Two outs and the count was full. Since he had already hit five home runs in this series, Colby imagined that the pitcher might intentionally walk him. But just in case this pitcher wasn't completely gutless, just in case, Colby would be ready.

The crowd was completely silent. Some were praying. Some buried their faces in their hands, unable to bear the suspense, unable to imagine the pressure on the young shortstop.

In his mind, Colby stared down the pitcher while hearing the announcer's voice.

*…and here's the pitch! Grayson steps, he swings! It's a long fly ball! Deep center field! It's going! It's going! It's…GONE!!!! IT'S GONE!!!! IT'S GONE!!!! HE DID IT!!!! HE DID IT!!!! GRAYSON DID IT!!!! IT'S A GRAND SLAM HOME RUN!!!! AND THE CINCINNATI REDS ARE THE 1949 WORLD SE-RIES CHAMPIONS!!!!*

Colby felt the familiar chills run up his spine and set his scalp dancing as he envisioned himself trotting around the bases, the crowd uncontainable, his grateful teammates waiting at home plate to mob him.

This was one of his favorite scenarios, one that he replayed at least once a week. He started to go back to the beginning to make a revision or two (he thought that maybe he should hit two home runs in game two), when a wasp flew nearly into his right ear, snapping him out of his reverie. He looked up. The sun was directly over his head. As it often did when Colby was deep into his fantasies, time had sprinted past him and he realized that he had already worked the morning away. He thought that he should be about halfway or more done with the front field. He looked around, gathering his bearings.

In a morning of nonstop work, he had hoed two rows and less than half of a third row. He was mildly surprised. He was sure that this job wasn't that big. He couldn't remember how long it had taken him and his father to do it. He had never before paid any attention to the time it took. He had never had to. That was what his father did.

As he walked back to the house for lunch, he decided that it was a good thing that he had started on the hoeing. At his current speed with his fantasies playing, it would take him a full week to finish the front field and twice that long to do the back field and the vegetable garden.

## CHAPTER 5

At four-thirty that afternoon, Colby was walking back to the house from the barn after putting up his hoe and moving to the afternoon milking. As he drew even with the front porch, he set the bucket down and watched as a car pulled into their dirt driveway, a rare enough occasion that it was chief event of the day.

He knew instantly that the driver of this car was a stranger. Only two people in town owned cars and both of those cars were black. Doctor Cardiff had one that he used for making his rounds, and Reverend Tannehill had an old, smoky, tragically unreliable Ford that he used for church business. Cars went by on U.S. 60 every day, but he wasn't sure if he ever remembered a strange car pulling up to his house. The car was as shiny green as the leaves of the magnolia tree that grew in the churchyard.

Dust from the car's wake ballooned around two men as they stepped out with a calm, steady diffidence. They both carried leather briefcases.

"How'do. You must be Colby. You wouldn't remember me. I haven't seen you since you were knee high." The speaker who stepped out of the driver's side had an open, easy face.

"I'm Colby. Who are you?" Colby said. He had been taught to always respect his elders, to say "yessir" and "nossir," but this man and the taller passenger, who now walked up beside the driver, was a stranger first, an elder second.

"I'm Maurice White and this man is Thomas Scott. We're from Morehead. Actually, we represent the Bank of Morehead." White hesitated, waiting for some kind of recognition and, receiving none, added, "We did business with your father."

Colby felt his heart quicken. The word "business" made him immediately nervous and alert. To Colby, business was what men talked about by themselves, while smoking cigarettes and drinking coffee, without women or children around. It had to do with money and signing papers and things. It was understood in the Grayson household that when Vernon said he had to talk business with whoever was present, everyone else cleared out of the front room and didn't return until the company was gone.

Colby stood in a silent, sustained panic, hoping that his mother knew at least a little about what "business" was.

White took a step forward but stopped, sensing Colby's uncertainty. Scott remained a step behind.

"We both knew Vernon real well, Colby. I surely was sorry to hear about his passing," White said.

"What kind of business you got now, being that Daddy's dead and all?" Colby asked.

"Well Colby, your daddy left some business behind and we have to talk to you and your mother about it."

"What kind of business?" Colby repeated. His uncertainty grew and he struggled against the urge to take a step backward. His heart started galloping. Then again, they might be the ones that bought the tobacco when it was raised. Were they farmers themselves? They didn't look like it. At least they had said, "you and your mother."

"It's about the farm, Colby."

"What about it?"

"Well, what are you going to do with it?"

"What do you mean?" Colby said, then added quickly, "It ain't for sale."

White looked at Scott and cleared his throat. Scott stepped forward.

"We don't want to buy it Colby but…there is, however, some…ahh… business we had with your father that isn't entirely…ahh…complete. That's why we need to speak with you and your mother."

Colby reached down and picked up the bucket of milk and looked out over his front field and into the afternoon sun.

"Well, then, I reckon y'all best come in and sit awhile." he said and stepped through the front door.

In the darkness of the front room Colby saw his mother in her rocking chair, singing softly, both of her hands gently rubbing her throat. The throat rubbing was new and Colby was inexplicably embarrassed by it. The curtains were drawn against the afternoon sun and the acute change from the breezy, bright outdoors to this brown and cheerless room silenced the bankers, stifling any inclination to make polite conversation with its mumbling, unfocused matron.

Colby left the men standing just inside the front door and carried the bucket to the kitchen. He set it on the counter next to the sink and returned to the front room. He stopped by his mother's chair and, when she failed to stop rocking, put a hand on her shoulder.

"Mama, this is Mr. White and Mr. Scott. They're from Morehead." Anne did not answer but looked up at Colby and stopped stroking her throat. Colby glanced up at the obviously uncomfortable men. "Y'all can sit on the couch over there."

The men nodded gratefully, and walked quickly to the couch and sat, facing her, their briefcases at their feet.

"How are you, Mrs. Grayson?" White asked with a slight nod.

Anne's eyes snapped suddenly into focus, as if some prankster had clapped his hands loudly next to her ears. She looked at White, at Scott then back at White.

"My back's much better but I think I'm catching a cold," she said.

White hesitated, opened his mouth to speak, closed it, opened it again and then spoke.

"I was very sorry to hear about your husband," he offered.

Anne's eyes began to melt back into the darkness of the room, becoming as lazy and without focus as her thoughts, when she remembered her manners.

"Would you gentlemen care for some coffee?" she asked.

"No thank you, Mrs. Grayson," said White. Anne looked at Scott, who shook his head with a slight, comfortless smile.

"You're here to talk business?" she asked.

"Yes, ma'am. We are at that," White replied.

With a surprising amount of grace, Anne rose out of her chair and started walking toward the kitchen.

"I'll keep the children out of here, Vernon," she said.

"Mama?" Colby said. One foot in the kitchen, Anne stopped and looked back at her son.

"It's Colby, Mama."

"Yes, I know," she said and glided quietly into the kitchen.

The two men watched her leave without comment, then turned their attention back to Colby. They waited, wisely and with unbiased patience, for Colby to speak first. They had seen many different kinds of people in their line of work.

"She gets sick a lot," Colby said. The men nodded. They could hear her rustling about the kitchen, singing delicately to herself as she took the cream off the milk.

"What's the business we got to talk about?" Colby finally asked.

The men looked uncomfortably at each other, unsure now of where to start. White raised his eyebrows at Scott, telling him without words that they had to at least try.

Scott sat forward and cleared his throat.

"Colby, I'm sure you know what a bank is, correct?" he asked.

"Yessir. It's where people keep their money if they got extra."

"That's right Colby, but it also does many other things. One of those other things is that it loans out money to people who may have a temporary need."

"Yessir."

"Well Colby, the way it…ahhh…is…ahhh…is that your father borrowed some money from our bank," Scott finally finished.

"Why would he do that?" Colby asked, growing irritated at Mr. Scott's 'ah's'. It sounded somewhat like charity to him and he absolutely could not form in his mind a picture of Vernon Grayson asking anybody for anything, ever.

"All the farmers around here borrow money from the bank, Colby. They borrow it to get their crops started and to buy groceries and things until they can get their crops in and sold. Then they pay us back."

"Why do y'all let them borrow it?"

"Well, Colby, because when they pay us back, they pay us a little bit more than what they borrowed."

Colby glanced away from the men, looking out the front door. He was actually relieved to hear this. The knowledge that these men were trying to earn money just like the farmers settled easily into Colby's sensibilities. He thought that maybe he had "business" figured out. People trying to make money any way they could. In any case, the fact that these two men weren't providers of shameful relief was comforting to Colby, because otherwise he would have had to revise his iron-wrought beliefs about his father and, by extension, the world.

"I understand," he said.

Scott took a deep breath and let it out slowly, doubting very much that Colby did see, but he put his doubts aside when Colby said, "The farmer needs the money and y'all wasn't going to do nothing with it any way, so by letting him use the money a while, y'all get back more than what you give."

The two men began nodding vigorously, eagerly. They glanced at each other, tacitly acknowledging that they were impressed. They both knew grown men with families who couldn't grasp the concept of interest. Those men just paid the bank what the bank said was owed, more often than not, signing the papers with an X.

"And Daddy borrowed some money from you, and when I bring the crop in, I'll have to pay you back that money, plus a little bit more."

The men shifted in their seats, awkward and uneasy again. They knew Colby was sharp but also that the boy didn't realize that he was in over his head, way over his head. White coughed once and took over from Scott.

"There's an awful daggone lot of work here, Colby," he said.

"Yessir."

"What I'm trying to say is that this farm, nice as it is, was as much as your father could handle." He shook his head with a slightly exaggerated sadness. "An awful lot of work."

"I reckon I can do what work needs to be done. I been helping him two years now," Colby said.

White started to reply but Scott put his hand on the other's sleeve and took over again.

"That's fine Colby and we both hope that you get plenty of rain. I just want to make sure that you…ah…know that there are other…ah, options, other things that you may want to…ahhh, consider."

"I'd like to hear them," Colby said without hesitation.

"Well, Colby, this is not a small farm, and considering the fact that you have only one mule, it is in fact, for this area, a fairly good-sized farm. You might want to think along the lines of…," Scott hesitated. "Selling it," he finished.

"Why would I want to do that?" Colby inquired.

"Well, you know how we told you about your father borrowing from us?"

"Yessir."

"The only way that your father had to pay that money back was to… ahhh…bring this crop in. Now I know that you're planning to bring it in yourself but what if you can't Colby?"

"What if I don't?" Colby asked.

Now it was White's turn again. He hesitated, then cleared his throat.

"Then we would have to sell this farm to pay off the loan," he said, resisting an urge to look at the floor. Scott closed his eyes.

Colby's heart began hammering. "Did Daddy know about this?" he asked, his rising desperation obvious to the bankers.

"Yes, Colby, he did. It's called collateral. All the farmers do it. It's just in case the farmer can't bring his crop in, then the bank will still get its money. It's how we protect ourselves and the money we loan out."

"I see. Y'all didn't ask Daddy to come in and borrow no money. It ain't your fault. You're just protecting what's yours, same as everybody. Fair's fair."

The two men had not even the smallest hint of an answer to this. They had, in fact, asked Vernon to come in and borrow money, just like they asked all the farmers to come in. They would likely have come in anyway, this being the only bank in the area, but Colby's unusual combination of intelligence and innocence made the men uneasy—even a little ashamed.

Scott opened his briefcase, retrieved a piece of paper and handed it to White.

"What we were thinking might be the best solution for you and your family, Colby, would be to sell the farm now so that you don't run the risk of losing it. You have twenty-one acres here. Farmland around this area sells for three hundred dollars an acre. That would be six thousand three hundred dollars to you if you sold. With this house and your barn, you could add on say another seven thousand. Now your father borrowed one thousand and two hundred dollars from us. After you paid that back you would still have twelve thousand one hundred dollars. With that, you could buy a smaller place and still have some money left over. I even know of some small houses in and around Morehead that you could buy for that much."

31

Colby looked at the small slice of outdoors visible through a slit in the curtains, and tried to act like he was thinking. These numbers were so high that he was unable to put them in any type of context relative to his own experience. Tens of thousands were the same to him as hundreds of millions. He had been one of the best math pupils in school and he could add, subtract and multiply in his head as quickly as most could do it with a pencil and paper, but these men were talking amounts so high that Colby had no hope of immediate comprehension.

He noticed that the men were now silent; watching him, but still Colby stared at the thin slice in the curtains. A shaft of sunlight stabbed through and began climbing the wall to Colby's left. He didn't really notice it until White lit a cigarette. Colby watched the smoke as it billowed and swayed in lazy, rollicking patterns seen only in the thin slice of sunlight. On more than one occasion, he had watched those vaporous designs as his father smoked in the late afternoon while they listened to the Reds. Colby felt the hammering desperation begin to subside. He had always been curious and pleased that he never noticed one or the other, the smoke or the sunlight, unless they combined at this time of day to produce a humble but mesmerizing show. Today, it made him think of his father and that calmed him. His heart slowed. Colby knew precisely what Vernon would tell him to do and he needed only to heed the unseen voice to be absolved of responsibility, or even the need for further painful thought.

Vernon rarely strung more than three sentences together, nor had a conversation that lasted more than a minute or two. It had not been unusual for Vernon to go a full day and never say a single word to Colby, other than issuing commands while they worked. The only time Colby ever heard his father speak with anything even approaching eloquence and passion was the previous summer when, after a hot and cheerless day of labor, Vernon put his hand on his son's shoulder and spoke.

"See this barn, Colby? This barn was built by your grandaddy Denton. See that house up yonder? That house was built by your great-grandaddy Jordan Grayson. He built it to replace a house that got hit by lightning and burned down. That house was built by Jordan's grandaddy, Andrew. See that fence over yonder? I built that fence before you was born. Ever Grayson that ever been the head of this farm has added something to it, built something on it, but that don't matter. What stands on this land ain't important. What's important is the land itself and the men what tend it. All these buildings going to fall down someday but this land is always going to be here and there's always going to be a Grayson tending to it. Right now that man is me. Someday it's going to be you. The land's all that really matters, Colby. It can feed you, it can give you lumber to build with, it can make you strong and it can give you pride. It makes you work hard but if you do it, if you work hard enough, can't nobody ever take this land away. You remember that, son. You hear?"

Colby had heard, although he didn't get the full gist of his father's speech until now and it gave him direction.

"Mr. White, Mr. Scott, I aim to keep the farm," he announced.

Slowly and with formality, Scott opened his briefcase and put the papers back inside. He closed it silently and set it back on the ground by his feet. White did the same with his briefcase.

"All right, Colby," Scott said.

"And I aim to pay you back your money, too," Colby pledged.

"I know that you do, Colby." Scott said. They rose and lifted their briefcases. "If we can be of any help, please let us know."

Colby stood up and started to speak, hesitated, then nodded. Scott extended his hand. Colby took a shambling step forward, reached up and shook Scott's hand, then White's. Colby felt that his hand was completely engulfed by both. The men nodded once again at Colby and turned to leave. Colby followed them out and watched from the front porch as they climbed into the car, and then turned back into the house.

## CHAPTER 6

The two men didn't speak until they pulled out of the driveway and turned back to Morehead.

"Sharp kid," White said, his eyes fixed on the road.

Scott rolled the passenger window down an inch and lit a cigarette. "You sound surprised, Maurice," he said.

"Aren't you? Vernon was a workhorse, but he wasn't the smartest man who ever lived." White knocked on the wood paneling on the dashboard because he was speaking ill of the dead. "And I knew that Anne was different, but..." His sentence trailed off.

"Yep, I didn't know it was that bad either," Scott agreed. "She had a rough, rough upbringing, didn't she?"

"Yes, she did. Her mother died young, her daddy was a bad awful drunk, violent the way I heard it, lost the farm, and disappeared."

"Well, it is a shame though. I do hate to see that boy broken. Vernon should have told him to sell."

"Well, sir, I imagine that thought would never have even entered Vernon's head. I'll tell you what though, if that boy gets even a little help and a good break or two, I wouldn't count him out," Scott said.

"How do you figure that, Tom?"

"Well, he's big enough to do the day-to-day work. I figure on it just being a matter of his being tough enough, and with Vernon Grayson being his father..." This time, Scott didn't have to finish his sentence. They both knew, as did anyone who knew the Graysons that Vernon's eldest son, whether through genetic blessings of physical inheritance or the ungentle tutelage of Vernon's leather belt, would be tough.

"And, like you said, the kid's sharp, sharp as a tack."

White nodded then checked his speedometer. He didn't agree with his partner and thought that Colby had no chance, but he didn't press the issue.

"There is one thing bothering me, though," he said.

"What's that?"

"Well, it couldn't have taken much more than five or six hundred dollars to get that crop started. That leaves six or seven hundred and it's not in the bank. Colby didn't mention it."

Scott dismissed this with a wave of his hand. "It's probably tucked up in a pillowcase. Either that or buried out behind the barn somewhere—" Scott stopped suddenly, looking at White with his mouth open. White looked back at him, eyebrows raised.

"That's right," he said. "It would be just about like Vernon to bury that money or hide it somewhere that it couldn't be found. What if he didn't tell them where it is?"

"Maybe we should go back and ask," Scott said.

"No. Let's give it a little while. Maybe Anne knows where it is or will remember when it comes time to buy groceries. If it looks like they're in trouble, we'll go back by and let Colby know that there's some money around."

What they could not have known was that the money lay with Vernon Grayson in his grave. Anne Grayson, with Doctor Cardiff's help, had dressed Vernon for his burial, as was proper, in his Sunday suit. Vernon kept all his money in the left-hand pocket of the coat. As Anne dressed the body, she had felt a lump in the pocket. But the pants weren't buttoned yet and she wanted to make him decent before she stopped to see what the lump was. After the pants, she had to get his tie straight and knotted and this task proved beyond her. By the time the doctor had taken over, her mind, as it so often did, had slipped, and taken her to the misty, music-filled realm where she dwelled most of the time, roaming directionless in a painless world that she could not describe.

## CHAPTER 7

David Grayson stood motionless in quiet, stunned awe. He knew that Colby and the banker men were talking about money but that wasn't the big deal. He knew what money and banks were but when the banker man had said "six thousand, three hundred dollars," David gasped loudly enough that he was sure that Colby and the men had heard him. He was standing just inside the kitchen door listening to Colby talk "business."

David, alone of the Graysons, possessed a keen and unquenchable curiosity. He couldn't remember ever seeing anything new and not being interested in it. *Where did it come from? How does it work? Why is it here?* He repeatedly asked himself these questions. These questions that most children stopped asking with repetitive frequency in their fourth or fifth year had never stopped their soft insistent demands. David knew instinctively that he was smarter than anyone else in the Grayson house, at least when it came to math or reading, but he also disregarded the fact, correctly figuring that one didn't need to read well to fulfill his apparent destiny: growing and selling tobacco. In his home, superior intelligence was as important as having larger feet or bigger ears. It never occurred to David to think of his intelligence as an asset. He had no pride in his superior ability to read and write, any more than he would belittle Timothy for having smaller hands than he did.

What he couldn't understand was that no one else seemed to share his curiosity, his defining characteristic, and that sometimes hurt him and even frightened him.

He had once asked Vernon how gasoline made a car move. Without looking at him, Vernon had answered, "Who cares?"

He wondered how the electric lights worked and once spent an hour clicking them on and off, trying to see if there was a delay between the 'click' and the lights coming on. He wondered why it was hot in the summer and cold in the winter, because the sun shined during both.

He wondered how Doris made all that milk, and one afternoon, inspected her after Colby finished the milking. He had started from the side and ended up crawling under her, between her back legs. He had lifted her tail when Doris apparently tired of his inquisitiveness, twitched her tail out of his hand and emptied her bladder in a gush. The hot stream hit David in the throat, soaking his shirt completely before he could scramble away. He didn't drink milk for a week but remained curious as to how she made it.

When he was seven, he began wondering why his parents' bed squeaked sometimes at night. The fourth or fifth time that he noticed it, he got out of bed and walked into their bedroom without knocking. It merely looked like his parents were playing, but that didn't bother or even interest him. He walked straight to the bed, got down on his hands and knees and began inspecting the mattress. It had stopped squeaking so he reached up with his right hand and began pushing down on it, trying to make it squeak again. David noticed that his parents were staring at him, so he smiled at them innocently, when Vernon delivered a stinging and loud backhand that caught David on his right cheekbone. David suddenly didn't care why the bed squeaked.

In David's life, the back of Vernon's hand remained the only thing that ever darkened his glowing need to know. Now, as he stood listening to his brother speak, his curiosity changed into something less familiar: he was spellbound.

Six thousand, three hundred dollars! Seven thousand more for the buildings! And it was Colby discussing these matters, not Daddy. David had no idea that this place could bring that kind of money, and it would be Colby making the decision!

David slowly shook his head in silent adoration, elevating his worship of his big brother to yet another level. His reticent Grayson nature kept David from letting Colby know that he was his idol. The twins had each other, Mama had her own world and Colby and Daddy were always working together or listening to baseball. David had friends at school but Colby didn't even go to school. He worked just like Daddy and, in the shortsightedness of his youth, David saw no way he would grow as big or as strong as his father. In Colby, however, David saw a possibly attainable goal. The total extent of his humble hope was to one day be as big as Colby and work the tobacco.

From the time the weather turned warmer and the talk in their community turned to yet another crop, David had been trying to work up the courage to ask if he could quit school and go to work, just like Colby. Then again, the summer break was coming up and maybe Colby would let him work then. Daddy had let David do some hoeing last year.

When Vernon died, David had guiltily thought that at least it would be easier for him to ask Colby to let him work than it would have been to ask his father.

But now, with Colby speaking of six thousand, three hundred dollars and another seven thousand…and with banker-men who carried leather cases…Like his brother, David couldn't grasp the concept of thousands of dollars. Finding a penny on the street was the luckiest thing that could happen in any given day and possession of a dime meant that he was wealthy.

He thought about the amount, thirteen thousand dollars and realized that he hadn't known there was that much money in the world.

"Dang," he muttered as the men shook hands with Colby. He was disappointed that he didn't know what kind of deal had been struck. As the front door closed, he sat down at the kitchen table and was delighted when Colby came in and sat across from him. Neither of them noticed Anne doing her work. Colby stared into the corner, gnawing on a thumbnail, a sure sign that he was still studying on "business."

"Colby?" David said.

"Hmm?" Colby returned, without looking up or taking his thumbnail out of his mouth.

"Them was banker-men, wasn't they?"

"Uh-huh."

When Colby still didn't look up, David knew he wouldn't get any information out of his brother. Then a thought hit him: maybe this was the time, while Colby was studying on something else, to ask if he could work. David's heart began to speed up.

"Colby?"

"Hmm?"

"Uh…you reckon that maybe…uhh…I could maybe…" His courage faltered. Now Colby did look at him and David felt shy and shamed and silly. No way he could ask now.

"Nothing," David said. He sat a moment longer and Colby went back to his thumbnail. David got up and walked out the front door.

## CHAPTER 8

Russ Traylor sopped up his egg yolk with the last biscuit, stood up from the breakfast table, stepped out onto his back porch and burped. A big breakfast eater, he loved his eggs and ate four of them every morning, fried, along with bacon and biscuits and, in the summertime, thick slices of tomato.

It was the second morning after Vernon's burial. A cool morning mist lay low over Russ's fields, dampening the freely turned earth to the point of muddiness. The sun was scraping its reluctant way into the sky behind a scud of clinging night clouds. The rooster had finished crowing and the wild song-birds were taking over. A damp early summer morning was Russ's favorite time to be alive in Kentucky.

He pulled a pack of Mail Pouch Chewing Tobacco out of his back pocket and put a good size chew in his mouth, sat down in his porch chair and chewed, spitting into an old, rusty J.F.G. coffee can. It had been his porch spittoon for four or five years. From here, he would watch the sun finish rising and wait for his hired hand, One-Eyed Zach, to arrive.

Dot hadn't exactly forbidden him to chew in the house but frowned on it. Russ preferred to chew tobacco rather than smoke after a meal, so another pleasant morning ritual had begun.

It was commonly known that Russ Traylor was better off than any member of the community and it was no coincidence that he was also considered the smartest and one of the hardest working.

Russ had been the closest thing to a friend that Vernon Grayson ever had. Russ understood that this was mainly due to the proximity of their farms, but he had been genuinely fond of Vernon. The other farmers in the community couldn't understand why Vernon wasn't as well off as Russ. Vernon's capacity for back-breaking, soul-stretching work was the stuff of minor legend. Each year, when autumn crept over the mountains, the farmers would stand around the churchyard after the preaching and discuss tobacco-cutting: which farm would go first this year (they all helped one another in the cutting and housing); the fastest way to cut it; and the best cutters they had ever seen.

Every fall, Vernon's name was the most mentioned, the only man among them to cut two thousand sticks in one day. Usually Vernon cut about

39

fifteen hundred and that was a good day for any two men. But he would cut two thousand at least once during a season, just to prove he could. He had first cut two thousand ten years earlier, and Russ knew it was because of a rumor about a cutter out of Lexington that went by the name of Silk. They heard that Silk had cut nineteen hundred in a day, so Vernon made it a quiet point to do two thousand.

When they started housing the tobacco, Vernon would run bottom rail all day, thereby handling every single stick. Russ knew that Vernon worked like a mule, but was also as stubborn as one. He would take neither charity nor advice. His demeanor was every bit as callused as his hands. He was level-headed, but far from shrewd. Although he had never spoken it aloud, Russ knew that Vernon could not see any further than the end of his own nose.

Russ had never cut two thousand sticks in a day, but he knew that he could if he had to. He had never run bottom rail all day, but knew that he could, and felt no particular urge to prove it to himself or anyone else. Vernon's brand of rock-hard, backward pride was not uncommon in Russ's experience, but Russ failed to understand Vernon's need to demonstrate the uttermost limits of his stamina. The only payoff Vernon received for his displays had been an early death and the pine box where he now lay. With or without Vernon Grayson, the tobacco still grew and still needed to be cut, housed, cured, stripped and sold.

Russ knew that the other farmers considered him the smartest man around, but he knew that he wasn't. What set him apart from many of the others, and especially Vernon, was that he never minded trying something new. Some ideas he came up with on his own, but the county Extension agent was full of suggestions. Some were good, some were not but, to Russ, it never hurt to try.

Potassium nitrate had been his biggest find to date. He had first used it seven years earlier and the powerful fertilizer had given him ten percent more tobacco per acre. Three years ago, a couple of other farmers picked it up. This year, every farm would employ it except, to no one's surprise, the Graysons.

Potassium nitrate was on his mind this morning as he chewed and waited for his help to arrive. The county Extension agent had suggested that Russ try a thinner mixture this year, applied more often. He had just settled on trying the method on one or two acres when One-Eyed Zach appeared, walking loosely across the back field.

One-Eyed Zach was an enigma to everyone, including his employer. For starters, why did everyone call him One Eyed-Zach? True, his left eye was gone, the lid permanently closed over an empty socket, but it was also true that he was the only Zach around.

The second part of the mystery was Zach's origin. He had just shown up at cutting time fifteen years earlier, looking for work. Transient labor was unheard of at that time in their community; no one would ever come there looking for wages. But Russ's oldest son had just died of meningitis and he needed help. One-Eyed Zach proved to be such a good worker that Russ put him on permanently.

Zach had never spoken of his past and Russ had never asked, although he was mighty curious as to how he had lost his eye. Zach had been an aging man then and was nearly an old man now; Russ guessed his age at between 64 and 69, just a few years older than himself. He was a good hand, never late and never complained, and that was good enough for Russ.

Third was the question of his breeding. He obviously had some Negro blood in him. He had skin as white as any man's but his nose was wide, he had curly hair and bigger lips than most. As it became clear that Zach would be staying on, his breeding became a silent issue in the community. They couldn't treat a black man like a white man, nor could they do the reverse. The issue never became a problem as Zach kept mostly to himself. He lived in a converted smokehouse connected to Russ's back barn. On some hot days, Zach could still smell the curing smoke from years past.

Finally, and of interest only to Russ, was the question of what Zach did with his money. Not that it was any of Russ's business, but he had been paying Zach forty dollars a month for the past five years and thirty dollars a month before that, but he had never known Zach to buy anything other than groceries and roll-your-own cigarettes. He even fed Zach lunch every day. Zach spent no money on improving his living quarters, he paid no rent, he didn't drink or gamble and had never, to Russ's knowledge, mailed anything, money or otherwise, to anyone.

Russ figured that maybe he was saving up to buy a glass eye.

"Mornin' to you, Russ," Zach said as he stopped at the bottom of the porch steps. He lifted his right foot onto the second step and began rolling a cigarette on his right knee. His shoes and the cuffs of his pants were damp from the morning dew.

"Morning, Zach. Have you done had your breakfast?"

"Yessir, I surely have. I fried me up some bacon and I toasted three of them biscuits that the missus gave me last night. I ate 'em with some of that molasses that y'all give me for Christmas. That surely is some good molasses." He lit his cigarette, took a drag and spit out stray bits of tobacco.

Russ spit into his can. "You know, that is some good molasses. The wife and I got a jar of it ourselves."

"Yessir. I do like the taste of good molasses," Zach nodded in agreement. They chewed and smoked in comfortable silence, Zach looking out toward the road, Russ looking over his back fields.

Zach finally finished his cigarette, crushed the butt with his heel and put it in his pocket. That night, he would unroll all the butts he had saved during the day and get enough tobacco to make at least one more cigarette.

Russ set down the coffee can, rose and walked down the steps.

"Well, I reckon we could do some hoeing today," he said.

"Yessir. I reckon we could," Zach answered and followed Russ to the tool shed.

## CHAPTER 9

There were, Zach supposed, worse ways to finish out a life. The work was hard but not so hard that his old bones couldn't take it. The summers were hot and the winters cold, but he had lived through more extreme conditions than Kentucky could ever throw at him.

Zach had lived in Arizona for the first four years of the century. Still a relatively young man at that time, a good horseman and handy with a rope, he had tried his hand at being a cowboy. His experience turned out not at all like he had imagined it during his Louisianna boyhood. Rather than long trails, big skies and snow-peaked mountains, it was mostly just hot, dusty, tedious work.

Mostly just hot, and not the sweaty, muggy Bayou brand of heat, but truly withering, dangerous heat. He could not to this day figure out why he'd stayed at it for four years.

Zach had also been to Greenland, something no man he'd ever met could claim. He joined the army during World War I when it became clear that the United States would be going to Europe; he joined up to see the continent but a small, isolated Army base on the southern tip of Greenland was as far as he got. He spent six months with a hundred other men doing not much of anything other than trying to stay warm. He never got to Europe but, as a volunteer serviceman, he was allowed to resign his position that spring.

As Russ suspected, Zach had seen and done many things, but he had decided that excitement just wasn't important. Maybe he was just being an old man, but he believed that the best things in his life were directly related to his personal comfort. He had a soft bed, a good wood stove that kept him warm in the winter, plenty of food and all he had to do in return was help Russ raise his crop. Not a bad trade.

Zach liked working for Russ; he got a quiet satisfaction out of raising the crops year after year. Starting every spring with just seeds and the knowledge of work to come, and ending with food and tobacco pleased him, even if the crops weren't his. He sometimes wondered if they were even Russ's crops. It seemed to him that God had a whole lot more to do with it than he or Russ ever would.

It was tobacco that they worked at now, Russ in one row, Zach in the next. They hoed up and back, sometimes talking, sometimes each in his own thoughts. The sun was shining but it was still cool—perfect working weather, in Zach's opinion.

"Well, Zach, I'm thinking about using that thin mix that the County man was talking about. It seems like a little more work but I can't see how it's not at least worth a try." This was Russ's way of eliciting Zach's opinion, an asset that Russ used as often as possible.

"It were me," Zach said, "I'd try it out on maybe just an acre. Last year's crop come out so good that maybe it might not do to go and change too much."

"That's about what I was thinking, one acre or maybe two, just as a test."

"Yessir. Reckon it wouldn't hurt too much to try."

Russ stopped chopping at the weeds and leaned on the handle of his hoe. He looked out over his fields. They were in order.

"Well, then, I reckon we'll try it out up on the south corner there." He nodded forward and to his left.

"Reckon that's as good a place as any," Zach said and went back to his hoeing.

The fertilizer wasn't the only thing that Russ wanted Zach's opinion on, but he was having trouble bringing the subject up. He wanted to help out the Graysons but didn't know how to go about it. He couldn't give them money, even if Colby would take it. Russ had a little less than two thousand dollars in a savings account at the Bank of Morehead, but it was strictly emergency money. There had never been a withdrawal made on the account in the twenty years he had held it. Russ knew that just one failed crop, for whatever reason, would eat up every bit of the money. When he was a boy, a rare, late summer tornado had completely wiped out his father's annual harvest and that winter, Russ had tasted true hunger. Luckily, that was the last tornado to hit the area and Russ had never lost crop. Still, that money would not be touched.

He knew that he could help Colby with work and the fact that Colby wouldn't let him frustrated him so badly that he couldn't see straight. He and Zach could, in fact, be there now, helping Colby hoe. The field they were now working could wait a couple of days. Russ had even considered not asking but rather just going over and starting to work. But the only way that would have worked was if he had not offered his help on the day of Vernon's funeral. Then, if he and Zach showed up to work, Colby might have been confused enough or at least flustered enough, to allow them to help. As it stood, however, any help forced on Colby would break his pride before it got a chance to develop.

Russ lacked the subtlety needed for a situation like this and he didn't mind admitting it. He thought that perhaps Zach might have an idea or two but he didn't want to just up and ask. It would be much better and more normal if it came up in conversation, however, because they didn't talk for more than three hours out of the ten they worked every day, he was wondering if the subject would ever get raised.

About an hour before lunch, Zach finally brought it up.

"Daggone shame about Mr. Grayson," he said. Russ looked up, surprised and relieved. Zach was still bent over hoeing. He was shaking his head. "A real daggone shame."

"It surely is a shame, Zach. Vernon was a good man."

"Yessir. He surely was one hard-working man."

"He was. Workingest man I ever saw. I just hope that his boy can work as hard."

Now Zach did stop his hoeing and looked right at Russ. "Russ, do you reckon that there's any way at all that boy can bring in that crop by hisself?"

Russ stopped hoeing too.

"Well Zach, I must say that, no, I do not think that he can bring in that crop by himself."

Zach nodded, unsurprised. "Reckon he don't want no help either," he said.

"Don't want it and won't have it. Sometimes Vernon could be right thick-headed."

"And I reckon he taught his sons to be the same."

"I reckon so, Zach. I offered help to him already, a mistake, I suspect. To be just honest about it, I'd still like to help that bunch, but I must admit that I can't really see a way to go about it."

There it was.

"Well sir, ain't nothing tougher than helping out someone that won't be helped. 'Bout like putting socks on a chicken."

"I'd say that is so," Russ agreed. He pulled his Mail Pouch out of his back pocket and took a chew. Zach decided that he could take time to roll a cigarette. He did and lit it.

"Well, Russ, he is still young," Zach said.

"He is."

"Well, I reckon about the only thing for us to do is to help him so maybe he ain't exactly sure that he's being helped."

Russ spit a dark stream of tobacco juice into the dirt and looked briefly up at the midday sun. He looked back down to Zach and nodded.

"That would be a possibility. I would hate to see that boy get broke down."

"Yessir."

"Well…" Russ let it trail off when it became clear to him that Zach had no immediate solution. He began chopping at the weeds. Zach crushed out his smoke, put the butt in his pocket and resumed hoeing.

"I reckon we'll think of something 'fore too much longer," he said.

45

# Chapter 10

Colby hoed. And hoed. And hoed some more.

He hated hoeing. Despised it. He hated hoeing with his whole body, heart and soul, with everything he ever was or ever could be.

For more than a solid, hard week, sunup to sundown, he had been hoeing and he hated it. He hated the word "hoe." He hated the weeds he hoed. He hated the dirt in which the weeds grew. He even hated the tobacco around which he hoed. He hated everything about the whole operation.

By the third day of hoeing, he hated hoeing even more than he hated the Brooklyn Dodgers.

He was now in his ninth day of hoeing and he hated it nine times as much as the first day.

When he had helped his father hoe, it hadn't been anywhere near this bad. It had been hard work but Colby remembered from last year that he and Vernon would start hoeing in the morning, they would talk a little, Colby would fantasize about playing baseball a while, they'd maybe talk a little more, then Colby would look up and they would be nearly done with a field. It didn't seem possible to Colby that his father had done that much more work. What drove Colby to nearly screaming frustration was the fact that he appeared to be getting nowhere. He would chop for hours and look up and it seemed that he was in the same row as when he started.

Worse, the sunny, moist weather caused the weeds to grow with a speed and purpose that truly scared Colby. The field in which he was working now needed hoeing badly and by the time he got to the back field, the weeds would be taking over, a fact that made Colby's stomach flutter, his heart race, and kept him working steadily through his loathing.

Tomorrow was Sunday and Colby wondered if it would be too big a sin to work after church. Reverend Tannehill said that Sunday was strictly a day of rest. Colby and his father had never worked on Sundays but, then, they hadn't ever needed to. Colby didn't want to sin and go to Hell, but he didn't want to sit around for a whole day watching the weeds grow.

He had just decided to ask the Reverend if it would be all right to work after church tomorrow when he heard a noise and looked up. David was on the edge of the field, under an apple tree, staring up into its branches. The noise he had heard was David poking cautiously at a branch with a stick, trying to run a robin out of its nest so that he could climb up and inspect the screeching nestlings inside. Colby went back to hoeing. David was always into something.

The baby robins were, in fact, of secondary importance to David. He had seen a robin's nest full of featherless baby birds before. No, he had been hanging around on the fringes of the field for most of the afternoon, trying to figure out a foolproof way of asking if he could work.

"Need some help Colby?" was all he had to say but he couldn't quite work up the nerve.

"Reckon that I might could try some hoeing Colby?" Naw. That wouldn't sound right either. David admired the ease and confidence with which Colby handled the hoe. He came so close to the tobacco plants each time that David wondered if Colby had to really concentrate on not hitting them. What must be going through his mind, David wondered. Was he thinking about the bank? About the weeds? About Daddy?

*Grayson steps back up to the plate. He looks like he's ready. The pitcher shakes off the sign. Again. He's ready. Here's the stretch, checking the runner at first. Here's the pitch. Grayson swings! It's a line shot to deep left center! The runner will score easily and and...here goes Grayson for third! He's trying to stretch it into a triple! Here's the throw from the center fielder! Grayson slides...and he's out! No wait, wait! He's safe! Safe at third and the Cincinnati Reds take a three to two lead! Colburn Grayson comes through in the clutch and the Reds surge in front in the ninth inning in this, the seventh game of the World Series...*

## CHAPTER 11

The next day, Colby stood in the churchyard, thinking. The preaching over, the congregation stood outside at the beginning of the socializing hour. The women stood together under the magnolia tree. From this spot they were still in sight of their men but were upwind and screened from the view of the mules and horses that pulled the wagons to church. The Reverend's car was parked in back of the church.

The children ran around screaming and laughing, unashamedly happy to be out of the church. Colby watched David and the twins play with an energy and raw happiness that they seemed to hoard for Sundays, as chores and the distance between farms made play during the week impossible.

The men gathered beneath the towering sweet gum tree in an imperfect circle and discussed their crops. The oldest man there, Elijah Settles, could not remember ever having a Sunday discussion that wasn't primarily about their tobacco crops.

The men rotated weekly magnanimity as they took turns providing the chewing tobacco. They would gather directly after the preaching, form their circle and exchange nods and greetings. Silence would ensue until one man would casually say, "You know, I wouldn't mind a chew of tobacco right about now." In their weekly stab at wryness, several would make an exaggerated show of checking their pockets. Then, after ten or fifteen seconds, one that hadn't provided the chew in a while would say, "Well, I might just have a little bit of chew on me here. You fellas care to join me?" He would open the new pouch and hand it to the man standing next to him. The provider of the week's tobacco would take his chew after it made it around the full circle.

The Reverend, although not a tobacco user himself, never spoke against their ritual. He realized that tobacco was the community's only source of income, and was in truth nearly the totality of their economy. While the women made a dramatic point of standing far enough away to avoid hearing the splatter as the men spit, the Reverend tolerated it with smiling good nature.

Asked once by one of the women why he allowed the men to spit on the grounds of the Lord's home, the Reverend mirthfully explained that the Sunday services conducted by his father's father in Virginia had sometimes lasted all day and included, as an integral part of worship, massive consumption of clear, unaged, sour mash whiskey. If the Lord could stand that, then surely He could stand a few men chewing on a leaf, couldn't He?

The Reverend didn't mention that his grandfather had also told young Lucas Tannehill, with a hand around the boy's neck, that more than one baby had been conceived behind the church after an all-day bout of semi-drunken Baptist worshipping, both copulators sweating and aglow with the rapture of the word of the Lord, or simple lust.

Bible in hand, he walked among the groups. Colby was trying to think of an acceptable way to ask the Reverend if he could work that afternoon. He had only one row left to hoe in the front field and was itching to get it done. Because it wouldn't take very long, Colby figured it couldn't be too much of a sin.

He was just about to approach the Reverend when the preacher suddenly turned and joined the men. Looking over at the tall figures, Colby realized that he had no group to join. He used to run and play with the other children but now that wouldn't be fitting. He wouldn't feel right standing among the men, and he most assuredly would not stand among the women.

Colby looked around and found, to his embarrassment, that he was standing alone, not a person within twelve feet. He felt that everyone was looking at him, wondering what kind of dang fool stands by himself after church. To his great relief, Reverend Tannehill left the men and approached Colby.

"How are you, Colby?" he asked.

"I'm alright, Reverend. How are you?"

"I'm fine, Colby. Thank you for asking." The Reverend smiled invitingly. It gave Colby courage.

"Reverend, there's something I've been aiming to ask you."

"And what would that be, Colby?"

"Well, you see, I might be falling just a little bit behind with my work and if that was the case, I was wondering whether or not it would be very sinful to work today."

"And what work is it that you would do on the Sabbath?"

"Well-sir, what I'd like to do is to finish hoeing my front field. I've only got one row left to do and I wouldn't really mind having it done today so that I could start fresh on the back field tomorrow morning."

"How much then is a man better than a sheep? Wherefore it is lawful to do well on the Sabbath days.' Matthew, 12:12. Are you doing well, Colby?" the Reverend asked.

"I reckon so, Reverend. There sure ain't too many weeds left in that daggone field."

The Reverend smiled at Colby and then walked silently away. Colby felt that he had maybe missed some point or another, but the Reverend had said that it would be lawful, so Colby's mind was eased.

49

That problem solved, he began thinking about his new dilemma. He knew he couldn't stand alone after church every Sunday, but he didn't know what else to do. He decided to study on it while he hoed this afternoon. His immediate solution was to simply leave the area, and so he walked towards the back of the church, hoping that anyone who noticed would assume he was going to the outhouse.

Russ Traylor watched him go and knew that Colby wasn't going to the outhouse.

The sounds of the children playing diminished as he walked down the side of the church. There was more shade back here and a cool, quiet serenity that Colby had never fully recognized. It was lonesome back here, lonesome but not sad. The trees were thick and just beyond the small clearing, the undergrowth grew heavy and tangled. The ground was shin-deep in dead leaves and stunted, shaggy growth. It smelled different back here too: cold but rich, dark but wholesome. He thought that out front was the place for people. Inside was the place for talking about God, but back here, amidst the cool green, was where God would probably rather be.

Colby walked to the Reverend's car and sat down on the back bumper. He could barely hear the people out front. To his left was the two-room add-on where Reverend Tannehill lived. Colby could smell the smoke from the Reverend's stove and the bacon that the Reverend had cooked that morning. From where he sat, he could see the few wagons, most drawn by mules. His own mule, Leviticus, stood in his stall in the big Grayson barn.

## Chapter 12

Six days later, Anne Grayson woke up alone in her bed with an odd feeling of chilly solitude. Was it the absence of Vernon or of little Annetta that made her feel so vaguely lonesome?

She was unable to luxuriate in the softness of her bed, to stretch and awaken slowly. She noticed how her stomach was fluttery and the shortness of her breath.

The music didn't come to her as it usually did upon waking. She hadn't felt this way in a long time, so it took a few moments for her to put a name on her feeling.

She was worried.

She was having, as the neighbors might call it, in low, guilty voices, one of her better days. She was quite lucid this morning and was suddenly keenly aware that her family needed help. They were in serious trouble. Why hadn't she realized it before?

With her sudden clarity, she knew that it would be nearly impossible for Colby to bring in Vernon's crop. Working this farm alone had made Vernon old beyond his years and he was the strongest man she had ever seen. It was that fact alone that had attracted her to him.

She knew that Colby possessed Vernon's strength, his stubbornness and, most importantly, his will, but he would need help. They all would.

Or maybe they should just sell the farm. She vaguely remembered the bankers coming and talking with Colby, but she had no idea what had been decided.

Anne rolled over in bed, pulled the covers up to her chin and looked out the window. Colby was doing the morning milking. What kind of deal had he struck with the bankers?

Already her head was beginning to hurt, and she longed for her smoky, undulating, soothing song.

Jason.

Jason would help. He would. He had to.

Jason was Anne's younger brother. She couldn't remember if he had been at the funeral or not. The last thing she heard was that he was living and working at Alladon Farm in Lexington, grooming thoroughbred racehorses. He was smart and, Anne knew, fond of her.

She was fond of Jason as well and, on days like this, even a bit envious. Of all the members of their dark and tortured family, only Jason had escaped to normality. She had no idea where her sister Lily was. Was it Florida? She wondered if Lily, too, listened to and used the song.

Jason didn't hear the song; he didn't need it. He would help. She decided to write a letter to him that afternoon. He would come down or write back, and he would know what to do. He was smart like that.

Sitting upright in her bed, with her clearest and most lucid thought in months, she decided not to delay, knowing that her mind could slip back to the musical place where things didn't count for real, where things were blurry, wispy and harmless.

She arose immediately and put on her robe. Armed with a pencil and a piece of David's school paper, she sat down at the kitchen table and, in surprisingly lovely script, she wrote:

> Dear Jason,
> As you mite no, Vernon is dead. I
> don't know what to do about the farm and
> other things and Colby is still yung. If
> you can make the time for it, wud you
> please come down to see us and tell us
> what we shud do? If not cud you pleese
> write? I am very worried.
> Yur Sister
> Anne Grayson

She folded the letter in half, then in half again, then walked into the front room and to Vernon's roll-top desk. It was a scarred but sturdy piece that had come from Vernon's father, Denton. It had so many drawers, slots and cubby holes that it took Anne a minute to find an envelope and a stamp. She addressed the envelope to Mister Jason Wagner, Alladon Farm, Lexington Kentucky.

Looking out the side window, she saw David leaning against the trash barrel. He appeared to be watching the barn. She walked to the front door, leaned out and yelled, "David! Come here, David. I've got a chore for you."

David stepped away from the trash barrel and looked more closely at the barn. His mother's voice bouncing off the huge barn's siding had confused him. It seemed as if she was calling from the barn where, to his knowledge, she had never once been. But David knew all about echoes and it took him only a second to figure out what was happening. He looked back at the house and there stood his mother.

This was the first time since his father's funeral that his mother had spoken to him directly or with any coherence. He ran to her.

"What can I do Mama?" he said as he reached the front door. Anne held the letter out to him.

"This letter here needs to be posted today. What I want you to do is to run over to the Traylors' place, give this letter to Russ or Dot and tell them to see that the carrier takes it with him today. You understand, David?"

"I understand Mama." He was so excited to have a job to do that he forgot to point out that the same mail carrier came by their house just after stopping at the Traylors'.

He took the letter and, waving it at her reassuringly, went off at a gallop. He noticed Colby coming out of the barn with the bucket in one hand and the lantern in the other. He slowed down enough so that Colby couldn't help but notice that he was off on an errand, then sped up again, envelope flailing conspicuously in front of him.

## CHAPTER 13

Just as Anne Grayson sat down to write to her brother, One-Eyed Zach began his morning walk up to the Traylors' house. He was ready to present Russ with a partial solution to the Grayson problem.

He had known pretty much what to do from the beginning, but he held back his idea for a couple of reasons. First, he wanted to see if maybe Russ would think of something. As the days rolled on, however, it became obvious that Russ was at a loss. They hadn't spoken of it but once, while hoeing. Second, for Zach's idea to work, he knew that Colby's pride had to be blunted, at least a little bit. Zach knew that there was nothing like working twelve or fourteen hours a day at a nearly impossible task to take the edge off a serious case of pride.

"Mornin' to you, Russ." Zach began rolling a cigarette as he reached the back porch.

"Morning, Zach. Did you have a good breakfast?"

Ritual dictated that Zach should answer affirmatively and describe what he ate, then he and Russ would discuss the merits or drawbacks of having that particular food in the morning, then they would talk about nearly anything unimportant while they finished their tobacco. But since this was Saturday, when they quit working at lunchtime, Zach wanted to give Russ plenty of time to consider the plan.

"Yessir, I did. You know Russ, I've kindly been studying on that Grayson problem and I just may have me an idea."

Russ spit into his coffee can and raised his eyebrows, inviting Zach to continue.

"Yessir and it's like this," Zach continued. "Even though Colby is now a farmer like you, he's still more of an equal to me, if you understand my meaning. But what I figure is that he's maybe thinking that he's an equal to you or the other farmers around here."

Russ nodded. "I would say that is so," he said.

"Well, sir, it seems to me that maybe it wouldn't hurt his pride so much taking help from me, as it would from you or another farmer."

"I'll say yes to that, Zach, but just to tell you the truth, I don't see him taking help from anybody. You've been around here long enough to know how that bunch is."

"Yessir and I reckon that's where it might get a little bit tricky. You remember what we was saying about helping him so's he don't really know for sure that he's being helped?"

"I do."

"Well, what we'd have to do is make out like he was doing you a favor by letting me work for him."

"And just how do you reckon we'd do that?" Russ inquired, intrigued.

"The way I got it figured is this. You and me ain't never run into so much work around here that we can't handle it. Ain't that true?"

"That is true," Russ agreed.

"Well, then, it's also true that along about cutting time, we got as much work as we can handle and maybe a little bit more." Zach paused, waiting for Russ to agree. Russ nodded and Zach continued. "Then what we got to do is to offer that boy a trade. What you could offer him is to swap me working for him now, for him working for you 'round about cutting time. That ain't charity on your part, nor does it even seem like it. It's a fair swap, fair enough anyway."

Zach took a deep drag off his cigarette and looked off to the side of the house. After fifteen years of working side-by-side with Russ, he knew that his employer couldn't really study on anything if you were looking directly at him. Zach remained silent, unacknowledged, until his cigarette was smoked and the butt was in his pocket. Still he waited silently. It usually didn't take Russ this long to make a decision. Zach thought that he knew what was bothering Russ about the proposal.

"The way I got it figured is that you just pay me half wages on the days that I help that boy. That way, we both be giving something."

Russ now looked directly at Zach, as if being snapped out of a daydream. "Naw. It ain't that Zach. It ain't that at all. I'll still be paying a full day's wage if you're doing a full day's work." Russ stood up with the coffee can, walked to the edge of the porch and threw the tobacco juice into the grass.

"It's a good plan and I'll bring it up to Colby at church tomorrow. Ain't a reason in the world I can think of that it won't work."

"Good. I think it ought to work, too but, if you don't mind me asking, I'm wondering what you was pondering for so long just now."

"Well Zach, I was thinking that it might not be a bad thing that it took so long to come up with a plan. I figure that after two hard weeks of hoeing and work like he's had, he won't be near so ready to turn down a deal like this. A couple of hundred or so hours of hoeing is bound to take some pride out of a young man."

Zach smiled as he began following Russ down the path to the tool shed.

"Yessir, I would say that is so," he said.

55

## Chapter 14

While Zach and Russ discussed him and as David ran to the Traylors' farm with his mother's letter, Colby was returning to the barn after delivering the bucket of milk to the house. Too wrapped up in revising his work schedule for the day, he failed to notice the clear and unfogged look his mother had given him.

Most mornings, Colby would bring the milk in, then relax until breakfast was ready and maybe listen to the farm report on the radio. Last night, however, he had taken a good look at the vegetable garden, which he hadn't touched in well over two weeks. In most of the rows, the weeds were far bigger and healthier looking than the crops. There was only a row and a half left to be hoed in the back tobacco field, so he decided now to finish the half row before breakfast, even if that meant eating cold eggs. By the end of the day, he must be finished with the back field and at least half of the vegetable garden.

The indisputable fact that he would soon have to begin hoeing again in the front field kept him from enjoying his temporary advantage over the weeds.

Then there was the matter of the chicken house. It was beginning to smell horrible, especially on the warmer days and he would have to clean it out soon. He had helped his father do this chore on at least three occasions but could not remember how it was done. Did they sweep it out and let it air? Did they use water and soap? Should he leave the nests be, or put in fresh straw? All he knew was that it took the two of them half a day to do it, meaning it would take Colby a whole day, time he hated to give over to the weeds.

Ten hours later, Colby had finished the back field and made a good jump on the vegetable garden. But the awful shape of the chicken house caused him to look nervously at all the other non-daily chores. The grass around the house would be up to his knees soon. During a heavy rain storm two days ago, Colby had noticed the barn roof leaking in more than a few places. Vernon had mentioned the work needed on the barn roof but there was never time. The trash barrel was rusty and worn through near the bottom. When Colby had burned their trash the day before, there seemed to be as many flames licking out the sides as spouting from the top. Colby hadn't a clue where to get new one or where to get the money to pay for it.

Money. Not having seen much of it, Colby had never given it much thought, but the sacks of corn meal and flour were shrinking and the pinto beans were going too. He hoped his mother had some money around somewhere, but he didn't ask her for fear that there was none. Every time he thought about money, he thought about the bank and the note due, and he always became sick with worry.

This continuous litany of worrisome items had charged him with enough nervous energy to make this his most productive day since his father's death.

It wasn't until three furiously worked hours after lunch that Colby was able to gratefully slide into the clear, raucous world of heroism on the baseball diamond.

How glorious it was to be back there, in the place where he was cheered and adored by thousands; where they chanted his name so loudly that he could feel the dugout vibrate; where the grass was green and mowed daily; where the flying dirt signified yet another diving, phenomenal play by Colby; where the pennants flew high and breezy beneath a sky that was so astonishingly blue that it was of itself enough of a reason to come to the ballpark; where he was more than a man, if less than a God; where Colby the baseball hero was the last, grasping hope of the desperately screaming fans; where he was among many, brandishing the Louisville Slugger, instead of here, alone in a field, holding the callous sanded oak handle of his father's hoe; where Colby the farmer found his only peace of mind.

In the predawn darkness of that morning, Colby had wearily and absentmindedly smashed his knee into the door of Doris's stall. It hadn't bled but a minute, but it did give him more fuel for his baseball fantasies.

It was game four of the World Series and he had sprained his knee sliding into home to win the game. His leg was swollen and painful and the doctors whispered sadly about ligament tears. They said that Colby would be out at least until the beginning of next season. The fans were understandably disappointed but held no ill will towards Colby. A man, after all, had limits. The hard-hitting shortstop had almost single-handedly given the Reds a lead of three games to one and he was satisfied—he didn't want all the glory for himself. His teammates could handle things from here; but the Reds lost game five in Brooklyn and brought their now one-game lead back to Cincinnati.

Game six was a colossal disaster. The second-string shortstop committed four errors and went zero for five. The game was a humiliating rout, ending 9-0, Brooklyn.

With the Series thus tied at three games apiece, Colburn Grayson hobbled on crutches into the Reds dressing room on the morning of the seventh and deciding game. To the astonished gasps of the assembled reporters and the boisterous cheers of his teammates, he set the crutches aside and began putting on his uniform…

"Colby! Hey Colby!" David was a few feet away, yelling loudly until Colby finally looked up.

"Boy oh boy! I thought you'd gone deaf, Colby," David said.

Colby smiled at his brother. "I was just thinking about something. What's wrong? Is supper ready?"

"No." David shook his head. "I was just wondering if you was meaning to do that," he said, pointing at Colby's feet. Colby looked down and saw, to his horror, that he had chopped the carrot tops out of twenty feet of the row. His first thought was that if his father was here, he would get a hard slap for not paying attention, then realized that he still wished his father was here. Only David's presence kept Colby from succumbing to the fierce tears that raged within him.

He put his back to the westering sun and looked off into the sad heights of the mountains. Despair, kept precariously at bay by baseball fantasies, crashed like wet thunder into Colby. How did he think he could bring in a huge tobacco crop when he couldn't even keep from stupidly chopping down the vegetables? He had barely an idea of how to clean the hen house and no clue at all how to fix the barn roof. Mr. White and Mr. Scott were right. He should just sell the dang farm and give up and buy a small…

"Colby?" For the second time in as many minutes, David interrupted his brother's desperate thoughts.

"It's all right David. I'm all right."

"Well, I know that. I was just thinking, though."

Now Colby turned towards David, again in full control of himself. "What?" he asked.

"Well…I just been kind of thinking you know, just thinking maybe that how school is almost…you know, over and everything…and how there might be some things that I could, you know, do, like maybe helping you hoe some. Since Daddy died, I know we got an extra hoe. So that's what I was thinking…" David finished mumbling, kicking miserably at the dirt, sure that Colby's silent stare meant that he was trying not to laugh. He had no way of knowing that his brother's silence signified precisely the opposite.

*Help. Help unlooked for and unhoped for and it had been in front of him the whole time. Willing help, willing and eager and here he stood, anxious to take at least some of Colby's burden.*

Colby had never in his life been so emotionally overwhelmed. He had to grit his teeth as he said thickly, "Sure, David. I could use some help. I sure could."

"You ain't kidding, Colby? There's lots I could do besides hoeing, you know. I know how to do the milking. And I could gather the eggs. Shoot,

Timothy could even gather eggs if you told him to be real extra special careful not to drop any. And you know what?"

"What?" Colby said, smiling at David's contagious enthusiasm.

"I know how to hook Leviticus up to the wagon and to the plow and he likes me 'bout as well as anybody, so most of the time I won't even have to fuss at him to get him to do what I want. Heck, school's almost over. I could even start tomorrow if you wanted me to."

Colby gave it genuine consideration. "How much longer exactly have you got left?" he asked.

"Next week is the last week but I think I've already learned about most of everything I'm supposed to learn this year. I got all A's," David said.

Colby was truly surprised. "You got all A's?"

"Heck, yes, I did. I always get all A's. I used to sometimes wish that they'd put me in with older classes but I figured it wouldn't be exactly right to be putting myself forward and all."

Colby thought a moment longer, then decided.

"Well, why don't you just go on and finish out the year but until it's over, I'll tell you what, why don't you take over the afternoon milking? You know how to milk and about the bucket and the stool and all?"

"Shoot, yes, Colby. I milked Doris lots of times. Remember when you got the influenza last winter? I milked Doris ten or twelve times then. And I won't mind getting up early to do the morning milking when school's over, either. Most mornings, I wake up when you do and can't get back to sleep anyway."

Colby was getting ready to respond when his brother's smile disappeared. "David," he whispered, "turn around real slow and look at that tree line that separates our farm from the Traylors'."

David turned slowly, as instructed and saw what had caught Colby's attention. Grazing under an oak tree was the largest buck deer either of them had ever seen.

"Geez, Colby. I ain't never seen a deer that big," David whispered. "You want me to go in the house and get the rifle?"

Colby continued looking as the stag lifted its head and sniffed the wind.

"Naw, David. I reckon not," he said, staring at the deer.

"That's an awful lot of meat on that deer, Colby."

"Yes, it is, but that rifle ain't nothing but a twenty-two."

"So?"

Now Colby finally did look at David. "So a twenty-two ain't enough gun to kill that buck shooting from here. I reckon I could hit him from here but it wouldn't do for me to put a couple of longs in him and him run off alive but suffering. That was one thing Daddy was always right clear about. He always told me that guns was for killing and nothing else. He said that I shouldn't even take it off the wall if I wasn't aiming to kill with it." Colby looked hard at David, motionless but decisive. "I reckon that's something you ought to remember, too, David."

"I'll remember, Colby. You ever killed with the rifle?" David asked. He knew full well that Colby had killed with the rifle, that he himself had eaten the meat provided by Colby and the twenty-two but David was anxious to keep the conversation alive.

"Sure I have. Possums and 'coons and a groundhog or two."

David still looked at him expectantly. Colby was pleased with the attention, but it didn't last long. The memory of the rabbit kept Colby from any thoughts of becoming a mighty hunter.

Two years ago, just as Colby had begun to help his father full-time, Vernon had showed Colby how to load and shoot the rifle. His father had told him that any animal with fur was food, except for a skunk or rats or anything smaller, and that if Colby could bring it down, they would eat it. Colby had gone out alone with the gun that night and seen a single rabbit grazing at the back field. Despite Vernon's admonition to shoot only if he was sure that he would kill his prey, Colby had fired.

He knew that he had hit his target when he saw the rabbit flip violently over in an inelegant, bloody somersault. Exhilerated with the knowledge that he had provided meat for his family, he had sprinted to the far edge of the back field to collect his furry prize, but he found only a few tiny drops of blood. There was no rabbit and Colby knew that it had limped away.

Colby found the rabbit about ten days later. He had been picking up rocks out of the back field and putting them in a wheelbarrow. He had already filled the wheelbarrow three times and it wasn't yet ten o'clock. He had just picked up the first rock of the fourth load when he saw the rabbit.

It was still alive. Its left hind leg was hairless and swollen and Colby could smell the rotten infection from ten feet away. He had stepped closer, wanting to make sure that it was breathing, hoping, praying that it wasn't.

It looked directly at him, eyes empty, vacant, its chest rising and falling rapidly. Was it longing for death or was that Colby's imagination? He knew with sickening shame that he could not release the rabbit from its suffering.

Demoralized and disgraced, he walked away, painfully aware of the rabbit's misery but no less aware of the necessity of hunting.

He had slept little that night and the next day went back to end the rabbit's suffering, but found only the gnawed and bloody skull and three of its four paws.

"I'll tell you what, David. Why don't you take that rifle out this evening? Maybe even take Tim-Bug with you. You shoot us a rabbit or a 'coon and Mama will cook it right up. You know how to load it and such?"

"Well, I seen you loading it and I reckon I could figure it out without too much trouble."

"All right, then, but just remember, don't go shooting at nothing for the fun of it. If you're going to shoot at something, you best be sure that you're going to kill it. Understand?"

"Sure I understand, Colby. And I'll take over on that milking tomorrow. Just see if I don't. I know you've got lots of things to do but milking's not going to be one of them anymore." David grinned, eager and proud.

"Sure, David. I know you will. Sure I do." he said.

## CHAPTER 15

The preaching was done, the women milled by the magnolia, the children played, the men gathered in their circle and again Colby was without a place. Unlike last week, when he had waited around for the Reverend, today he had no place to be and was left with only the awkwardness. The Reverend was nowhere to be found, and he was just about to walk back to the cool and peaceful spot behind the church when he heard his name.

"Colby. Hey, Colby. C'mon over here a minute, will you?" Russ said with a beckoning hand, inviting him to join the circle.

Colby was seized with an intense shyness that he hadn't felt in years. He was intimidated by the pack of tall men. Still, being there would be better than being alone. He walked over, looking as many in the eye as he could. He reached the group and Russ brought him into their discussion.

"Well, Colby, we were just talking about hoeing. Every one of us here and you, too, I suspect, ain't been doing too much besides hoeing the last two, three weeks," Russ said.

"Nothing but hoeing," Colby agreed.

"Well, what we were discussing was how often is often enough to sharpen your hoe. Now myself, I have One-Eyed Zach sharpen my hoes twice a week. Big Tom there says he don't do it but maybe twice a month, while Old Man Tom there says he don't never sharpen his hoe, says it makes it last longer."

"It's the truth," Old Man Tom said. "I've been using the same durn hoe for twenty-three years. It's on its third handle, but I'd just bet a man that it'll last another twenty."

"And I'd just bet a man that you won't last another twenty," Big Tom said, getting a laugh from all.

"Well Colby, how about you settling this for us. How often ought a man to sharpen his hoe?" Russ asked.

Colby looked up at him, grateful and nervous. "Wellsir, I do it the way Daddy taught me to. I sharpen it every day, but I don't hone it like I would a knife. I hit it a lick or two with the file, just enough to bring out some fresh metal. Daddy said that way you could have it sharp enough to work with but you weren't wearing it out for nothing," he said.

The men made a grand performance of agreeing with Colby, acknowledging the wisdom of the departed Vernon.

"The way Vernon worked I'm surprised he didn't use up a hoe every day," Elijah Settles said through a sad and toothless grin.

"Yessir," Old Man Tom agreed. "Only Colby there could say for certain, but I heard it said that when Vernon hoed a field, it stayed hoed. The daggone weeds were too scared of him to grow back." This turned the grins into laughs. It was an old joke, said about many a stout man but it made Colby proud and he laughed the loudest.

They talked on, discussing the toughest type of weed to kill off, the quickest growing, the thickest growing and the most damaging. On every point, someone, most often Russ, made it a point to ask Colby his opinion.

He was so glad to be an accepted member of the group that he didn't hear E. E. Robinson remark on how good a chew would be right about now. Colby became aware of his predicament only when Spencer Kirk pulled a bag of Mail Pouch out of his back pocket, saying, "Well I might just have me a little here…"

Spencer was directly across the circle from Colby but still only eight men remained between Colby and the tobacco pouch that was making its steady way toward him.

With a steadily rising panic, Colby watched as one man after the other took a modest chaw and passed the pouch down.

The men were still cutting up, pleased with their success at including Colby in their group, as Russ had asked them to do, and none noticed the white look of raw, barely contained panic on Colby's face.

The boy was thinking that, if he were to be a member of this group, he should participate in its rituals but he had never tried tobacco. Often told tales of boys getting violently sick, combined with the stingingly sweet smell, had made Colby duly wary of chewing tobacco.

Mr. Robinson had the tobacco now, next would be Lawrence Norvell, then Elijah Settles, then Russ, then Colby.

It was passed to Mr. Norvell as Colby looked around for the Reverend. He could tell the men that he had to speak with the Reverend about something and thereby avoid chewing without losing face. The Reverend was with the women, deep in smiling, tranquil conversation. There was no help there.

As it was passed to Mr. Settles, Colby looked toward where the children played, briefly considered abandoning his new status for running and playing with the kids, anything to avoid the shame of vomiting because of a nicotine overdose in front of these men. He had miserably decided to take a chew and act like he had an outhouse emergency. They would know he was faking but that was better than relinquishing his current station. So deep was his panic that for the second time in a week, he didn't notice Russ looking at him.

Russ knew what it was like to be sick on tobacco. It had happened to him two or three times when he was a kid no older than Colby and it was a type of sick that he wouldn't wish on anyone.

"You know what? I believe that my breakfast ain't exactly agreeing with me this morning. I think I'll take a pass on the chew," Russ said, handing the pouch to Colby.

Colby was not so panicked that he failed to recognize his sweet deliverance, like a cloudless dawn after a black and hopeless night.

"You know what? I probably ought not to have eaten that third egg this morning because my breakfast don't seem to be sitting just right either. I think I might take a pass, too," Colby said and handed the tobacco carelessly to his right. Big Tom took it, wondering why Russ had passed. It had never happened before. Some even said that a good chew settled an upset stomach.

Big Tom, steady as any if slower than some, opened his mouth to ask Russ why he didn't take any when he felt an elbow thud harmlessly into his ribs.

"Either take a chew or pass it on, Big Tom," James Caudill said. He was next in line, owner of the elbow and fully aware of what had just occurred. "You think I got all day to wait around on free chew, especially free chew provided by Spencer Kirk? Why such a thing ain't happened in my memory, Spencer Kirk being rich enough and all to buy tobacco for all his poor friends," he said and winked plainly at Spencer. Big Tom looked at Spencer, then at James, then at the tobacco. It dawned on him.

"Sorry James," Big Tom said. "It's just that with Spence providing it and all, I was wanting to make sure it wasn't some old maple leaves with sorghum poured on top. Y'all know how tight Spence is," Big Tom said, grinning and taking his chew. Spencer grinned back.

"Don't reckon you'd know the difference, Big Tom," he said.

Colby smiled, then laughed watching the tobacco make its round.

Later, he couldn't say how long he stood among them. It seemed both eternally slow and lightning fast. He was one of them, laughing with men, nodding in sage agreement with men, his opinion sought and valued and the respect that he gave candidly returned. It was one of the chief moments of his life and he had only one regret, small and insignificant though it was. Most of the men chewed and Colby determined to learn how to chew also, so that his place among them would be authentic; official and without question.

Thirty minutes later, their chews spent, the men began herding children, nodding at wives and organizing for the trip home. Colby didn't want the circle to end, but knew that it must. He looked over at the running bunch of children, trying to catch David's eye so that the younger boy would go collect Tim-Bug and Baby-Anne.

The group of men had dispersed, and Colby was ready to walk over to his mother when he felt Russ's hand on his shoulder.

"Colby, before you go, could I have a word?" he asked. Colby looked once more for David, then looked at Russ and nodded.

"Well, surely, Mr. Traylor," he replied.

"Colby, I was wanting to talk a little business for a second. It's nothing too serious, so I reckon the Reverend wouldn't mind, even if he knew."

Colby looked over the rapidly thinning crowd, finally caught David's eye, then realized that Russ was waiting for a response. "Okay, Mr. Traylor. What is it?"

"Well, Colby, I was maybe wanting to offer you a bit of a trade if you were willing."

"Don't reckon I have much to trade with, just to tell you the truth."

"I wouldn't say that is so. See, what I'm thinking about trading isn't goods but labor," Russ said, trying hard to treat Colby as judiciously as he would any other man. He was concerned when Colby waved his hand with a helpless laugh.

"I couldn't help you now for any amount of money. I'm putting in a good amount of hours every day and I still ain't on top of my work."

"That don't surprise me much," Russ answered, "Not because you ain't working hard but because I know that there's a right smart work to do over at your place, especially if a man is working alone like you are. But I got help at my place. You've seen One-Eyed Zach before."

"I have."

"Well sir, once we get on top of these weeds, I won't have too durn much for him to do. But at the end of this summer, there'll be enough work for him, me and a man or two besides."

"Ain't that why all the farmers kick in and help one another cut and house?" Colby asked.

"That is so. We all help one another when it comes to cutting and housing but I'm talking about even before that. Both my barns are older than yours and I have a good bit of work to do on them every year before housing. Plus, I like to do some cutting on my own, before everything really gets going. It wouldn't seem quite fair if I didn't, seeing as how I raise a good bit more tobacco than most."

"So you was thinking I could help you then?" Colby inquired.

"I was."

"And in trade you'd what? Help me now?"

"Not me. I'd send Zach over for the day, say on Tuesdays and a half day on Fridays."

Russ watched Colby while trying to appear only marginally interested in whether or not Colby agreed. Had he made the offer a little too generous?

"Reckon I'd be feeding Zach his lunch on Tuesdays. Fridays too?" Colby asked.

Russ pondered this but not for the reason that Colby thought he did.

"I think it would be fitting for you to feed him on Fridays after he's worked for you all morning. I can tell you for sure that he don't really eat much at lunchtime. He's like me, big ole breakfast and even bigger supper and not a whole lot in between. What do you say, Colby? We got us a deal?"

"No, we ain't traded just yet, Russ." Neither of them noticed his use of the first name. "I don't mind admitting I could use the help now but the way I see it is that I might have just as much work at summer's end as I have now and I'd be obligated to help you."

Russ hadn't thought of this and wondered if Zach had.

Colby looked around again and saw that David had Tim-Bug and Baby-Anne corralled and standing next to Mama. Russ saw where he was looking.

"That is so, Colby, but let's do this. That oldest boy over there, his name's David, isn't it?"

"It is."

"Looks like he's old enough to work."

At this, Colby brightened.

"Sure is. I'm going to start him on the milking and some hoeing right after school's over," Colby said proudly.

"That's fine, Colby. I would say that he looks like a stout boy. What I would say is to leave him in charge of your place when you're gone or to bring him along when you're working at my place. That way you'll pay me off twice as fast."

Colby glanced up at Russ, thinking. He was exhilarated yet uncomfortable thinking of David as an asset. He wanted to pretend that he was pondering the offer, weighing the pros and cons in a shrewd and businesslike manner but he knew that he would accept. He had an uneasy suspicion that he was being given more than he would give back but to have help, a man's help, for however long each week, was more than he could turn down.

"I'll do it, Russ. We'll keep track and swap out day for day, me and Zach and if it's work that David can do, we'll swap out two days for one."

"That sounds like a good deal for both of us, Colby," Russ said. "I'll send One-Eyed Zach over this coming Tuesday."

"That sounds about right to me. How did Zach lose that eye anyway-he ever tell you?"

"He never did tell me Colby and I never had the occasion to ask."

## CHAPTER 16

When Tuesday morning rolled around, Colby was nervous about his appearance for One-Eyed Zach. Although he was running a farm, he was still only thirteen years old and not ashamed to admit, if only to himself, that he would feel uneasy issuing orders to a grown man. What would he do if Zach was disagreeable about whatever work Colby proposed they do? Even more worrisome, what if Zach came in, looked around and then tried to tell Colby what needed to be done? Surely Zach's experience and views would be an asset, but Colby had strong ideas about what he wanted done first.

The sun was struggling up to the fence tops and Colby, done with the morning milking, was sitting at the kitchen table. David sat there, too. He had noisily left his bed at the same time Colby had, just as he had done yesterday, proving to Colby that when school let out at the end of the week, it would be no hardship on him to do the morning milking.

Colby was only vaguely aware that he was chewing nervously on his thumbnail and even less aware that David was chewing on his own thumbnail, solely for imitation.

Mama was shuffling efficiently around the kitchen, cooking breakfast while singing so softly to herself that she may as well have been underneath the quilted bedspread that had covered her and Vernon's bed since their wedding day.

Neither Colby nor David even noticed her singing, any more than they would notice someone else's breathing. It was simply part of what made Anne their mama.

"Mama?" Colby said.

Anne looked around at Colby. She didn't answer but did stop singing. That was answer enough to Colby.

"We're going to have an extra at lunch today. Hear? I got a hired hand coming today and we'll need to feed him lunch. Okay?"

"I'll make some extra beans, but they won't last forever," Anne said. Colby took his thumbnail out of his mouth and chuckled.

"Well, they don't have to last forever, Mama, just till lunchtime," Colby said, looking over at David to see if his comment was worth a laugh. David shook his head uneasily and pointed at the bean bag in the corner. Colby was shocked to see no more than two or three pounds left of the fifty-pound bag.

Colby wearily realized that he had been purposely avoiding the corner where the bean bag was kept. He knew that they had been eating beans every day for at least a week but hadn't had the energy to wonder why.

"Mama? How much cornmeal we got left?" Colby asked. Anne cracked eggs into the skillet and sang.

Colby looked at David, who shrugged his shoulders and grinned uncertainly. He wasn't sure whether they were having fun with Mama or not.

"Mama?" Colby said, sitting up straighter.

"Yes?" she said finally.

"How much cornmeal we got left?"

"Plenty of cornmeal, but when you go into town to pick up the beans, you should also get some sugar. We're near out. Also salt. It wouldn't hurt none to stop by Old Man Tom's place and get us a good big bucket of lard either. I can't make any decent corn cakes without lard."

Old Man Tom was the only hog farmer within walking distance of town.

Colby opened his mouth to ask Mama where Daddy had kept the money but just then Baby-Anne walked sleepily into the kitchen and sat down. He surely didn't want to find out in front of David and Baby-Anne that there might not be any money. He felt his heartbeat quicken and the panic rise.

"I'm hungry. What's for breakfast?" Baby-Anne asked.

Despite his concern, Colby smiled at Baby-Anne. There was food now and there would be food for lunch and tonight. As soon as he could get Mama alone, he would ask her if there was any money.

"Well, Baby-Anne, we're having possum tails for breakfast, but don't you worry none, the way Mama cooks them, they taste just like eggs," he kidded.

David laughed and Baby-Anne looked at Colby sleepily, willing to play along. "You telling me Mama's got some nasty old possum tails in that skillet?" Baby-Anne knew, as she often knew things, that Colby was in his state of barely controlled panic.

"She surely does but these is special possum tails. They look just exactly like fried eggs," Colby added.

"That's right, Annetta." David added, smiling broadly. "Tastes just exactly like a fried egg. It's the durndest thing. If you didn't know you was eating possum tails, you'd swear it was fried eggs."

Colby was getting ready to embellish his story, trying to add to his success, when Tim walked in. He was already quite awake, although still wearing only the flannel underwear pants that he always slept in.

"I bet we ain't having no possum tails for breakfast," he argued. "Possum ain't barely fit to eat, and I know when you clean a possum you leave its tail with its skin and guts."

"What do you know about cleaning a possum?" Colby asked.

"I helped Daddy clean one once. Well, I watched him clean one and…well, it wasn't no possum. It was a squirrel, but I bet there ain't much difference. And you know what else, Colby?" Tim asked.

"What?"

"David said you was going to give him the rifle and let him hunt and I'm going to go with him and clean whatever he kills. You reckon we might could go hunting this afternoon?"

"It's fine with me. David, you said you know all about the rifle, right? How to load it and carry it and all?"

"Sure, I do, Colby."

"Good. You be sure and show Tim-Bug how to use it, so's I don't have to worry about y'all none. Okay?"

"Sure, I will. And I won't shoot at nothing unless I'm sure to kill it." David turned seriously toward Tim. "It's very important to remember that, Tim. Don't shoot at nothing unless you're going to kill it. Remember that." He had almost called him Tim-Bug but that was Colby's name for him. "I'll bet we bring home a rabbit or two at least, won't we, Tim?"

Tim nodded vigorously. "Yessiree. Cleaned and ready for the skillet. Colby?"

"What, Tim-Bug?"

"To properly clean a rabbit, you need a good sharp knife," the boy replied.

"Yessir. That's a fact," Colby agreed.

"Well, Daddy's good pocketknife has been sitting there on his desk since…well, since, you know, he went away and all and I know you got your own knife. If I was to have that knife, I'd keep it sharp and clean and oiled up and slicker'n a whistle. I sure would."

Colby thought for a minute. It was true he had a knife of his own, his grandfather Denton's knife, a gift from Vernon last Christmas. He wondered if the knife should go to David, as the next oldest but saw no jealousy in David's eyes.

"So then, David will shoot them and you'll clean them with your new knife. That's how it's going to be?"

Tim could only nod excitedly. He didn't notice David smiling and nodding, too.

"Okay then. The whetstone's out on the workbench in the barn. After you get done sharpening the knife, you make sure to put the stone right back where you got it, understand?"

"I do. I will!" Tim said, then jumped up and ran into the front room. He came back carrying the knife, looking at it and nothing else.

Colby watched him with his new prize, delighting in Tim-Bug's delight.

Colby had forgotten his nervousness about Zach coming to help.

Mama put the eggs and biscuits on the table, then went back into her bedroom. Colby and the children ate the food and drank the milk that was still warm from Doris.

## CHAPTER 17

"Well, sir, I reckon that you'd be Colby," Zach said.

"Yessir and you're Zach, I reckon," Colby said, looking up from the workbench. He had been sharpening the other hoe, the one he himself once used.

Zach stood silently just outside the barn door, a smile on his face. Colby froze for a minute, unsure. Should he walk over and shake his hand, go back to the task at hand, or instruct Zach to finish sharpening the hoe?

"Gettin' you a good edge on that hoe, are you?" Zach asked.

"Yeah, I reckon I am. I was thinking that maybe we might could do some hoeing today," Colby said and nervously and redundantly held the hoe up as evidence.

"Yessir, them old weeds do want a minding, don't they?" Zach said with a chuckle.

"Boy, do they. Can't hardly seem to keep up with 'em sometimes." Colby said, starting to chuckle a bit himself, yet not wanting to admit that the work was getting to him. He was relieved when Zach laughed out loud and stepped through the door and into the barn.

"Well Colby, I'd say that you surely aren't the only farmer in these parts that do some mighty battlin' with the weeds. If I could just figure me out a use for them weeds, I swear to you that I'd get me some land and not never even try to grow tobacco, I'd just harvest weeds. Know I'd have me one heck of a crop, too," Zach said. He stopped two steps from Colby and held out his hand. Without thought or hesitation, Colby handed him the hoe.

"Yessir," Zach said, "I've held one of these a time or two before. Reckon you have, too."

"A time or two," Colby said, then stepped to the wall where the tools hung and retrieved his hoe—the one that Vernon used to use. He turned and looked at Zach, still reluctant to issue an order. Zach waited a moment before motioning with a nod of his head toward the Traylor farm.

"I noticed walking over here this morning that your back field looks to be in right good shape," he offered.

"You know I'm going to feed you your lunch today, right?" Colby asked, as if just remembering.

"Well, sir, I kind of figured you was."

"And Mama makes real good beans, too."

"Can't think of anything I'd rather eat for lunch than a good big bowl of beans. Them brown beans seem to have a way of sticking with a man through the afternoon, keep him from getting hungry before suppertime," Zach said.

"Well then, I reckon we'd best start chopping some weeds in the front field. I got a good jump on them yesterday so I figure that with the both of us working we might just get it half done today. I wouldn't mind if we did. I swear I wouldn't mind at all," Colby said. He nodded and started walking out of the barn. Zach stepped back to let him pass, then fell in behind him and they walked up the slag path with their hoes over their shoulders.

Colby's initial nervousness turned gradually into relief, and then gratitude as he worked with Zach. Colby found that he enjoyed working with the one-eyed old man. He was surprised to find that just talking and even laughing and cutting up a bit while you worked made the day slide by even faster than baseball fantasies did.

Zach was not what Vernon used to call a jabberer, but he did like to talk with an unassuming, easy air while he worked. He could ask questions without being nosy; tell interesting stories about places he had been without bragging and state his opinion strongly but with humility. Before they had worked even two hours, Colby was completely at ease, talking and even laughing at some of Zach's tales.

A few minutes before noon, Colby looked up and around the field. They had made enormous headway. If they did as much work that afternoon, they would have hoed nearly three-quarters of the field. He would easily be finished with it by Thursday, and when Zach came back for his half day on Friday, Colby could easily find other work for him.

Zach seemed smart and able, and Colby had no problem tapping Zach's experience. It was, after all, an even swap with Russ, and Colby acknowledged that he was in a position where he had to fully utilize all of his assets, and Zach's experience was now one of Colby's assets. Colby guessed that Zach knew how to clean a hen house and fix a barn roof. The vegetable garden wasn't looking as it should and Colby decided to tackle that task on Friday. If the worse came to worst, he knew that his family could live a long time on the cucumbers and yellow squash and green beans that were nearly ready to pick, but the corn wasn't doing so well and the tomato plants were small.

The thought of food reminded Colby of the nearly empty bean sack and the empty lard bucket. Mama could make corn bread with milk and eggs and they wouldn't miss the lard but would Zach notice? They sure couldn't have biscuits without lard. Thinking of the lard made Colby think of the hams that Old Man Tom sold or traded and realized that his mouth was watering just thinking of it. His family had not eaten meat in a while.

If David didn't have any luck hunting, then he would go out himself and bag a rabbit or a raccoon, maybe even a groundhog.

"Well, Zach, you about ready for some lunch?" Colby asked.

"I sure am, Colby. I can smell those beans from way out here," he said with a laugh.

"Let's go, then. What I usually do is just to lean my hoe up against the house next to my shoes. Mama ain't too particular about most things but she does like to keep her floors clean."

## CHAPTER 18

The first thing Zach noticed upon entering Colby's house was that the curtains were drawn shut, shutting out the sun on such a bright, breezy day.

The second thing he noticed, as they walked through the front room and into the kitchen, was Anne, who appeared not to notice their entrance. She was preparing lunch while whispering a song that Zach could almost identify, like a song he had heard years ago and forgotten entirely until hearing this delicate reminder. Somehow the song made him uncomfortable.

"Mama? This is Zach. I don't think you ever met him before. He's the one that I hired on part-time, the one I told you was going to be eating lunch with us today."

Anne went on singing for a moment, long enough to put some home canned tomato relish in a bowl and a pickled onion on a saucer. She was about to put both the dishes on the table when she stopped her song and looked directly at Zach.

"Yes. Lunch. We're having beans. Won't you sit down? I made this relish myself, last year I think," she said. She seemed frozen to the floor, halfway between the counter and the table. The frightened, nearly panicked look on her face and her posture made Zach more uncomfortable than the singing had. He quickly sat down on the far side of the table.

"Yes ma'am. Relish. I do like a good relish on my beans. I sure do," he said with a slow nod and a smile. Anne did not move, her eyes on Zach.

Zach realized that he was making the poor woman nervous, so he looked down at the ground, then turned his head slowly to look out the kitchen window. Colby sat down and Anne finally made her way to the table. She set down the dishes and turned to the oven.

"We're having cornbread too, and Mama makes real good cornbread. And fresh butter, too. Mama always adds a little extra salt to it, makes it real tasty. Ain't that right, Mama?" Colby asked but noticed, as his mother opened the oven door, that she had resumed singing. He saw the coffeepot, on and steaming, next to the beans on the stove. Colby was both relieved and shocked that she had thought to make coffee.

74

"Zach, would you like a cup of coffee with your lunch?" he asked.

"Yessir, don't mind if I do," he said, then asked quietly, "Should I get it or…"

"No, no, Mama will…well, I'll get it for you." Colby got up and poured Zach a cup of coffee. As he set down the pot, he saw the little pitcher for fresh cream and remembered that they were nearly out of sugar. What if Zach wanted some in his coffee? Colby wanted to make a good show of keeping a generous table but thought that he should probably keep the sugar for his own family. He didn't know when or if he would be able to get more. Worst of all, he thought, was that he was standing there with a hot cup of coffee in his hand, looking stupid in front of the company.

He had just reached for the sugar bowl when he heard Zach speak.

"I usually don't take nothing in my coffee. But I think I see some fresh buttermilk over there by the butter churn. You reckon I might could get me a glass of that?" Zach said.

Colby walked to the table and set the coffee in front of the old man. "Well Zach, I'd say that you could have just about all the buttermilk you could ever want. Leastways, I won't be fighting you over it none. Matter of fact, Daddy's the only one that drinks it regular…well, you know, before and all. Used to drink it, I mean. Now only Tim-Bug drinks it at all."

Zach took a steaming sip of coffee.

"Don't care for buttermilk?" he asked. Colby shook his head as he sat down.

"Not now, not never. I've smelled milk that's done turned and it don't seem to me any different at all from that buttermilk. Never have been able to stomach it. Tell you the truth, most times Mama ends up just dumping it out in back of the hen house. Mrs. Traylor don't churn her own butter, does she?" Colby asked.

"No, sir. She's buys it at Lawrence Norvell's store along with all her other groceries. They got shut of their milk cow when their youngest son moved off."

They stopped speaking as Anne put bowls in front of them, took the kettle from the stove and served the beans. Colby picked up a small paring knife and diced the pickled onion. As they spooned the relish and onion onto their beans, Anne retrieved the cornbread from the oven and set it on a dish-rag on the table. Colby used the same paring knife to cut the cornbread into squares and offered the pan first to Zach, who took a piece, then Colby took a piece for himself. They both loaded the cornbread with butter and Zach was about to pick up his spoon when he looked over towards the oven at Mrs. Grayson. He wondered if she was going to eat with them. She turned to face the table, now silent and Zach noticed her hands were folded in front of her. He looked at Colby and saw that his hands, too, were folded. Zach quickly bowed his head and folded his hands, embarrassed and a little ashamed that he had, for some reason, assumed that these folks didn't say a blessing over the food before eating.

"Lord, thank you for this food," Colby began. "Please let it put strength in our bodies, gratitude in our hearts, peace in our minds and hope in our souls. Amen."

"Amen," Zach echoed, moved suddenly and deeply by the simple prayer over the simple meal before him. He took a spoonful of beans and they tasted better to him than any beans had for as long as he could remember.

"I like that grace you just said, Colby. Just make that up did you?" Zach asked, then took another bite of beans.

"Nossir. That's the prayer that my daddy's daddy always said before a meal. You probably remember him, though? Denton? He's the one built the big barn. I never sat down around a table without him reciting that prayer. Course, Daddy wasn't much of a prayer but with him gone and all…well, I figured it would be the thing to do, praying over the food and I always was partial to that prayer."

"I'm gonna remember it, I'll tell you that. Next time it falls on me to offer grace, that's the prayer I'm going to use," Zach said.

Colby smiled as politely as he could around the mouthful of beans.

"Well-sir, I know that would make Granddaddy happy."

The day was nearly spent and the front field was over three-quarters hoed. When he saw his brothers and sister walking up the road on their way home from school, Colby realized that this was the first day in weeks that he wasn't completely done in by the day's labor. His body was tired as always but with the knowledge that David would do the afternoon milking and Zach would return for a half day on Friday, Colby was free of the bone-deep, mind-numbing weariness that had been his only afternoon companion for weeks.

"Well, Zach, I usually quit hoeing about the time that the kids get home," Colby said.

Zach looked at the approaching children, took a deep breath and nodded. "Reckon they about done with school for the year, ain't they?" he asked.

"Yes, they are. That biggest one there, David, has done said he wants to start helping out, doing some hoeing and things. I already got him started on the afternoon milking. Does a right good job of it, too."

"Fortunate thing, having a boy that wants to work. When I was his age, I wasn't good for much more than frog-gigging and tree-climbing."

The mention of frog gigging turned Colby's mind to fried frog legs and his mouth began watering. He didn't know until then how much he liked frog legs. He was about to ask Zach if he knew of any good frog ponds nearby when the kids stopped beside the workers.

"Did y'all get real smart at school today?" Colby asked with a smile.

Baby-Anne and Tim-Bug laughed, glad only that Colby had the energy to acknowledge them. David didn't laugh. He merely stared at Zach in dumbfounded awe. As much as he worshipped Colby, the thought that he could employ a grown man had seemed unthinkable.

Even Daddy had never had a hired hand and here Colby already had one. Colby saw David staring at Zach and misunderstood the reason.

"This here is Zach," he explained. "He works for Mr. Traylor, but we're doing a swap. He's helping me on Tuesdays and half of Fridays now, and I'm going to help out Mr. Traylor this fall. Maybe you could help Mr. Traylor some, too, David—this fall, I mean."

David looked eagerly at Colby, then at Zach, then back at Colby.

"Sure, I could! I mean...sure! And by this fall, I'll be really handy with a hoe, but I reckon there won't be much hoeing to do this fall. But I learn things quick, you know that, Colby. Shoot, yes, I can help out."

Colby smiled at David, then looked at Zach, who was smiling too. Colby saw that Tim had pulled his new knife out of his pocket and was examining it. Baby-Anne wasn't paying much attention to the goings-on.

"What're we having for supper tonight, Colby?" she asked.

"Well, beans, I imagine, plus cornbread and butter," Colby said.

"Can't we have something else, Colby? I'm sure pretty durn tired of beans," his sister said.

Colby looked at Zach, then at the ground, suddenly ashamed. Zach tried to smile in understanding, but his smile failed and he wished that he could walk away without making things harder on Colby. There was a silence until David, knowing full well what was occurring, began singing.

"Beans, beans. They're good for your heart, the more you eat 'em, the more you—"

"Ththpthpth!" Tim supplied the appropriate sound on cue. They all cracked up laughing, Zach the loudest of all and he used the laughter as cover to begin walking back to the house. With the others behind him, he slowed just enough to let Colby lead. At the front door, the twins ran in to play one of their odd, private games. David darted in just long enough to drop off his books and change his shirt. He had milking to do.

Anne stepped out of the front door and handed Zach a sealed Mason jar full of buttermilk.

"It's fresh," she said, then walked back inside.

"Thank you so much, ma'am," Zach called after her. He handed Colby his hoe. "Yes sir, that sure is a fine hoe," he said.

"It surely has seen a few weeds," Colby said and they exchanged the companionably weary smile of co-workers, still here after yet another hard day's work. Zach nodded once more and said, "Well, then..." and turned away.

"Zach?" Colby stopped him.

Zach faced the boy. Colby had no real idea why he called the one-eyed man back and was on the verge of embarrassment. He tried to think of something to say but he had no words.

So he simply stuck out his hand, Zach grabbed it, shook it and walked away.

## Chapter 19

That night after supper, David decided to try his hand at hunting. Having heard Baby-Anne complain earlier about eating beans every day, he proudly and with a smug wink announced to the supper table that they would be eating rabbit the next night. Timothy nodded in serious agreement. Colby nodded, ready for a change himself.

About half an hour before dark, David and Timothy were still out, Baby-Anne was in bed with Mama, and so Colby sat alone in the front room. He languidly rocked in his Father's chair, gazing without focus out the front window and idly wondering if his brothers were near. He had heard no shots, although there were a good many rabbits about already this year. He had also seen more than one raccoon in the early, pre-dawn darkness. Maybe they would luck up on one if they stayed out until sunset or later.

Colby let his eyes wander to the tobacco field that he and Zach had hoed that day. They had made great progress, such great progress that it bothered Colby a bit. Mathematics wasn't one of his better skills, but he figured that he and Zach had done roughly three times the work that Colby could do alone. What bothered him the most about this was that Zach hadn't hoed anymore weeds than Colby himself. From the start, Colby had made sure to pace himself so that he was doing every bit as much as, if not more than, Zach.

How, then, was it possible that two men could do three times the work of one man? It didn't make sense to Colby and he did like things to make sense.

Maybe it was just some kind of math problem and he could ask David about it later.

Colby couldn't bring himself to stew on the problem for too long. All that really mattered was that the weeding would be caught up tomorrow. The tobacco plants were doing well, over twice as big as they were when Colby took over. He decided that he would look at the plants on neighboring farms on the way to church on Sunday to see if his tobacco was getting along as well as theirs. He was fairly sure that it was and he found that he was actually eager to get back in the field.

Eager to hoe: ten days ago he wouldn't have thought it possible. If he could get the field done tomorrow, then he could get Zach to help him in the vegetable garden on Friday. As little as he knew about tobacco, he knew even less about the vegetables. Every one required different handling and they matured at different times.

Colby recognized that the corn wasn't getting along as well as it should. He remembered thinning the plants out with Daddy last year but had no idea how to space the plants.

"Well." Colby said to the empty room. Friday would be soon enough to start in the vegetable garden. With that thought, two further ideas occurred to him. First, the sodden, thick blanket of fear and sustained panic that had been strapped to his chest since Vernon died wasn't there this night. A day's labor of a one-eyed old man had lightened Colby's load so completely and quickly that he hadn't noticed until now. It actually seemed easier to breathe.

Second, he had not once today slid silently into his baseball world. The fantasies that got him through so many days had not come, nor had they been missed. Moreover, he had not listened to the Reds in over a week. He had been too busy during the days and too tired and worried at night. So lax and behind was his fandom that he did not even know if they had played today or were to play tonight.

He reached over and clicked on the radio. Serving as the perfect ending to a perfect day, not only were the Reds on, they were playing in Brooklyn and beating the Dodgers seven to nothing in the third inning.

Colby let the sun go down, the front room lit only by the radio's dial, and quietly enjoyed the evening.

The only thing missing was the smell of cigarette smoke. Daddy usually smoked while listening to the games and the smell had been part of the entire experience for Colby. There was still some of Daddy's tobacco and cigarette papers in the roll top desk, and he considered trying to roll one up and light it, just for the smell.

The thought of tobacco reminded him of his predicament at church and he began studying on this so much, that he forgot about the smoke and the baseball game.

It was a lucky thing that Russ had that upset stomach last Sunday or Colby would have been embarrassed, but he probably couldn't count on that kind of luck two weeks in a row. He couldn't chew tobacco because he knew he might get sick, but he couldn't stand with the men and not chew. And he couldn't learn to chew in just five days.

He'd just have to learn, that's all. Maybe he could plead illness again this Sunday and get away with it, maybe next Sunday, too, but not forever. Where was he going to get any tobacco for learning? He couldn't just pick a plant out of the ground and learn that way. He'd have to buy some at Lawrence Norvell's grocery store. Then he remembered he probably had no money and the thick, wet blanket of worry settled with smug indifference back onto his chest, his breaths getting shorter and more difficult.

Colby fought it by trying to involve himself in the game, but the Reds had upped their lead to nine to nothing and so it just wasn't enough to occupy his mind.

He had nearly resigned himself to trudging off to bed, prepared to spend a worrisome and largely sleepless night, when he heard the unmistakable popping sound of the twenty-two. There were three quick shots, a long pause, then one more shot.

Colby sat up straighter, listening. He wanted them to bring something in, partly because he wanted meat, but mostly because he knew how proud the boys would be if they succeeded.

As Colby sat forward, listening and expectant, he heard another shot, a pause, then the triumphant whoop of his brothers and Colby knew that they had brought something down. He silently hoped it was a rabbit.

He turned off the radio. He knew they would be running home with their prize. The door slammed open and David ran in, carrying the rifle. He skidded to a stop in front of the rocking chair and silently, comically pointed at Timothy, who was running through the door holding a large rabbit up by his hind legs.

"Got him! Got him!" David yelled.

"Sure did. Sure did!" Timothy yelled, nodding, holding the rabbit up for inspection and validation. Colby stood up and walked over to Tim. He turned to David.

"So, you're a pretty good shot with that rifle after all," he said with a grin. David shook his head and pointed at Tim-Bug.

"Not me, him. We seen this rabbit about thirty yards away and I musta shot at him five times and couldn't hit him. Tim says for me to give him a try and durned if he didn't hit that rabbit in the head on his first shot. Durned if he didn't!"

Colby was impressed. When he hunted, he never aimed for the head, always for the body. There was a better chance of hitting that way. He inspected the bullet hole. There was very little blood; the head shot had immediately stopped the rabbit's heart.

"Was you aiming for his head, Tim-Bug?" he asked.

"I sure was, Colby and it wasn't no lucky shot neither. I knew as soon as I aimed where I was going to hit him. Swear to goodness I did!" Timothy was proud and beaming.

"Well, sir, I'd have to say that it was a mighty fine shot, then. It's a good thing he sat still that long," Colby said, grinning. He looked at David, who quit laughing but instead smiled knowingly and nodded at Tim-Bug, urging him on.

Timothy looked at his brothers, stretching out the moment as long as he could. "It wasn't sittin' still," he said.

Colby wondered if this was a post hunt-joke but he could see the truth in their eyes. He looked back at Timothy.

"You meanin' to tell me that you hit a running rabbit in the head from thirty yards with a twenty-two?" he asked.

"Well, actually, by the time David got done chunkin' away at him, I reckon he was more like fifty or sixty yards out," Timothy said. David nodded his agreement.

"At least," he agreed.

"Well, I'll be durned." Colby said. He looked again at the hole in the rabbit's head. "You still aimin' to clean him with that new knife of yours?"

"I sure am. I'll take him out back right now. We gonna eat him tomorrow, right?" Timothy asked.

"Sure we will," Colby said.

"How's he going to keep until then?" David asked.

"Well, sir, as soon as Tim-Bug gets him cleaned and cut up, what we'll do is to put him in a big bowl of saltwater and then put him in the icebox. Mama'll know what to do with him tomorrow."

## CHAPTER 20

The next morning, Russ was out on his porch a full twenty minutes earlier than usual. He hadn't seen Zach the night before and wasn't ashamed of his eagerness for news about how the Graysons were getting along. Dot had felt him flopping and turning in bed and finally got up, wondering aloud how anyone was supposed to sleep when someone was doing somersaults in the bed. But she knew the reason for his unease and cooked him an early and unusually hearty breakfast. It wasn't often that she made him sausage gravy during the week and this was gravy made of Old Man Tom's sausage, by general acknowledgment the best sausage one could ever hope to eat.

Russ gobbled the big breakfast down, regretting that he couldn't enjoy it more, took an absurdly large chew and stepped onto his porch to await Zach. He was about to sit down in his chair when his lack of proper courtesy struck him. He walked back to the kitchen door and stuck his head in.

"Dot?" he said.

Dot stopped clearing the table and looked at her husband, silently. She knew what he would say and why he had not said it earlier. He had been thinking of the Grayson boy and what Zach's news would be. It was also why she still loved Russ Traylor thirty-eight years after they had walked down the aisle.

"That sure was a mighty fine breakfast. If that gravy could only be gotten in heathen lands, I reckon I'd just have to become a sinner." he said, grinning. It was an old joke between them.

She smiled at him, genuinely amused by his simple jest. "I'm glad you liked it, Russell. You be sure and tell Old Man Tom that last fall's sausage may have been his best ever. Now you go on out there and wait for Zach. When he gets here, you make mighty sure that you talk plenty loud. I want to know how that boy's getting along myself, you hear?" she said.

"I hear. Why don't you just come on out here, though? Zach ain't shy of you, you know that."

"I don't want to have to listen to you spit nasty tobacco juice in that smelly old can. I can hear fine from in here with the door open and I've got to clean up these dishes."

"Suit yourself." Russ said and sat down in his chair.

The sun had not shown its upper edge to the horizon when Zach walked through the back yard and up to the porch. Russ wondered if maybe he couldn't sleep either or if maybe he knew that Russ would be waiting.

"Mornin', Zach," Russ said.

"Mornin' to you, Russ. I saw your light and figured I might come on up."

"Have you done had your breakfast?"

"Yessir, I have. I went ahead and fried me a couple of eggs, toasted me a couple of pieces of white bread and washed it all down with two big glasses of buttermilk, courtesy of Mrs. Grayson."

Zach pulled out his tobacco and papers, rolled a cigarette and lit it.

"Then you ain't had no coffee yet this morning?" Russ asked.

"Well, sir, no I haven't, to speak truthful. I maybe figured I'd best get on up here this morning."

Russ looked at him, then at the promising eastern sky, quietly appreciating Zach.

"Dot," he called. "You reckon Zach here might get a cup of—"

Dot swung through the door with a steaming mug of coffee before Russ could finish his sentence. She handed the mug to Zach, smiled guiltily at Russ, then went back inside.

Zach blew on it once, then took a loud sip.

"Ah…thank you, Mrs. Traylor," he said.

"You're welcome, Zach," she called from inside.

Zach took another big sip, took a drag of his cigarette then looked directly at Russ.

"Well, then," Russ said.

Zach nodded. "Reckon you may be wondering just how they're getting along," he said.

"I am," Russ replied.

"Well, sir, first of all, them kids seem to be doing good enough. You know how kids are. Bounce back from most anything pretty quick. Those young'uns, they ain't gonna take no permanent hurt from their daddy dying. They young and they healthy. Only thing that might give me a worry at all is the fact that they ain't been eating no meat. Now they got milk and they got eggs and that's a durn sight more than many have, but I think they ain't been eating nothing but beans for dinner and supper for more than a week now. That little girl, the one they call Baby-Anne? She was even complaining about it and you know well as I do that them Graysons ain't complainers."

"Colby can hunt," Russ said.

"Colby ain't got time to hunt, but that next oldest boy does. David. That's his name. Colby said that he was going to try his hand at hunting. I heard some shots last night. Maybe he had some luck. Hope so anyway. But I

84

don't reckon a rabbit or two gonna help them as much as they need helping, Russ. I looked around their kitchen as much as I could without being obvious and their bean sack's about empty. Unless they got some cornmeal stored back somewhere, that's about gone too. I don't think they have any flour and the sugar's so low that Colby was fretting about offering me some to put in my coffee. I also saw two empty lard buckets in the corner and not one full one."

"But they're eating, right?"

"Yessir. Like I said, they got milk and eggs, but Russ, I'm thinking that they sorely need a trip to Mr. Norvell's Grocery Store but I'm also think- ing that if they could have, they would have gone already. I'm thinking maybe there ain't no money around there or if there is, poor Mrs. Grayson has done forgot about it."

Russ spit loudly into his can, then looked out over his fields. The sun was making its slow, lazy way up to the fence tops.

"I'm afraid that that might be exactly what happened, Zach. Vernon didn't ever like to run accounts anywhere, so he usually kept enough cash around to pay for things between crops. It'd be an awful shame if there is money around and they just don't know where to look."

"Yessir, that would be a shame and an awful waste too," Zach said.

Russ sat back and began rocking again. "I'm just about a hundred percent sure that Lawrence Norvell wouldn't mind for a minute if Colby were to start buying a few things on credit," he said.

Zach agreed. "I don't imagine he would mind at that. Most everybody got some kind of account with him. He's a real decent sort. I bet that Colby could have an account just for the asking," he said.

"I would say that is so but there again, getting him to ask might be a right smart task," Russ said. He spit again into his can, then asked, "His tobac- co doing good, is it?"

"Looking right good, Russ. It could do with some ammonium, but that Grayson land has some good soil on it and I was maybe a little surprised. Taking care of that much tobacco would be a chore for any man, let alone a boy, but he had it all in right good shape. Now, the vegetables wasn't looking none too good, but I think he's planning on us getting into that on Friday."

"I'd say that's a good thing. A good garden full of vegetables will car- ry a family a long way. Durn shame that the only fruit trees they got are those old apple trees."

"Russ, you reckon you might could speak to Mr. Norvell about them getting some credit? They gonna need beans and flour and sugar."

"Well, sir, it may be that I already got me an idea about that," Russ said, with a wry smile on his face. "By Sunday afternoon, I'd say Colby's going to have an account that he feels no shame using. About that money though, you reckon you might think up a way of mentioning it to him? Kinda casual like?"

"I reckon so, Russ. Seems like an easier job than yours." Zach was crushing out his cigarette when an idea struck and he had to hide from Russ a wry smile of his own. He had suddenly seen what to do, how to mention the money to Colby and how to offer a different kind of help—one he wouldn't tell even Russ about.

"Well then," Russ said rising, "I thought we might replace a few rails in the front barn today."

"Well, sir, that is surely a task that ain't gonna do itself," Zach said and followed Russ to the tool shed.

## CHAPTER 21

Zach arrived at the Grayson farm early on Friday morning. He was about to make his way up the slag path to the house when he saw Colby walking toward the barn.

"Morning, Zach," Colby greeted him.

"Mornin', Colby," Zach said and nodded toward the front field. "Looks like you kept that hoe busy the last couple of days. Might just be that you done worked poor old Zach right out of a job," he said, laughing.

Colby chuckled. "No sir, I reckon I could always find work around here for willing hands. I just figured I'd go on and get that field done so's we could put in the morning working on the vegetable garden."

"Yessir, I seen that garden the other day. My mama used to call 'em kitchen gardens. I've worked in a right good many."

"I kind of figured you had," Colby said. "I was counting on it. You've maybe seen a lot of them but this one here would be my first. It don't bother me none to admit that I ain't exactly sure if I'm doing things right."

"Well, sir, from what I seen, it looks like it's doing good but could be doing a sight better."

"That's about the way I had it figured. Maybe we ought to grab our hoes and walk on up."

They grabbed their hoes from the barn and made their way to the garden, where Zach made a close but unjudgmental inspection.

As they worked, Zach pointed out to Colby what needed to be done, carefully explaining why, while cautiously avoiding anything that could be mistaken for an order.

"Now these corn plants of yours, they looking good and healthy but maybe a might small. Now, I had a grandaddy used to grow corn and he every year raised up pretty near the best corn I ever tasted. If this corn was mine, what I'd do is to thin them out a little the way my grandaddy used to."

"How'd he do it?" Colby asked.

"What he did was to plant a bit too much corn, then thin out the smallest plants, just leaving the bigger ones. What he always said was to thin them out to where the plants was as far apart as the length of your foot plus the width of your hand. He had a pretty durn big foot, so you may want to go the length of your foot and the width of both your hands."

And later, "Now, these tomato plants, as much sun as we've had, these things gonna shoot right on up. They ain't quite as easy to grow as those cucumbers over there. Those cucumbers grow themselves if a man can manage to stay out of their way. But these tomatoes here, they look to me like they doing just fine, big leaves and strong looking stalks. Some folks will tell you not to pester them until they're at least above your knee but some would tell you it never is too early to sucker these puny limbs off the bottom, like this one here or that one there," he said, kneeling and pointing to the bottom of the tomato plants.

"How'd your grandaddy do it?" Colby asked.

"He suckered his tomatoes early and often," Zach said, standing up and awaiting Colby's decision.

"Grow good tomatoes, did he?"

"What're you talkin' about? Tomatoes so big it took two men to lift them! Plants so bent over he had to tie them up like a grapevine. I swear, just as sure as I'm standing here, I one time saw a tomato plant of his that was taller than he was."

Colby grinned at Zach's excited descriptions.

"Well, Zach, it's hard to argue with such success. Let's do it his way."

Under Zach's gentle, sometimes comic tutelage, Colby learned much that morning. He learned that the cucumbers and the squash liked to have a couple of weeds growing near and that the reason Vernon planted eggplant every year was because beetles preferred it to most other things and would thus leave the other plants alone. Hearing that vegetable plants needed far more water to thrive than tobacco did, Colby decided to assign David the task of carrying well water or, if the well ran low, pond water, to the garden. He learned, too, that this garden needed constant hoeing—not the fervent, sweaty hoeing of the tobacco fields but a simple quick and daily scraping, keeping the dirt turned and alive and not allowing it to settle and pack.

About a half-hour before Zach was to leave, they were both still chopping and turning the dirt in comfortable silence. Colby was reviewing his new knowledge, thinking that he might let Tim-Bug do the light daily hoeing of this garden, when a brand-new Cadillac went by noisily on U.S. 60. To Colby, the word "Cadillac" was utterly without meaning. To him the car was simply big, blue and shiny.

Zach, however, whistled appreciatively. "Hoo-wee," he said. "Can't hardly even imagine having enough money to own something like that. Makes me wonder what a fella would have to do for a living to make that kind of money."

"Nothing around here," Colby replied. "Probably not even in Morehead. I'd bet that car come from either Lexington or Ashland, although what he'd be doing out this far is more than I could guess."

"Well, sir, rich folks got rich ways. Could be they out just burning up fuel having themselves a joy ride, and on a workday, too," Zach said. He waited for Colby's response and getting none, looked over at him. Colby was already bent back over his hoe, working at the soil.

Zach was surprised. He was sure that Colby, like all boys, would be interested in talking about money, wealthy people, opulence and riches. And, if not money, what boy didn't want to talk about cars? A few years ago, Russ's youngest son had gone through a stage where he was blinded to most other worldly matters because of his obsession with cars and here Colby was not only unimpressed, he was apparently completely uninterested in them.

Zach persisted, "Yes, sir, people like that got so much money they walk with a limp because their fat old wallet pokes a hole in their butt." He sensed without seeing that Colby had smiled.

"That'd be one limp I wouldn't mind taking on," Colby said, and Zach laughed too loudly, eager to keep this conversation going.

"I had that kind of money, I'd carry two wallets and have a hole in each side of my you know what," he said.

"That kinda money, I believe I'd hire me someone to carry it and they could have the hole in the butt," Colby said laughing.

The moment over, Colby was bending back to his work when Zach said conspiratorially, "Colby, I'll let you in on a little secret, if you're willing. Might be of great benefit to you someday."

"Yeah?" Colby said with doubtful amusement.

"There's been times in my life when I was hard-pressed for money. Not often, mind you, but sometimes. I reckon I haven't never needed much more than what a few dollars could buy me, but cars like that, people like that, with more money than good sense? Drinking beer and carrying on? Well, sir, the secret is this, they ain't too awful careful with their money. I'm standing right here to tell you that many's the time I just went walking up and down the road and found me quarters and dimes and dollar bills. Whether you believe it or not, I one time found me a twenty-dollar bill on the side of a road, stuck to the bottom of a blooming thistle."

Colby looked sidelong at him, not willing to think of Zach as a teller of tall tales but with an instinctive mistrust of money gained without toil or dishonesty.

"And you just kept it? What I mean is, they didn't never come back looking for it? I believe that if I lost a twenty-dollar bill, I'd spend the rest of my life looking for it."

"Like I said, rich folks got rich ways. Any man can afford to buy an automobile like that ain't gonna sweat over losing no twenty-dollar bill, even if he was to notice it missing. I wouldn't never keep nothing I thought someone would miss but these rich ole car owners, well, sir, I gotta say about them, finders-keepers, losers-weepers," Zach finished with a grin.

"Twenty dollars..." Colby marveled, temporarily caught up in fantasies of riches and ease.

How long he could feed his family on twenty dollars went through his mind. Beans, flour, cornmeal and lard, maybe some factory canned fruit—peaches or even pineapples, a treat Colby had only had twice in his life. Sugar, bacon, perhaps even some chocolate or other sweets to be portioned out with caution and cheerful stinginess.

Maybe he would buy Annetta some new ribbons for Mama to tie in her hair or a bow that she could wear as a sash. For Tim-Bug, a new whetstone to go with his new knife; maybe an Arkansas oilstone, the best whetstone going. David would get a shiny new hoe, polished and presented with casual indifference, rendering his younger brother speechless.

And for Mama, what for Mama? Something. But what? He simply didn't know.

For himself, there was not the slightest bit of doubt. In the back of Mr. Norvell's store, on a low, forgotten shelf, dusty and unremarked, Colby had seen a baseball glove.

It was a Wilson infielder's model, not brown like most gloves but shiny black, stiff and unwrinkled. Lined on the inside with supple suede, it had a soft, white, wool band lining the strap that ran over the back of the hand.

Colby had seen it and immediately desired it, despite knowing that it was as unattainable to him as a place on the roster of the Reds.

He let go of the thoughts after realizing that he had been standing there daydreaming long enough that Zach might think him odd. Besides, Colby now had another element to add to his fantasies: the Glove. Colburn Grayson, the Cincinnati Reds' hard-hitting shortstop, was undeniably and inarguably, by virtue of his magical glove, the best infielder in the league—perhaps in the history of the baseball. Colby knew that he would spend all afternoon giving birth to this new fantasy.

He put his eyes on Zach. "Well Zach, I believe I could say in complete honesty that I don't know a man who wouldn't welcome a free and clear twenty-dollar bill," Colby said, and Zach again laughed too loudly.

"Maybe one day me and you gonna be rich enough to toss money out the window of our shiny new cars. You reckon?" Zach asked, still laughing.

"Well, sir, I'd settle for getting this crop raised up and sold," Colby said and was immediately sorry. It sounded like complaining. Zach made a quick attempt to laugh it off but knew he couldn't. Colby reddened a bit and Zach thought about pretending that he didn't hear it but thought that might add insult to injury for Colby.

"Well, Colby, I guess I helped raise a good many crops of tobacco, and there ain't but three things that it really needs. It needs a few sunny days, a few rainy days and someone that don't mind tending to it every day. Now

God gonna give it the first two things and from what I've seen of you and your work here, I know you're providing the last. I know things run through a man's mind unbidden, but I was you, I'd surely try not to spend too much time worrying."

"You think?" Colby asked.

Zach nodded. "I do. I surely do. You doing just right."

"You think?" Colby repeated, unexpectedly hungry for Zach's assurance, while ashamed that he needed it.

"Shoot, yes I do." Zach kindly couched his earnest reply in a light-hearted chuckle. "I bet ole Vernon's up in heaven with a big silver hoe in his hand, begging to come back down here and chop some weeds but God won't let him 'cause He knows you doing the job."

Colby smiled, thankful and sad. "I reckon it'd take God to keep Daddy from doing just exactly what he wanted," he said.

Zach was respectful in his answer. "I knew Vernon and I'd say maybe it'd take God and four or five angels, too. Reckon I never saw a stronger man."

## CHAPTER 22

The kids arrived home from their last day of school that afternoon, the boys excited not about freedom from the schoolhouse but rather about having time to pursue their newfound passions.

David had already retrieved Doris from her small pasture. He did the milking quickly and correctly, with consistently fewer complaints from Doris than Colby had received.

Timothy was inside the house with the barrel of the rifle in his lap. A school friend had told him about the importance of cleaning the inside of the gun, how to break down and how to clean carefully the spent powder out of the barrel using a piece of baling wire and an oily rag.

To Colby's surprise, Baby-Anne was out in the vegetable garden, closely and curiously inspecting the progress he and Zach had made. She wove in and around the plants, sometimes kneeling down and laying hands on rough, broad leaves, occasionally smiling. Colby was about to walk over and ask her what she thought but remembered that he had not yet picked up the day's mail.

He had no genuine interest in the mail, but his father had made it a point to walk out to the mailbox at the end of every day and collect the contents. As often as not, there was no mail, but Colby thought that it was a simple enough thing to do that would, perhaps, give the others a sense of consistency. This could be one less thing to miss about Vernon.

He walked up the driveway and stopped at the galvanized steel box, which sat atop a creosote-soaked cedar post. On both sides were hand-painted words:

Vernon Grayson
Route 2
Cox Co. Kentucky

The box opened with a worn, protesting screech. There were two envelopes. One was from The Bank of Morehead. Colby's heart began its familiar pounding and he felt fresh sweat begin popping out on his forehead. This first physical reminder of his debt to the bank caused his stomach to lurch, and he was sure for a moment that he would vomit there in the driveway. His brothers would see however, so he swallowed the gorge. Colby opened the letter right there and saw that it was a Statement of Account. It listed what they owed, how much principal and how much interest. Colby recalled enough of his conversation with White and Scott that he felt he didn't need to read the statement and felt he couldn't anyway. He folded it back up and put it back in the envelope.

The second envelope bore a return address reading:

RCEC
Rowan County Electric Co-operative
Morehead, Kentucky

It was the electric bill. While Colby had known with fair certainty that the electricity wasn't free, he had been numbly hoping that perhaps it was paid yearly and that his father had already paid it. He had known his hope was a slim one. He didn't even open the envelope. He had not the beginning of an idea of how much electricity cost and he truly didn't want to know. He had enough to worry about.

He put both envelopes in his back pocket. It was what Vernon had always done. When he got back to the house, Colby would put them in the upper left slot of the roll-top desk. That was where all outstanding business documents were kept. The slot was filling up ominously.

Colby took two steps toward the house when something caught his eye. A spark of sunlight had reflected off something between the road and Colby, about thirty feet from the mailbox.

Colby, with the psychic weight of the letters on him, had nearly lost his capacity for curiosity but he felt inclined to investigate. He wandered over to where he had seen the flash and walked casually around the area, head down.

An old delivery truck rumbled loudly past and Colby's embarrassment won out. He turned back to the house when his right toe nudged something that caused another reflection. There at his feet was a shiny quarter. He bent down, picked it up and whistled in mild awe and appreciation.

Colby dropped to his knees, searching through the weeds. In less than a minute of searching, he found three more quarters, two dimes and nine pennies. Another truck passed while he searched, but Colby didn't notice, nor would he have cared if he had.

One dollar and twenty-nine cents! Free and clear! There for the taking. So One-Eyed Zach was right. The owners of those fancy cars were so durn rich that the money just fell out and wasn't missed.

Hadn't Daddy known about this? Maybe he had but it would be Vernon's way to just ignore the money and let someone else find it. Colby, however, although he spent every second trying to live up to the standard set by his father, knew he was in no position to turn his back on this unforeseen bounty.

He recounted the money, already calculating and prioritizing what he needed to buy in the way of groceries. They could eat for a week on a dollar twenty-nine. Maybe two weeks, if Tim-Bug's hunting luck held out.

Colby again began walking back to the house, the coins clasped tightly in his hands. He was so busy spending the money in his head that he almost missed it. He happened to glance down at his shoe as he stepped on a young thistle and there, punctured by the fresh thorns, was more money than Colby had ever seen.

"Oh," Colby whispered, stunned and immobile. The coins clasped tightly in his right hand, he bent down and, with his trembling left hand, retrieved a silver certificate ten-dollar bill.

He picked it up by one corner, wondering for a moment if it might be a fake. He probably wouldn't be able to tell if it was, so limited was his experience with folding money. The closest he ever came to large quantities of paper currency was in the church collection plate and with rare exceptions on Christmas or Easter, it held at most one-dollar bills.

Colby transferred the coins to his right front pants pocket and held the bill up in both hands, letting the sun shine through it. It had a look and feel of authenticity and Colby finally allowed himself to believe his luck.

"Dang me, dang me, you could take a rope and hang me!" he laughed. He leaped into the air with a celebratory yell and took off running down the road towards Mr. Norvell's store. He was a hundred yards down the road when he remembered that he should tell someone where he was going. He turned around and began running towards the barn. He crossed the front field, then remembered that the store closed at six on Fridays.

He drew even with the house and collected himself, chuckling in self-deprecation that he had taken off so excitedly, like a kid that found a nickel in front of a candy store.

Better anyway that he ask Mama what she needed and make up a list. He'd go to town in the morning and he would take Leviticus and the wagon.

Town was the crossroads of U.S. 60 and the newly paved and numbered Route 1465. Three miles from the Grayson place in the direction of Morehead, it consisted of Lawrence Norvell's grocery store on one corner; the one-room Post Office—of which Mr. Norvell was the Postmaster—on another; and E. E. Robinson's Fencing and Farm Supply Store on a third. On the fourth corner was a building so old and gravely dilapidated that all who passed by it on a regular basis made a point of slowing to see if they could discover any new promise of its imminent collapse.

In its day, it had been a blacksmith's shop. It was owned by Big Tom Lainhart, the son of the last man to make a full-time living as a blacksmith in that area. Big Tom said from time to time that he was going to build a gasoline station on the site.

All the farmers called this crossroads community "Town," as if the name of their town was Town.

Colby put the bill carefully in the same pocket that held the coins. He entered the house. Mama was in the kitchen and Colby smelled boiling beans as he saw the now empty and folded bean bag on the pantry shelf, along with other empty—but perhaps still useful—bags, jars and cans.

Colby noticed that his mother was singing again, louder than ever, in a fevered, grating whisper to herself. He could hear an unmistakable undertone of quiet desperation and a raw, harmonic hopelessness.

"Mama?" he said quietly, with fearful discomfort. Mama went on singing and Colby noticed that she was dicing up a leftover rabbit leg. She threw it into the pot with the beans, including the bone. Colby took two steps forward.

"Mama!" he said more loudly.

She stopped singing or at least lowered the volume so that Colby couldn't hear her. This was all the acknowledgment he received from her.

"Mama, I'm going to the grocery store tomorrow morning," he told her, and finally Anne turned around to face her son. He saw that her lips were indeed still moving but now spilled a silent song.

Colby watched her, ready to prod her to snap out of it and speak but he didn't. For reasons undefined and unknowable to him, he instead let her come to him.

After thirty or so uncomfortable seconds of expectant, leaden silence, Anne nodded.

"We're out of most everything, Colby," she said.

"I know Mama," he said, silently grateful that she was looking him in the eye and calling him by his name. "That's why I'm going tomorrow. I was thinking maybe you could make me out a list of sorts."

"Have you heard from Jason?" she asked suddenly.

"Jason who, Mama? You talking about Uncle Jason?" Colby asked, wondering if she was slipping back so soon. Anne shook her head dismissively, perhaps reading the worry in Colby's brown, sharp eyes.

"Never mind. Go now and get me a piece of the children's paper. And a pencil, too," she said and walked to the pantry to inspect its woeful emptiness.

Colby returned with the pencil and paper and sat at the table with his mother. She studied and wrote for less than five minutes then handed the list to Colby. It was surprisingly short:

Pinto beans
Flour
Corn meel
10 pounds Sugar
Baking Powder
Vinegur
Salt crakers

Balonee
Sliced bred
Salt
Frute
Maybe Mustard

She handed the list to Colby and he read it quickly, relieved that it was so short. He had a renewed sense of appreciation for the chickens, and for Doris and the kitchen garden.

"We got to have lard, too, Colby, so you go by Old Man Tom's place and get us a bucket, or two if possible," Anne said.

Colby nodded. "Sure, I will, Mama. What kind of fruit you think we should get?"

"Bananas and oranges if they got them. I'd like to see these kids get some oranges in them. Oranges is good for them. They come from Florida you know."

Colby smiled at her, as happy as he had been in a while.

"I know, Mama. Those ones we got at Christmastime had those little red and blue stickers on them that said 'FLORIDA,' remember?"

"Yes. Yes, I remember. I have a sister that lives in Florida."

"Yes, Ma'am, Aunt Lily. She hasn't written in a while," Colby said, eager to keep the conversation alive.

"No, I don't reckon she has. She was smart, Lily was, smart like you."

"Shoot Mama, I ain't smart. David, now he's the smart one. He gets all A's," Colby said.

"I know how smart David is but that ain't the kind of smart I'm talking about. Lily was smart like you. She always knew what to do, smart like that. She always knew what to do and the best way to go about doing—"

David noisily opened the front door and stumped into the kitchen with the full bucket of fresh milk. It was enough to cause Anne to lose her hold on her thoughts and the conversation. She silently took the milk from David.

Colby was sorry that their talk was at an end. It was the most she had said in weeks and his most lucid conversation with her in perhaps a year. He folded the list and put it in his pocket along with the money.

"Okay, Mama. I'll get all this tomorrow."

David sensed that he had interrupted something important.

"You going to town tomorrow, Colby?" he asked.

"Sure am. Want to go?"

"Sure, I do but I gotta milk first thing, you know."

This made Colby smile. "I do know that. How about if I come out with you and I'll hook up Leviticus while you're milking. Then we'll go after breakfast."

"You reckon we might ought to take Tim?" David asked and Colby thought it over.

"No, I don't believe so. Him and Annetta ought to stay here," he said.

David glanced at their Mama, then nodded. "Well, sir, Tim can just go in with you next time," he said.

Colby nodded, appreciating his brother's ability to grasp the situation. "That'd be the way," he replied.

## CHAPTER 23

The next morning, the sun was well up, the boys had stomachs full of fried eggs, and Leviticus, with silent, gray indifference, was hitched to the wagon. David was itching to go but, for some reason, Colby was in no apparent rush. He checked the harness a time or two, told David that he had to visit the outhouse, then went to check something in the barn. Now he was back in the front yard calling for Tim-Bug.

David didn't understand why Colby was deliberately stalling their departure. David couldn't know that he was the reason Colby was stalling to delay long enough to ensure that the store would be open.

Colby had awakened earlier than usual that morning but had feigned slumber for a few minutes, waiting to see if David would wake himself up in enough time to complete his new chore.

Colby had been pleased and admittedly a little surprised, when David rose from his bed earlier than Colby normally did and began to dress in silence. At that point, Colby made a show of yawning loudly and asking what time it was.

"I don't know what time it is, Colby, but I'll do the milking and hook Leviticus up, too, if you want," David had said.

Colby had swung his legs out of bed and began dressing also.

"No, no. I'll hook up the mule. You just worry about Doris."

"Wouldn't be a bit of trouble, you know."

"I know it wouldn't cause you no troubles, but I need to get on up anyway." So their premature morning routine had begun.

Now David watched as Colby called again for Tim-Bug. Finally, Timothy came out. He had been sharpening his knife and, stepping into the yard, he closed it and slipped it into the front pocket of his pants with smooth, mindless grace.

"Yeah, Colby?" he said.

"You know me and David are going to town, right?" Colby asked.

"Well, I reckon you done told me ten times already," he said with a chuckle. Colby and David laughed too.

"Is that a fact?" Colby said.

"I'd say," Timothy answered.

"Well, then, the reason I called you out here is to tell you that you probably ought not to do any hunting this morning, at least until we get back," Colby said.

"I was planning on staying around, Colby."

"That's good. You see, it's just that…with the way Mama…"

"He knows why, Colby. Let's just go on and go," David interrupted his older brother. Timothy nodded and averted his eyes.

Colby stood in silence, maybe both his brothers were smarter than he was. He had a hopeful sense of mild shock. He looked over at the kitchen garden where Baby-Anne was already moving about, plucking the random weed, touching the plants.

"Well then, let's go," he said. He and David climbed up into the wagon and fussed at Leviticus until he turned toward the road.

They were less than halfway to town when Colby, without turning to look at David, said, "David, I've got in mind a dollar figure of how much I'd like to spend today. Now I know how smart you are and all, but I'm wondering if you're quick smart. Can you figure numbers real fast?"

"You mean just arithmetic?" David asked.

"Well, sure I do. What else is there?" Colby asked with a laugh. David didn't bring up the geometry book that he had seen at school.

"Yeah. I can add and subtract pretty quick and right in my head, too. I don't even need pencil and paper unless it's really big numbers."

"Well, I'm wanting to spend no more than nine dollars. Mama made out a list of things we need, so what I want you to do is figure up how much we've spent and keep a running total as we go. You understand?"

Colby knew that he could perform this task himself but thought that David could to do it more quickly. Plus, it would make him feel useful.

"Sure, I do, Colby. That shouldn't be no trouble at all."

"Good, then. What you need to do is to just tell me real quiet-like how much we've spent each time we get something."

David nodded with a thoughtful, serious expression designed to let his brother know that he would approach this job with appropriate studiousness.

Colby was glad to have David along and not just to keep the totals for him. Although he had been in the store hundreds of times, he had never been there as a money-holding decision-maker. He had his list but was nervous nevertheless.

They reached the store and Colby reined Leviticus to a stop in front. There was another wagon, horse-drawn and two pick-up trucks parked haphazardly along the side of the road. One of the trucks was a Ford and the other a Chevrolet, although the distinction was wholly lost on the boys. To them, the only difference was that one was black and one was a dirty, rusty red. They knew that the trucks were not owned by a member of their small community. They recognized the wagon as Spencer Kirk's.

They dismounted, and Colby, trying in vain for a confident swagger, led the way through the door.

The lack of a window in the east wall produced a dusty dimness in the mornings. Although the building was wired for electricity, Mr. Norvell refused to use the lights in the daytime.

Colby wanted to stop just inside the door, long enough to acclimate himself but David was behind him. He walked on in and looked quietly around.

Mr. Kirk sat in a rocking chair on one side of an old, empty pickle barrel, casually studying his end of a checkerboard. The game in progress had been interrupted by the arrival of the drivers of the pickup trucks. Mr. Norvell was behind the plywood counter, ringing up the purchases of one of the strangers while the other stood patiently in line. It would be the only time that day and perhaps the third or fourth time that week, that Mr. Norvell would have someone standing in line to make a purchase.

He looked up when Colby and David entered.

"Well, good morning to you, Colby. How's life on the farm?" This was his standard, well-used greeting to any of his regulars.

"Morning to you, Mr. Norvell," Colby said, then turned to the man in the rocking chair. "Morning, Mr. Kirk. You ain't gonna let Mr. Norvell beat you this early on a Saturday morning are you?" he asked with a grin, nodding at the checker game. Mr. Kirk yawned elaborately.

"Well Colby, Reverend Tannehill preached about charity last Sunday and truth is, that sermon went straight to my heart. Why, the thought of it still nearly brings a tear to my eye and so I think I could not bear to go through this day without letting old Lawrence win at least a game or two. It is, you understand, the Christian thing to do."

"The Lord does love a charitable man," Mr. Norvell said to the two strangers. The strangers, aware of the overblown irony in Kirk's speech, laughed at Mr. Norvell's retort. They didn't know that Mr. Norvell was, without question, the best checker player around. He would probably win the game in progress, just as he won nearly every game he played. To battle him to a draw was considered an accomplishment.

Russ Traylor was, by general acclamation, the second-best player around and could manage a draw once out of about every five games. He even managed to win one out of every thirty or so.

Colby laughed and tried to act at ease.

"Thought I might pick up a few groceries," he said to Mr. Norvell, who replied without looking up from the register, "Help yourself," and then, to the first stranger, "Looks like two dollars and twelve cents." The man took two one dollar bills off a small roll, laid them on the counter and added a quarter.

He didn't wait to watch Mr. Norvell count out the change. There were four aisles in the store and Colby led David down the first, where bags of beans were displayed. Colby stopped in front of the pinto beans.

"Colby," David whispered.

"What?" Colby answered.

"Mr. Kirk can beat Mr. Norvell."

"Well, he'd be about the only one that could," Colby said.

"No, I mean in the game they're playing now."

"Now how in the world could you know that?"

"I don't know how. I just know that if Mr. Kirk forces a trade out of the pieces on the left side, then in eight or nine moves, he'll end up with two kings and Mr. Norvell will only have one, with no hope of getting more because Mr. Kirk will have him on the run," David said confidently but eager for Colby to believe him.

"And you can tell all that just by looking once?" Colby inquired, dubious and even uninterested in what he considered David's exaggerations.

"Sure, I can. I'd bet every bean in this store that I could play Mr. Kirk's position to a win."

"Well-sir, why don't we start out with this twenty-five-pound bag here. You see that price tag?"

"Sure, I do."

"Well, start adding," Colby said and picked up the bag and set it down by the front door. He returned to the first aisle to continue shopping.

It seemed to Colby that it took at least an hour to collect the items on Mama's list but in reality less than ten minutes had elapsed by the time they collected everything except the fruit.

Colby led David to the fruit bin and they looked in.

"How much we spent?" he asked.

"Eight dollars and ten cents." David answered.

Colby nodded. "Good. Now what I'd like to do is to get us all an orange and a banana. Is ninety cents enough to do that?"

"Sure, it is. We could even get two bananas apiece."

Mr. Norvell, now reseated across from Mr. Kirk and beating him in checkers for the third straight time, saw them picking up the bananas.

"Colby, if you're going to buy those bananas, be sure that y'all eat them tonight or tomorrow. They've been there four days, and if they get much riper, they won't be fit to eat."

"Yessir," Colby said. He and David carried the fruit to the counter and laid it next to their other goods.

"I reckon that's gonna 'bout do it, Mr. Norvell." Colby was relieved that they had stayed within their budget. They still had to go to Old Man Tom's, who lived with his hogs a mile up Route 1465, and buy two buckets of lard. Colby didn't know for sure how much a bucket of lard cost but was confident that he could get two for less than a dollar.

Mr. Norvell walked behind the counter and began ringing up their purchases.

"Looks like nine dollars even, Colby. That going to be cash or do you want to put that on your account?" he asked.

Colby, who was about to ask how much Old Man Tom charged for a bucket of lard, was taken wholly by surprise. Account? Colby was fairly sure that an account meant that he didn't pay now but later on. Would Mr. Norvell charge interest like the bankers? Did Daddy know about this? Colby had never seen Vernon purchase anything on account but, even if he had, he wouldn't have done it in front of Colby. Colby couldn't imagine Vernon buying anything on credit, but Mr. Norvell had asked so casually, like it was completely normal. Colby pulled out the ten-dollar bill and held it up.

"Reckon today I'll just pay cash," he said.

Mr. Norvell nodded as Colby handed over the bill, then handed him a single dollar bill back.

"David, why don't you start carrying out some of these things?" Colby requested.

"Sure, Colby." David grabbed the beans and walked out. After the door closed behind him, Colby said, "Mr. Norvell, how much does Old Man Tom charge for lard, do you know?"

"Fifteen cents a bucket and you got to promise him to bring the bucket back when it's empty."

"And another fifteen cents if you make him promise to wash out the bucket before he fills it up again," Kirk joked from his perch by the pickle barrel and both he and Mr. Norvell laughed. Colby tried to join in but was, for a moment, concerned that it wasn't a joke. He was also enjoying a sense of relief at the relatively low price of the lard. It left him enough money to attack another problem.

As David came back in, gathered another load of groceries and walked back out, Colby stepped quickly over to the tobacco rack and picked up a pouch of Beech-Nut Chewing Tobacco. It was either that or Mail Pouch and Colby faintly recalled hearing somewhere that Beech-Nut was a milder chew.

He walked back to the counter and flipped the tobacco casually onto it, quietly hoping that the men wouldn't think it out of the ordinary or want to talk about it. He said, "Let me get this too."

Mr. Norvell poked once at his register and the bell sounded.

"That'll be a quarter," he said. Mr. Kirk smiled and looked down at the checkerboard. Colby fished a quarter out of his pocket, laid it on the counter and pocketed the tobacco just as David walked in to get the last of the groceries.

"Wait just a minute and I'll get y'all a box for that fruit and bread and baloney," Mr. Norvell said.

# CHAPTER 24

Colby and David were home well before noon. Old Man Tom had sold them two buckets of lard and told Colby that he was planning his summer slaughter in six weeks or so.

Old Man Tom had, for the last thirty years, received help from his neighbors at slaughtering time by bartering out lard, sausage and ham. He needed three or four men to help him and the trade was a full day's help for one smoked ham, ten pounds of sausage, five buckets of lard and two pounds of bacon. He would also throw in all the pickled pig's feet that anyone wanted, although it was only the older helpers who wanted them.

He also offered head cheese for free, but it had been a while since anyone had taken him up on what he considered a generous offer.

The brains he would save for himself to mix with fresh, scrambled eggs and sweet butter, served steaming hot and teeming with salt and black pepper and, in the right season, thick, white slices of tangy, juicy onion.

Colby, who had recent experience in swapping out labor with Russ, eagerly volunteered to help in the slaughter and Old Man Tom took him up on his offer.

As they left the hog farm with two buckets of lard, Colby pondered how long the food provided by one day of his own labor would last. They were halfway home when Colby realized that he should have volunteered David's work, as well. He was sure that David would jump at the chance to help—in fact had probably already thought of it—and it would be twice as much food in payment.

He considered turning around to offer David's help to Old Man Tom but he didn't want to seem anxious. At church tomorrow, he could casually mention that David was a good hand and might be able to help out.

They stopped the wagon by their front door and the twins ran out to meet them.

"David, why don't you take these beans on in? I'll get Tim-Bug to help with the rest," Colby said. The groceries were quickly unloaded, and Mama silently put the dry goods away. The fruit she put in the middle of the table in a green, factory-made, ceramic bowl. Colby couldn't stop looking at the fruit and saw that his sister and brothers were also staring. He was pleased to provide them something they so obviously wanted but was also saddened somehow. He could see that David craved the fruit but kept his pride firmly in control. Annetta was wavering but she knew to wait. Timothy, however, pointed at the bowl and looked questioningly at Colby.

"Mr. Norvell said that we ought to eat these bananas today or tomorrow or they might go bad. It looks like we got ten, so why don't we each have one now and another tomorrow," Colby said. David, Timothy and Annetta all jumped forward and grabbed a banana and Colby had to stop himself from doing the same.

"Mama, c'mon and let's eat us a banana," he offered.

Anne shook her head, but Colby could tell by the way she stared at the bowl that it wasn't because she didn't want fruit. It wasn't until later that he noticed she wasn't singing her wounded song.

"Mama, we got us each two bananas and an orange. Now, why don't you come on and eat something?" Colby asked.

"I ain't never been over-partial to bananas, Colby. I want y'all to take mine and split it up between you now. Do as I say," Anne said.

The younger children, giddy with their unexpected windfall, hastily peeled another banana and began arguing over the proper way to divide it.

Colby, fully aware of what was going on, reached for his banana. "Y'all just divide that one on up into thirds. This one here's going to be enough for me," he said and peeled his banana and took a full-mouth bite of sweet, soft fruit.

He had eaten bananas before, but had never so fully enjoyed one, nor been so aware of its flavor, texture and rich, unique aroma.

David, the uneaten half of his banana in one hand, began running wildly around the kitchen making gorilla sounds, mashed banana pulp smeared over his front teeth.

Even Mama laughed at his performance as she began making baloney sandwiches.

# CHAPTER 25

After lunch, Timothy picked up the rifle and began loading it.

"Colby, I only got about a half box of bullets left. Might be you could pick some up next time you're in town," he said.

Colby rose from the table. "I'll see about it. You going on out now?" he said.

"Sure am. I'll be in before dark," Timothy replied and stepped outside. Colby had noticed a slight change in his youngest brother in the few days since he had started hunting. He wanted to spend more time with Colby and David, he complained less, the youthful whine was gone from his voice and he had started to walk with a straight posture, proudly and purposefully. Colby understood better than most that Tim-Bug felt good contributing to his family's well-being.

He had not yet talked to Timothy about killing, as he had with David, but it didn't worry him. He trusted that Tim-Bug intuitively understood the grave responsibility a hunter has towards his prey.

David rose from the table just after Colby and waited for directions. Colby finally turned to him. "Well, David, you about ready to try your hand at hoeing?"

"Sure I am, Colby," he said happily.

"Well, then, let's us just go on down to the barn. We'll chop around for a couple of hours in the back field today, kind of get you used to hoeing before Monday. Besides, the Reds play at three-thirty today and I sure wouldn't mind getting to listen to a whole game for a change. When they play during the day, I miss the first half or more and when they play at night, I either miss it all or fall asleep on it before the fifth inning," he laughed with a small shake of his head.

Colby showed David how to sharpen and hold the hoe and once in the field, demonstrated the short, economical chopping motion that worked best. He set a pace that he considered slow enough for David to easily match. Colby wasn't working a third as hard as he could but after thirty minutes he looked over and noticed that David, although grimly and proudly trying to keep up, was already breathing hard, sweat dripping off his nose, while Colby wasn't sweating at all.

Colby was proud of his brother for not saying a word of complaint and gamely trying to keep up. Colby remembered that he was two years older and had been doing farm work for two years. He slowed his pace a little more.

"You ain't got to fight that hoe, David. Daddy always said to let your tools do the work for you. Otherwise, you'd just as soon be out here with nothing but your hands and a long day ahead of you. Here, let me show you," he said and stepped over to his brother. David finally stopped chopping and wiped the sweat from his face with his shirt sleeve. He stood back and watched Colby's smooth, seemingly effortless strokes. His worship of his brother aside, David was amazed that Colby could cover so much ground without working up a sweat or breathing heavily.

"You just got to find you a pace you can live with, David. Don't even worry about how fast I'm going or how fast you're going. You just gotta get your arms and back used to the motions. It don't take long."

"Were you ever able to keep up with Daddy when y'all were hoeing together?" David asked.

Colby pulled a look of clownish exaggeration over his face. "Shee! What're you talking about? I couldn't no more keep up with Daddy hoeing than I could run as fast as a deer or climb trees fast as a squirrel. Couldn't nobody work like Daddy. That's why he told me to just work at my own pace and not try to match his." This last statement wasn't entirely true, but Colby hoped it might convince David to work at his own pace. It appeared to work because David started chopping more slowly at the weeds but still with a sidelong look at Colby's hoe. It wasn't long before David's motion was nearly as smooth as Colby's, although not nearly as fast.

The afternoon passed slowly, the words between them few. David kept watching Colby, hoping that Colby wouldn't notice, and Colby continued to watch David, moving fast enough to gently push David while staying well within David's range.

The breeze blew the worst of the sun's heat off of the boys as they finally found a pace to suit them both. David stopped sweating and even attempted conversation every so often, just to show Colby that he had enough energy to talk and work at the same time.

Colby knew that he couldn't continue to work at this slow pace after today, but it didn't worry him. On Monday, Colby would simply remind David to find his own pace, then go on working like he knew he should. He was confident that David would understand and not let it hurt his pride.

As the sun began falling toward the western horizon, Colby's mind slid into his world of baseball. He had recently heard talk on the radio of the All-Star Game. He was trying to decide if he should be a starter or a last-minute addition to the team, batting in the ninth inning with the bases loaded.

"You reckon he's in heaven?" David asked suddenly, without looking up from his work. Colby stopped hoeing.

"Who? Daddy?" he said.

"Yes, Daddy. You think he went to heaven?"

"Well David, I don't see why he wouldn't have. He went to church regular and was about as honest as any man could be."

"I guess so," David said, still hoeing. Colby stood a moment longer before it occurred to him that it wasn't heaven David wanted to talk about but Daddy. Colby felt a twinge of guilt that he had rarely thought of his father since that one awful morning on the lumber pile. He had simply been too busy with the business of his family's survival to think much of the dead.

"You know David, I ain't had much time around the twins lately. How are they getting along with thinking about Daddy dying and all?" he asked.

"I reckon they're all right." David paused in his work, then remembered where he was. He chopped harder.

"Truth is, I think they were mostly just scared of him and didn't really know what to think. I think they know they're supposed to be sad but maybe they ain't. Might be they're just scared. Hard to tell really," David said, unable to look at Colby.

"Shoot, I was scared of him too," Colby said, trying to laugh dismissively but failing. The figure of Vernon was still too fresh and imposing to laugh away. "Well, it might be better to say I was awed by him. Everybody was, though. And don't tell the twins but now I get scared a lot of times, too." Colby stopped and waited for a response.

Getting none, he looked more closely at David—clever, cheerful David—who was now back to hoeing at a pace far too fast. Colby saw a drop of water fall off the end of his brother's nose and land in the soil. He realized that David wanted to work up a sweat in order to pretend that it wasn't tears falling onto the ground. Colby turned away and resumed hoeing.

"What you might could tell the twins is that it don't really matter if they're scared. Everybody gets scared. The important thing is to not give in," he finally said.

"I wouldn't never give in," David mumbled, still hoeing and ashamed of his tears while also proudly, solidly defiant.

"I know you wouldn't David. Truth is, I was counting on it."

"You can count on me, Colby."

"I know it. I know that I can. And what you need to remember is that scared don't matter. With Tim-Bug doing his hunting and Annetta helping Mama and you helping me with this and doing the milking and all…wellsir, that's us fighting against that scared feeling. What we're doing here today, right now, working and keeping going and all, is really just the opposite of fear. It's just exactly the opposite."

Colby didn't turn around but knew that David was nodding his head in silent, sad agreement.

## CHAPTER 26

The next day, after the preaching, the men gathered in their circle. Colby was more comfortable this week, even looking forward to it a bit. Colby knew that he could pick up valuable tips as the men discussed their crops. The only thing making him nervous was the chewing tobacco problem. He still couldn't chew but still he didn't want to lose face.

He hadn't seen Russ speaking to Big Tom before church.

Mr. Norvell had just finished giving a comic account of two drunken young men who had come into his store earlier that week, absolutely certain that they were within ten or twelve miles of Ohio. Mr. Norvell had assured them that they were a solid hour and forty-five minutes from Ohio and sent them with gentle, country firmness on their way—watching in amazement as they drove back the way they had come.

After the laughter died, Russ reached into his back pocket.

"Reckon a chew might hit the spot about now," he said. He opened the pouch, took a small chew and handed it to his right, directly into the hands of Big Tom. Big Tom had been so cheerfully eager to play his role that he had made a worrisome point of standing right next to Russ.

"Think I'll have to pass today," he said. "I bit the daylights out of my tongue the other day, tried chewing afterwards and thought my head was gonna explode it hurt so bad." He spoke loudly and too fast, obviously rehearsed.

Russ looked at the ground, then closed his eyes and shook his head in resigned amusement. Subtlety was a skill that Big Tom neither had nor recognized. Next week he would ask one of the older men to pass on the chew. He just hoped that Colby hadn't noticed Big Tom's overacting.

Colby didn't miss much.

Russ glanced at Colby as Big Tom handed the chew on. Colby was talking to E. E. Robinson and conspicuously unable to stop himself from stealing quick glances at the tobacco's progress around the circle. He knew that something wasn't quite right about Big Tom's statement, but he wasn't exactly sure what. He thought it may have something to do with him, but he didn't suspect that their benevolent performance was wholly for his benefit. What he noticed was that nobody cared that Big Tom had declined the chew.

Russ watched Colby watch the tobacco. The conversation had picked up again. Spencer Kirk took the tobacco and glanced quickly at Russ, who discreetly shook his head. Kirk nonchalantly handed the tobacco on and began telling the circle about a solid white raccoon he had seen the previous week.

When the tobacco got to Colby, he handed it dismissively to his right, using his feigned interest in the white raccoon to hide his relief that nobody seemed to notice or care that he hadn't chewed again this Sunday.

The discussion went on, the plugs nearly spent, and Colby thought it high time to prepare to go home. Not yet comfortable enough to be the first to leave, he was hoping that one of the men would say something about heading home. Colby looked over at the playing children, trying to catch David's eye and didn't notice Russ nodding at Lawrence Norvell. When Colby brought his attention back to the group, Russ said, "Do much business to speak of this week Lawrence?"

"Well, sir, other than those two drunks, I can't think of but one other thing of any interest that happened all week."

"Don't tell me you beat Spencer now did you?" Big Tom said. He, like most of the men there, were in on this one too.

"You know better than that. No sir. Something even more remarkable happened. Something I can't recollect happening in ten or twelve years at least."

"You dusted your shelves," James Caudill said, his deadpan delivery earning a laugh from everybody, Mr. Norvell included.

"No sir, even more unbelievable than that. A local farmer, who attends this very church and is among us now, came into my store yesterday, bought some groceries and actually paid cash money for them instead of putting them on his account. Durndest thing I ever saw," he said and winked at Colby.

"You can't mean it!" E. E. Robinson said, acting comically shocked.

"I do mean it. Y'all might want to think about taking a lesson from him, too. Take a step forward, Colby," he said.

Colby almost stepped forward before he realized that he wasn't really supposed to. Colby thought that Mr. Norvell was talking about him, especially after the wink and was surprised and glad that he had done something worthy of notice. What hit him hardest, however, was knowing that all these men apparently bought groceries on account regularly.

Finally the circle broke, Colby walked over to Mr. Norvell and touched him on the shoulder. He wanted to confirm what he heard.

"Mr. Norvell?" he said.

Mr. Norvell turned around. "Yes, Colby?"

"Yesterday you mentioned me buying those groceries on account?"

"Sure."

"Well, sir, I do have an account then?"

"You surely do, Colby. The Graysons have always had an account with me." He didn't add that Vernon had never once used it. "I carry accounts on most every farmer around here."

"And we pay you off after we sell our tobacco?"

"Then or whenever is convenient. I sometimes kid 'em about it, but all the people around here are honest sorts. Having an account for them is just like money in the bank for me."

"You charge interest?"

"Interest?" Mr. Norvell asked.

"Yessir. Like at the bank. It's almost like you're lending money, so it seems to me that it would be fair of you to charge some interest."

"Nossir. I don't charge interest. Never have. Me giving credit ain't nothing more than what you'd call a business courtesy. All stores do it. Even old E. E. will give anyone he knows credit at his store, if you find yourself in need of fencing or lumber or other farm supplies. Around here, all the income comes in big lumps during the tobacco sales, so running things by accounts is just the way we have of making things work out for everyone, me included."

Colby nodded, trying to hide his overwhelming relief. He would use his account only if necessary but feeding his family would no longer be one of his major concerns. He stuck out his hand and Mr. Norvell shook it.

"All right, then, I appreciate it. I'll see you next Sunday, if not before."

"Yessir Colby, see you then," Mr. Norvell said and walked away.

Colby looked at his parked wagon. It was one of only two left. Mama was already in the front seat, looking silently ahead; the twins were in the back. David was on the ground talking to Reverend Tannehill. Something he said made the Reverend smile.

The last two or three Sundays, Reverend Tannehill seemed to be taking more of an interest in David and Colby was glad to see it. The Reverend was the closest thing to an educated man in their community. His only adornment was a ring that bore the words "Asbury Seminary" above a small red stone and below it, "1924." Colby knew that this was a college ring of some sort and had occasionally wondered why a college-educated preacher would choose a church so far from a larger town or city like Lexington or Ashland.

As Colby made his way toward the wagon, the Reverend said something that made David laugh out loud. The Reverend rarely cut up with anyone like this. Colby wondered whether, as an educated man, Reverend Tannehill recognized David's sharp intelligence and that was the reason why he paid David more attention.

Colby reached the wagon and nodded at the Reverend, who was about to put his hand on David's shoulder. He drew his hand back at Colby's approach.

"Reverend," Colby said.

"Ah, Colby. David here has been telling me that he has become a full-fledged farmer."

"Yes, sir, Reverend. He does all the milking now and he's going to start helping me out with the hoeing and things."

"That's wonderful. It's a good thing to keep children busy when they're not in school, for as we all know, 'lazy hands make a man poor but diligent hands bring wealth.' Proverbs 10-4."

"Yes sir, Reverend. I can tell you for certain that there ain't too many lazy hands around our place," Colby replied and climbed up onto the wagon, followed by David.

"That is well. For, staying in Proverbs, we learn to 'train a child in the way he should go and when he is old he shall not turn from it.' Chapter twenty-two, verse six." he said, eyes half-closed and smiling with composed serenity.

Colby looked behind at children, checking to see they were settled, then nodded at the Reverend.

"Good day to you, Reverend," he said.

"And to you also, Colby," Reverend Tannehill said and watched them drive away. When the wagon was well out of the churchyard, David raised a hand in farewell.

Reverend Tannehill waved back and swallowed hard, breathing deeply, with his eyes on David. He didn't know why he had quoted so much Bible to Colby. Only the women liked to hear him quote verses. He never understood if they really enjoyed hearing them or they wanted constant, gentle reassurances that their preacher knew his Bible frontwards and backwards.

He watched David until the wagon was out of sight. Such a bright, special child, shining with intelligence, wit and spirit. It had been five years or more since Reverend Tannehill had noticed such a glowing, perfect child. He wondered if Anne or even Colby, recognized how exceptional David was. He lifted his Bible and with trembling hands, turned slowly to the tenth chapter of Mark. It had been far too long since he had read verse sixteen.

111

## CHAPTER 27

The following week passed uneventfully. It rained most of Monday night but dried out enough Tuesday morning for them to get out into the fields. Although only his third day in the fields, David had already discovered the easiest way to hoe and maintained a pace that, while slower than Colby's, was respectable.

Zach worked with them on Tuesday and he and David hit it off immediately. They talked to each other nearly all day and Colby was frankly glad. He was accustomed to the silently productive workdays with Vernon and was content to listen in or sometimes pretend to listen and let his thoughts wander.

With David helping full-time and with Zach's help on Tuesday and half of Friday, the crops were in better shape than they had been since Colby took over. The tobacco got six days bigger. The weeds were completely under control. They would be eating fresh cucumbers out of their kitchen garden soon and the corn, though still small, had doubled in size since Zach had helped thin it out. Things were in such good shape that Colby thought he and Zach might begin fixing the barn roof on Zach's next full day at the farm.

On Thursday, about an hour before sunset, Colby walked out to check the mail and walk down the side of the road, hoping to repeat his good luck. In less than ten minutes, he found a crumpled-up dollar bill, three quarters, a buffalo nickel and five pennies. He decided to make another trip to town on Saturday. He could use this money to buy groceries and stop in E. E. Robinson's supply store to confirm that he could buy things on account there. He needed supplies for the barn. If he kept finding money and paying cash for his groceries, maybe he would have just the one account to pay off in the winter.

Things had gone so well that week that when he and David returned from town a little before noon on Saturday, Colby decided to give them the afternoon off from working the fields. David was improving daily, but Colby didn't want to risk wearing him out and Colby knew that he, too, would be none the worse for a free afternoon.

The Reds didn't play until that night. When David went off to hunt with Tim-Bug, Colby decided to use his time off to try chewing tobacco. He had held the pouch of tobacco for a full week but the most he had brought himself to do so far was to open it and take a big whiff. The sweet, molasses smell was encouraging but it also made his mouth water in a backward, unpleasant way.

The tobacco was on the work bench in the barn, not exactly hidden but purposefully placed behind an old coffee can full of nails. Colby reached behind the can, pulled out the pouch and opened it, smelling again the cloying, syrupy aroma. He extracted what he judged to be the proper amount. Held between his thumb and first two fingers was enough shredded, richly brown leaf that, when compressed into a wad, would be bigger than a robin's egg but smaller than a chicken's.

At church, he had observed the men putting the loose tobacco into their mouths and forming it into a wad with their tongue and jaws. Because this was his first time, Colby balled it up in his hands before putting it into his mouth. The process made his fingers brown and sticky. He held the wad up between the thumb and forefinger of his right hand and smelled it again before sticking out his tongue and taking a hesitant, fearful taste. He looked at the ball some more while running his tongue around the inside of his mouth, trying to decide how bad it was.

He heard Doris lowing out in the small paddock beside the barn. The sound reminded him that he wanted to complete this whole business before David returned for the milking. If it was going to make him sick, he wanted to be sick alone.

He popped the plug into his mouth and worked it over into his right cheek, creating a bulge. Whatever else was to come, Colby knew from watching the men at church that at least he looked like a tobacco chewer.

He stood perfectly still, fully experiencing his first real chew. It tasted every bit as sweet as it smelled, like molasses. After a few seconds, Colby felt a sharp, stinging sensation that made his mouth water so much that he nearly drooled.

"So that's why everybody spits so much when they chew," he thought, the realization somehow elating him. He spit a copious stream of brown tobacco juice onto the dirt floor of the barn.

"That's why they spit," Colby said aloud, grinning messily and still overly amused by his discovery. He spit again and had to wipe his chin with his shirt sleeve. This wasn't so bad. Chewing tobacco wasn't difficult. Apparently you just slobbered it around in your mouth and when it got really wet, you just spit. It was no big deal, really. He stood there for a few minutes, excited that he was actually chewing tobacco. If it was this easy, Colby thought he might chew with the men at church tomorrow.

He realized that he was standing in the middle of the barn, staring out the door and spitting in the dirt. The thought amused him and made him feel silly at the same time. Feeling that he should be doing something, he walked around the barn, making a mental list of the things that he, Zach and David would do on Tuesday and probably Friday, too.

Colby knew of a couple of things that for sure had to be fixed. Several of the metal sheets that comprised the roof were rusty, derelict and leaky and would need replacing. Many of the rails above his head were warped. He looked around on the ground. That lumber pile was a mess. He could have David straighten it up and make a neater stack of those tobacco sticks.

"Tobacco sticks," Colby said and laughed. He had no idea why those words were funny, but they were. He wondered why he should even bother spitting out the tobacco juice. His mouth was nearly numb and some of the juice had trickled down his throat, numbing it, too. He wasn't sure if it was against the rules to swallow but he was flying high enough that it seemed to be the very thing to do. It was the last even partially coherent thought that he would have that afternoon.

"Tobacco sticks," he said and swallowed a burning mouthful of thick, brown tobacco juice.

He walked into the back of the barn then stood still, looking at the wall in front of him. The buzzing high of moments ago had turned instantly into dizziness. The wall seemed to be breathing. In fact, Colby thought he could *hear* it breathing, then realized that it was the roaring in his ears. Why had he come back here?

He swallowed again.

"The rails," he mumbled wetly. The rails, upon which the tobacco sticks would rest while the tobacco cured in the fall, needed attention. Many needed to be replaced. Colby looked up at them with half-open eyes, his mouth hanging open. As he tilted his head back, he felt his mouth flood with saliva. So far gone, he couldn't even recognize that he was sick.

Luckily for him, the saliva began flowing unnoticed from Colby's mouth, taking the plug of tobacco with it. Colby's chin and the neck of his shirt were stained brown as the drool continued coming.

Colby couldn't know that the nicotine in the tobacco was absorbed much faster and in vastly greater dosages through his stomach than through the lining of his mouth. Because he had swallowed, Colby had enough nicotine crashing through his veins to make even an experienced chewer ill.

Colby finally looked back down. His mouth still hung open and dripping and thin, runny snot streamed from his nose. His skin had gone cold and moist. He knew that he had to get off his feet before he fell down in the dirt. Spinning limply around, he saw the lumber pile and reeled drunkenly in its direction. It was about twenty feet away but it seemed like miles. He staggered, using every bit of will he possessed to make it to the pile in a straight line. His stomach gurgled with sickening intensity.

Three feet shy of the lumber pile, he fell to his knees, retching with a fury that brought no relief.

Colby crawled as he vomited and finally reached the lumber. He raised himself just enough to flop face down onto the pile and settled uncomfortably in for the most miserable two hours of his life.

He threw up for five minutes, then dry-heaved for the next ten. The only mocking relief it brought was the capacity for coherent thought, as if the vomiting cleared his head just enough to let him experience the full depth of his misery.

Colby had never, ever been this sick. Never even close, nor had he imagined that this level of anguish existed. Three winters ago, he had contracted a bad case of the flu and that had been his previous standard for judging how sick he felt. He had thrown up a lot then and had been very ill for two weeks but he had slept feverishly through much of it and never felt anywhere near this bad.

As he lay there motionless, unable and unwilling to move, his nose running freely and his eyes watering, vomit and tobacco juice drying on his shirt and throat, he simply could not believe how bad he felt. Wave after nauseating wave of dizzying illness coursed through his inert body. Despite his immobility, his heart hammered away as if he had just completed a footrace. How could men voluntarily chew tobacco? It was impossible that there was in the world a substance that could make someone this sick.

And it just went on and on.

If Colby thought, even for a second, about the smell of the tobacco, the dry heaves would start all over again. He heaved so much and with such prolonged force that his stomach muscles ached and his neck grew stiff. He wondered idly and without really caring too much, if he would pee in his pants, maybe he already had. Directly beneath his face was a crack between two boards and much of his vomit had puddled among the lower boards, so at least Colby's face wasn't resting in it. It was, at that point, all that Colby had going for him.

He began to actually appreciate the smell of the vomit, because that kept him from thinking about the smell of the tobacco.

And it just went on and on.

It was a sickness that robbed him of all will. He was faced with the simple knowledge that he would never feel better. He didn't even have the strength to hope that he would feel better. So overwhelmed with illness was he that he couldn't even remember what it was like to feel well.

His body was exhausted, as was his spirit. He had not an ounce of pride left in his young mind, only a desperate, pathetic desire for sleep. But the nicotine, in a final, taunting insult, acted like caffeine and kept him wide awake to endure every last scrap of wretchedness.

And it just went on and on.

## CHAPTER 28

Colby became aware of a raging thirst. Various excretory fluids had dried into a disgusting, crusty mess on his face and he realized that he must have finally dozed off. He raised his head a bit, no longer dizzy and, miraculously, his stomach felt settled. His muscles were sore and his left leg was asleep. His right shoulder ached, though he couldn't remember doing anything to it.

Drained and shaky, Colby swung his legs around and sat up on the lumber pile. He held his right hand up and watched it tremble like an old man's. He took a deep shuddering breath, then another. Doris was lowing and Colby was disoriented. Was this the same day? Could he ever recover from that level of illness in just one day?

He looked out the barn doors and saw that the sun was just beginning its trip across the western sky. He correctly judged that it was between two-thirty and three o'clock. He had recovered in a little over two hours and more importantly, he had not been discovered. Wobbling, he made his unsteady way to the workbench and grabbed the can of lantern oil. He poured some over his vomit by the lumber pile. It masked the smell quite well and Colby could just tell David that he had spilled it.

He took off his shirt and headed for the well. The sun was shining and a cool breeze blew. Colby felt stupid for having made himself so sick, but he also felt mildly elated and even a bit triumphant. The worst thing he could imagine happening with the tobacco had happened and he had survived it.

He drew up a bucket full of water and took a long, cool drink from the tin cup tied to the bucket with baling wire. The water soothed his raw, aching throat. He drank another cupful and stood quietly, willing it to stay down.

Obviously, he had done something wrong. Chewing tobacco didn't make others that sick. He considered it as he washed his throat and chest. The wad he had chewed wasn't too big. Maybe it was just a matter of getting used to it, in which case Colby knew he would never be a regular tobacco chewer.

He drank another cupful of water before rinsing his shirt in the bucket. As he took in the cool, clean mouthful, he remembered swallowing tobacco juice. He was pretty sure he had never seen anybody swallowing the juice.

That's why Mr. Norvell kept an old brass spittoon next to the pickle barrel in his store, so they could chew inside and not have to spit on the floor. He had seen many men drink a Coke or an Ale-8-One while chewing, but that was still a long way from swallowing whole mouthfuls of tobacco juice. He would watch them at church tomorrow, but he became convinced that swallowing had been his mistake. He wouldn't chew tomorrow morning but decided to give the tobacco one more try, probably tomorrow afternoon and this time a smaller plug, no swallowing and he wouldn't leave it in long. If he became sick again, he would give up completely on chewing and make up some tale to tell the men at church. He dunked his shirt in the bucket, rinsed it out and dumped the water onto the ground. Rounding the back of the house, he hung his shirt over the clothesline to dry.

Colby's stomach was already rumbling with hunger. In the kitchen, Mama had laid out the rabbit meat to fry up for supper. Colby had always liked rabbit, but they had eaten it nearly every night since Tim-Bug began hunting. He was grateful for the meat, but the truth was he was getting tired of it. Tim was such a good shot that he no longer bothered with possums or squirrels, concentrating instead on rabbits and birds. The icebox was well stocked with cut-up rabbit pieces, soaking in salt water.

Although it was next to impossible to hit a bird with a rifle, there were also four dove breasts and two quail in the icebox. Another three or four of either and they would have a mess of them.

He looked again at the rabbit meat on the table and an idea hit him. He wondered if David hadn't already thought of it.

117

## CHAPTER 29

An hour later, Colby was sitting in the front room with the radio on. The Reds game was still a couple of hours away and he wasn't really listening to the music that was playing. Mama was in the kitchen starting supper. Along with the rabbit, they were having biscuits and a big mess of polk and wild mustard greens, steamed and covered with vinegar, boiled egg, salt and pepper. Mama and Annetta had picked them that morning at the back of the Grayson property.

Annetta was now out in the kitchen garden, though Colby didn't know why. He and David kept the weeds out of it and there was nothing more that could be done there. But she was showing an interest in the vegetables, so Colby just left her to it. Maybe he should show her how to hoe and turn the kitchen garden over to her, at least for the summer.

Colby's stomach began rumbling again, this time not so much in hunger but in queasiness. He went to the kitchen and poured himself a glass of milk, stirring the cream in and downed the glass in two long swallows. He stood at the sink, making sure that the milk would stay down, then returned to the front room.

Just as he was sitting down, Timothy walked in the front door, holding two skinned and cleaned rabbits in his left hand and the rifle in his right hand. He stopped when he saw Colby and held the rabbits up for inspection.

"David hit one of these," Timothy said.

"Is that right?" Colby replied.

"Well…winged one. I had to finish it off, though. It was right smart away from us and I was scared that it might get down its hole before David could put another bullet in it."

"Sounds to me like you done just right."

"Reckon so, Colby."

"David gone to do the milking?" Colby asked.

"He sure did. We came up through the back, so he just stayed to do it. Barn smelled funny."

Colby nodded. "Is that right?" he said.

"Sure is. I think maybe that the coal oil got…" Tim hesitated, realizing that David was the most likely to have spilled the oil and he didn't want to

118

get him in trouble with Colby. "Well, I don't really know what it was. Maybe it was nothing."

"Maybe," Colby said.

"Colby?"

"Yeah?"

"Did you, was you able to get me more shells today? I'm 'bout out, you know."

"They're on the desk there but from now on, you might want to think about buying your own," Colby said and grinned.

"Now just how in the world did you reckon I could do that, Colby?" Timothy said, not sure whether or not he was being made fun of. "I don't have a single durn nickel. Wouldn't even know where to keep one if I had one."

"Well, sir, I reckon you've seen how much rabbit we've got in the icebox, haven't you?"

"I sure have. Probably a durn sight more than any other icebox around here," Timothy claimed proudly, almost wanting Colby to deny it so that Timothy could argue the point and win.

Colby's grin widened.

"I can just about guarantee you that. Mama puts much more rabbit meat in there and it's going to start going bad before we can eat it all."

Timothy thought for a moment.

"Maybe we ought to start eating it for lunch, too. That way you wouldn't have to buy baloney or peanut butter," he offered earnestly, nodding in self-approval at his solution.

"Maybe we could but I was thinking of something else."

"Well Colby, it ain't easy to hit them birds. Unless I'm right sure of a hit, it's just a waste of bullets shooting at them."

Colby laughed.

"That ain't what I was thinking about either, Tim-Bug. I reckon I trust your judgment on that hunting more than I'd trust my own. I was just thinking that maybe you ought to try selling some of those rabbits to the folks around here."

"Selling 'em?" Timothy asked, then looked at the two in his hand.

"Sure, sell 'em. Just about everybody likes some good fried rabbit every so often but no one has much time to hunt during the summer."

"Sell 'em. For money?"

"Sure, for money. There's fifteen houses within walking distance. There's plenty of rabbits around. As good a shot as you are, you'll have plenty to sell."

"How much you reckon I could sell 'em for?" Timothy said, looking at his rabbits with a new respect, born of his realization that they had value other than as food for the family.

Colby shrugged his shoulders. "I don't really know, just to tell you the truth. I'd have to say that that much beef would sell for a dollar or more, so I'd have to guess…fifty or seventy-five cents apiece."

"You reckon?"

"I do, although I'd also reckon that a whole bunch depends on how much a man is willing to pay. You'd just have to work it out."

"I ought to take David with me," Timothy suggested, looking at Colby for approval.

Colby was surprised and pleased. He saw that, not only did Timothy recognize that David was better suited to handling a transaction like that, he wouldn't selfishly demand to be in charge and receive all the credit.

"You could. Probably have to give him part of the money then."

"Some of the money," Tim repeated.

"Well, sir, after you bought some more shells, took care of your cost. I should have said you might have to give him some of your profit."

"No, sir. David don't get none of it."

"What?" Colby asked. He had never known Tim-Bug to be hoggish.

"I don't think I'd give David none," Tim repeated.

"Well, come on now, Tim-Bug. If David helps you out, you got to share your profit with him. Fair's fair. You oughtn't to keep it all for yourself."

"I ain't going to keep none of it, either. If I make a profit, I'm going to give it to Mama. Well, I guess I'd really be giving it to you, but you know what I mean."

Colby's smile dropped from his face. He was ashamed to see how badly he had underestimated both of his brothers. He was about to tell Tim-Bug that it wasn't necessary to give over his profits when it occurred to him that contributing to the family's well-being was just as important to Tim as it was to him and David.

"I reckon that would help me out quite a bit, Tim-Bug. Sure would." Colby said, trying to act as if his brother had offered nothing more than to hook Leviticus to the wagon. "I know it'll make Mama happy."

Timothy bit his lip, waiting to make sure Colby was through, then nodded toward the kitchen.

"That's why, you know," he said quietly.

"Mama?" Colby said, equally as quiet. They could both hear Anne on the other side of the wall, preparing supper, singing.

Timothy nodded.

"You know how she's singing all the time? That song that kinda makes you sad but you don't know why?"

Colby nodded, heavyhearted that Tim-Bug knew all about Mama's song.

"I know, Tim-Bug."

"Well, sir, the other day, Annetta was telling me that Mama sings like that when she's scared or worried."

"I'd say," Colby agreed.

"Seems that she's been singing a whole lot more since Daddy died."

Colby noticed that Timothy had no problem speaking about Vernon's death.

"Could be. Annetta told you that?"

"She did. She's quiet sometimes Colby, but she don't miss much. She knows things, things like what's gonna happen. It can get right spooky sometimes. She always knows. Anyways, I'm thinking that Mama's worried more about money than anything else. I'd sure not mind putting her at ease just a little."

"That's a mighty fine offer, Tim-Bug, one I'd be proud to take you up on." Colby stared at Timothy, wanting suddenly to share with him that afternoon's experience with the chewing tobacco. He could make it into a funny story. Timothy would somehow understand it. More so than One-Eyed Zach. More so than even David. More than anyone Colby knew, Tim-Bug should be the one to hear the tale.

But not today. Soon but not today.

"Good then," Timothy said. "I'll go get David and we'll run on over to the Traylors."

"David's got milking to do. Besides, it's almost suppertime. It'd be more polite to wait till after."

"But then they won't be hungry anymore," Tim responded.

Colby shook his head with finality. "Nossir. I promise you that Mrs. Traylor's done already got their supper cooked and halfway to the table by now. Even if they want to buy those rabbits, they wouldn't eat them tonight. Just wait like I said, and you and David won't have to be in no hurry."

"Alright, Colby. I'll wait. I'd not really mind sitting down for a while anyway." Tim walked to the kitchen and laid his rabbits on the counter next to the sink.

"Colby?" he called.

"Yeah, Tim?" Colby called back.

"You reckon I ought to just put these in a grocery sack?"

"I'd say so. At least to carry them around in tonight."

Timothy pulled a brown paper sack out of the closet. He shook it open and carefully placed both rabbits in the bottom, then rolled the bag closed and set the bag next to the front door. Picking up the rifle, he checked to make sure there was no bullet in the chamber and hung it on the gun rack. He sat down on the couch.

"I'd say them rabbits got to be worth fifty cents apiece," he said, and Colby smiled.

## CHAPTER 30

Russ and One-Eyed Zach smoked peacefully on Russ's back porch. The late spring sun was sinking slowly. Both were quietly pleased by the lengthening days which, full and eventful, bestowed strength and hushed hope on nights like these. The men silently cheered the sun on its daily losing battle against the crickets and the stars.

As on more Saturday nights than not, One Eyed Zach had accepted an invitation to eat his supper with Russ and Dot. Dot had made mustard fried pork chops, buttery mashed potatoes, sliced fresh cucumbers covered in green onions and drizzled with apple cider vinegar, cinnamon fried apples, biscuits and cream gravy. For dessert, she carried three plates of peach cobbler onto the porch and handed one to Zach and two to Russ.

"You hold onto mine and I'll get the coffee," she said and turned to go back into the kitchen.

"Good thing you didn't hand me that extra plate, Mrs. Traylor. Wouldn't be none left for you when you got back out here," Zach said, crushing out his cigarette and smiling.

"Even you'd have a problem eating cobbler that fast, Zach," Dot said from within, then returned with a tray holding her coffee decanter, three cups with matching saucers and her matching cream and sugar service. Upon setting the tray down on the small table, she served first the men, then herself. Russ handed Dot her plate and they all took their first bite of fresh peach cobbler. Zach, as always, made the loudest fuss.

"Great day in the morning!" he burst, nearly a moan. "Mrs. Traylor, you just get better and better at this baking. I keep thinking that you can't top yourself and then you go and do it. Got to be some trick to it," he said, shaking his head in exaggerated amazement and took another bite.

"First rate, Dot," Russ said, more understatedly. He took a second bite just to make sure of his assessment. "Yes ma'am, I'd say that it surely is first rate."

Dot smiled in amusement. She knew that they were just as likely to carry on like this if she had cut up some green apples on day-old biscuits and called it apple pie but she also knew that this cobbler was especially good and enjoyed the flattery all the more because she knew that it was sincere.

They ate awhile in companionable silence, the only sound the clink and scrape of forks on plates, until the sun sank low enough for the crickets to begin their nightly, whirring song.

"Looks like the lightning bugs are back in business," Dot said, her fork held with dainty politeness in front of her mouth.

"You know this is the first time I've seen a lightning bug this year?" Russ said. "They surely are running late this year. That mean anything, Zach?"

Russ had discovered years earlier that Zach could authoritatively read the signs of nature. He could tell with fair accuracy a day in advance if it was going to rain merely by sniffing the wind or how harsh winter would be by the length of the woolly worm's brown stripe. With less seriousness but still with a grain of believability, he had told Russ that if you heard an owl hooting after sunrise in the spring, it would be a hot dry summer; the same omen in the fall signaled a cold, wet winter.

Zach also claimed that if it thundered in February, the same day of the month in May would bring a frost. Or, if you saw more than six or eight buzzards circling clockwise, you should guard your children for the next few days. Buzzards circling clockwise while others circled counterclockwise over the same spot meant you should watch out for yourself.

A squirrel that didn't run from you meant a good vegetable crop while a squirrel that ran towards you was bad news. If you heard a cricket chirring when there's frost on the ground, summer would be cool and wet.

"Well, sir, this is sure enough right late for the lightning bugs to be showing up," Zach said thoughtfully. He took a sip of coffee and put his empty cobbler plate on the tray. "You remember the second or third year I was here? The lightning bugs never showed up at all that year. You remember?"

Russ and Dot both nodded. Russ put his plate next to Zach's. Dot had a small bite of cobbler left but she cut it in half, turning it into two bites. She would make it a point to finish well after the men.

"Yes sir, I do remember. You remarked on it in July and I watched for the next seven, eight weeks. Never did see a lightning bug," Russ recalled.

Zach nodded knowingly. "You remember what that fall was like?"

"I do. Fall came early and hard with winter right behind it. Way I remember it, we were lucky to get the tobacco out of the field and in the barn as early as we did."

"We were at that. But the way it was told to me, better that the lightning bugs not show up at all than to show up late." Zach shrugged. "Can't really claim no knowledge about 'em showing up late and all though, never happened in my memory."

Russ combed his memory for a year the lightning bugs showed up late. He suddenly felt sick, troubled and, for some odd reason, hungry.

"Y'all want to buy a rabbit?" a cheerful voice called.

Russ, Dot and Zach all looked up, surprised. There at the bottom of the porch steps stood Timothy Grayson, holding a rabbit carcass up by the back legs. David was behind him.

"I got this'n and one more right here that's not much smaller. Killed 'em just today," Timothy said.

David closed his eyes and shook his head in frustration. On the walk over to the Traylors', he had explained to Tim-Bug why they should raise the subject of the rabbits slowly. They should, he said, make the Traylors want to buy a rabbit before they even knew that he and Tim-Bug had a rabbit to sell.

David had it all planned out. He was going to ask them what they had eaten for supper and if they had enjoyed it. The Traylors would naturally ask David what they had eaten, and David would tantalize them with the description of lean, salty, fried rabbit. One thing would lead to another and David would eventually say, "Well, we just happen to have a couple of extra rabbits here if you was maybe interested in buying them. But if not, we'll just enjoy them ourselves."

Tim-Bug had gone to pieces upon their approach and foiled David's plan.

"David?" Dot said, the first to recover. "Is that you, David Grayson? And Timothy with you. What are y'all doing out past dark like this?"

Timothy held the rabbit up higher, as if that was answer enough.

"Howdy, Zach," David said. "Mr. and Mrs. Traylor."

"David. What you got there, Tim?" Russ said, recovering from his surprise.

"Rabbit," Timothy said proudly. "Already cleaned and shot through the head. No buckshot to break your teeth on. Got him with a rifle. This other one, too."

"Is that a fact?" Russ said.

"Sure is. Tim-Bug here is a plain crack shot," David said. There was a brief silence. His plan for creating demand ruined, he dove right in. "The truth is, Mr. Traylor, Tim-Bug here has got us about as much rabbit as we can eat. We was thinking that maybe y'all might not mind eating some fresh rabbit. We'd sell it to you cheaper than you could buy beef or even chicken. Fresh-killed today."

Dot watched Russ for a moment as he looked at the boys. He didn't nod or even move but she knew his decision.

"Excuse me, boys," she said and took the tray of dishes back into the kitchen. She laid them by the sink and walked to the small, roll-top desk in the corner and counted out three dollars in quarters from the top drawer. It didn't matter how much the boys wanted for the rabbits; she knew Russ would pay it.

Outside, Russ was secretly elated that he had an opportunity to help the Graysons. He knew that what happened here would be reported to Colby, so he didn't want to be too obvious. He didn't want to simply give them far more that what the rabbits were worth. The boys were obviously excited, proud. Russ decided to haggle a bit.

"What are you asking?" Russ said, frowning seriously.

"Well, sir, at least…I'm thinking, if this was beef, you know, then…" Tim-Bug stammered, looking at David and wondering why he hadn't let his older brother handle it from the outset.

"We was asking a dollar apiece for them, Mr. Traylor. They're fresh," David interrupted.

"Well, sir, I was thinking that I might give you seventy-five cents for one of them," Russ said. "Don't know as I'd want two of them."

"Hawww," Timothy said, ready to lay the rabbit at Russ's feet. Seventy-five cents!

David put a restraining hand on Timothy's shoulder. "Ninety cents for one. Dollar seventy-five for both," he countered.

"I just want one," Russ said.

"I'd like to take the other, Russ," Zach said. "It's been six months or more since I fried me any rabbit."

Dot came back outside and handed Russ another cup of coffee on a saucer. Also on the saucer, unseen by the boys, were the quarters. She went back inside to get more coffee for Zach.

Russ sipped his coffee and looked hard at the boys, as if deliberating.

"Fresh are they?" he asked.

"Shot not two or three hours ago," Timothy said.

"And with a rifle? I ain't got to worry about no lead shot breaking my teeth?"

"Shot in the head. None of this meat is harmed," said Timothy, again holding the rabbit up for inspection.

"Well, Zach. Would you be willing to give eighty-seven and a half cents for a fresh, head-shot rabbit?" Russ asked, turning toward Zach.

Zach nodded. "I surely would," he said.

Russ set down his cup on the floor behind him, palmed the quarters and pretended to pull them out of his pocket.

"Well then, I would say that we have got us a deal. We'll take them both," he said and counted out seven quarters. He handed them to David and Timothy handed Russ the rabbits. Russ in turn gave one to One-Eyed Zach and the other to Dot, who took it inside and laid it on the counter. Later, she would cut it up and put it in saltwater.

Their business completed, Russ regarded Timothy.

"Crack shot are you?" he asked him.

"Well sir, if I aim at it, I generally hit it," Timothy answered with a nod.

"Generally, nothing!" David interjected. "Truth is, Mr. Traylor, I never seen him miss. Friday morning, Zach saw him hit a dove on the wing, didn't you, Zach?"

"I surely did, David and you ain't lying either. Ole Tim there is 'bout as good a shot as I've ever seen," Zach replied.

"Plenty of rabbits around here," Russ said.

"Don't seem to be no lack," Tim agreed.

"Might be you should ask around. Can't buy rabbit at the grocery," Russ said.

"That's what Colby said! He said that no one has time to hunt but everyone likes rabbit."

"I would say that is so," Russ said with a slow nod.

Dot came out again, this time carrying two small plates of peach cobbler. She handed one to each of the boys.

"Thank you, Mrs. Traylor." David said.

"Yes, ma'am, thank you," echoed Tim.

David held the plate uneasily, looking at the adults and shuffling from foot to foot, while Timothy watched David. The adults looked on, wondering what the boys were waiting for. It was Zach who understood first.

"Mrs. Traylor, you reckon I might could get me another small piece of that cobbler?" he said.

"Me, too, Dot, if you don't mind." Russ said, realizing that the boys didn't feel right eating alone at another man's house.

"Yes, I'll just get it." Dot said. "You boys just go on and dig in now, I won't be long."

David and Timothy devoured their cobbler in a way that saddened Russ, but he pretended not to notice. When Dot returned, she handed Russ and Zach their plates and they ate slowly enough for the boys to each get second helpings.

The boys finished their cobbler, thanked the Traylors politely and walked home in the dark.

## Chapter 31

On the way, they saw two raccoons scuttling about in the moonlight.

"You know, David, I might ought to have brought my rifle," Timothy said.

"How so?" David asked.

"Well-sir, if a rabbit's worth ninety cents, I'd say a 'coon got to be worth at least sixty."

"Could be," David mused.

When they entered their house, Colby was in the rocking chair with a glazed look in his eyes, apparently listening to the ballgame. David stood in front of him and, finally getting Colby's attention, silently dropped the seven quarters into his hand with a big grin. Colby grinned back.

"Mr. Traylor said he only wanted to give seventy-five cents apiece for these Colby, but David bargained with him and got near ninety cents apiece!" Timothy said, eager, excited.

"That's just great. It sure is. Just great," Colby said.

"Yes sir! And I'm going to keep on selling 'em too. I mean, we are, ain't we, David?"

"You bet we are," David agreed.

"Well, sir, since y'all are putting in money for groceries now, is there anything in particular you'd want me to get next time I go?" Colby asked.

"Peanut butter," Tim-Bug said.

"Canned peaches so Mama can make us a cobbler," David added. He had enjoyed Dot's cobbler more than he allowed to anyone, even Timothy.

"And Annetta loves that chocolate syrup that you can mix in with milk. Remember when Daddy brought some home a couple years ago?" Timothy said.

"I remember and I'll get some when I go. I'm pretty sure Mr. Norvell carries it," Colby said.

"Really? You will?" Timothy asked happily.

"Sure, I will. I might even go before next Saturday, depending on how the weather is."

"Good! I'm gonna go tell Annetta," Timothy said and ran into the kitchen.

127

"Colby?" David asked.

"Yeah, David?"

"Even Daddy never bought chocolate syrup but that once and that was in the winter, right after he sold his crop."

"I know. I'll just buy it this once and then we'll see." Colby watched David, waiting for his reaction. David simply looked at Colby with a concerned look on his face.

"You know you ain't got to worry none, don't you? I mean about us having enough to eat and things. You just ain't got to worry about that at all," Colby said reassuringly, aware of what was bothering his brother.

"Well, maybe I do sometimes," David admitted.

"Well, don't," Colby said, a bit harshly. It frustrated him to realize that David was worried. Colby had done enough worrying for the whole family. "We got things going pretty good around here. We got meat. We got eggs and milk. This money's enough to buy flour and I'm going to help Old Man Tom with his next slaughter, so we'll have plenty of lard and bacon and ham. A can of chocolate syrup ain't going to make or break us, so don't you worry yourself, now."

"Okay, Colby, I won't," David said.

"Good."

David pointed at the radio. "Reds winning?" he asked.

"They sure are. Up by one," Colby said.

## CHAPTER 32

Colburn Grayson limped out of the dugout using his bat as a cane. His right knee was badly swollen and nearly incapable of supporting his weight. He hobbled to home plate, the thunderous cheering of the home crowd a mere, trifling distraction. The men in the stands, war vets, understood pain and forbearance and nodded in sage admiration and commiseration.

The women, on the other hand, were stunned, some overcome by emotion, holding lacy handkerchiefs before their powdered noses and dabbing at misty eyes, wondering, "What could make a man do this to himself? What could drive him so? Could the competitive inferno rage and roar so profoundly in a man's soul? Could it burn so brightly, so hot and pure and liquid that he would endure, even ignore, such staggering pain?"

These fans knew that they were privileged on this day to witness the radiant collision of a hero and his destiny. And oh! How they roared! How they loved and admired him!

Colby was aware of the admiration but was unable to acknowledge it or dwell on it. It would distract him from his true purpose. He didn't see himself as a hero but simply as being true to his nature. If, by merely fighting through some annoying pain, he could help his Reds win one more game, then he would. He must. There was simply no other choice. If he could come through for his team this one last impossible time, the name of Colburn Grayson would be the name by which all future baseball greatness would be measured.

He nodded at the home plate umpire and then looked out at the pitcher as he took a few practice swings. He saw the slightest trace of fear in the eyes of the pitcher.

The Reds were down a run in the bottom of the ninth. Big Klu was on first, having lined a single to center.

"Batter up!" the umpire yelled.

Before stepping into the batter's box, Colby glanced into the stands behind home plate and there, hands folded as if in prayer and with tears of fear and love in her cornflower blue eyes, was the girl with yellow hair.

For reasons not altogether clear to Colby, the yellow-haired girl was a new character in this fantasy—indeed, in all his baseball fantasies. She was

Colby's age, maybe a year or two older, but Colby was an inch taller. Her face was vague and indistinct; Colby knew only that she was pretty. She wore a blue sundress, the color matching perfectly the color of her eyes and the pale blue ribbon that held back her flaxen hair.

In this scenario, she had come to the locker room before the game and begged Colby not to play, pleading with him not to ruin his future good health for the sake of one ballgame, however important.

Colby tipped his hat to her, threw her a wink and stepped to the plate, calm but eager to keep his appointment with the greatness that resided somewhere beyond the pain.

He stepped in, cocked the bat and waited for the first pitch. Big Klu was taking a short lead off of first base. The pitcher went into the stretch and threw a fast-ball, low and away for ball one.

The second pitch was a slider that just caught the outside corner: strike one. Colby knew that the pitcher would be coming with some heat on the third pitch, trying to get ahead in the count.

He dug in, waiting for the fastball. The pitcher went into the stretch, kicked—

*"On Jordan's stormy banks I stand and cast a wishful eye, To Canaan's fair and happy land…"* the congregation sang. Colby realized with a start that the sermon was over and the parishioners were singing again, hymnals open and held in front of their faces.

He peeked around to see if anyone had noticed that he hadn't been singing. Mama held a hymnal with Annetta singing on her left and David on her right. Tim-Bug was on the far side of Annetta, not even pretending to sing. Colby leaned over to look at Mama's hymnal and began to sing along with the congregation. He had been fantasizing throughout the whole service and hadn't the slightest idea what Reverend Tannehill's message had been.

The song ended and the collection plate was passed around. When it came to Colby, he held it low in his left hand and noisily dropped one of the quarters that Tim-Bug had brought home into it. It was the first time in weeks that he had anything to offer and, even though he knew that pride goes before a fall, he wanted his neighbors to know the Graysons were able to contribute.

There was not a single man there who did not know where the quarter had come from. Russ had arrived at church early again this Sunday to tell the men what needed to be done and assign them their lines and roles.

Today it was Russ himself, still mindful of Big Tom's woeful performance, who declined the chewing tobacco. Like he had the previous Sunday, Colby casually passed the chew on to his left, as if it was the most natural thing in the world to do so.

The men spoke a little of that week's weather, then Elijah Settles spoke to Colby. "Cole, Russ here tells me that that youngest brother of yours has rabbits to spare."

Colby didn't know what to be more excited about: the fact that there would apparently be a market for Tim-Bug's rabbits or that Mr. Settles had called him Cole. Colby liked the sound of "Cole." It made him feel more like an equal. Cole was the name that a farmer should carry, not Cole-bee. He hoped that the new name would stick.

"Yessir, Mr. Settles. Timothy. That's his name. He surely is a crack shot. My other brother David says that he's never seen Timothy miss."

"Well-sir, why don't you just send him 'round my place early this week. I know we oughtn't to talk business at church and all, but I'll give him a fair price. I do love a good fried rabbit," Mr. Settles said.

"And if there's any to spare, Cole, I wouldn't mind getting me one either," E. E. Robinson said.

"But Old Elijah said that he'd give a fair price and every man here knows that you wouldn't do the same, E. E.," Big Tom said and laughed, proud of his unscripted line.

Colby laughed with the rest of the men.

"Well, sir, it's Tim that shoots 'em but I believe it's David that sells 'em. You'd have to deal with him, I reckon. And I will say this, there don't seem to be no lack. I reckon that the foxes are going to starve to death this summer because Tim's taking all the rabbits."

"Sure enough, Cole, send your brother around this week. And speaking of foxes, now, if he could bag one of them, their skins sell for upwards of thirty-five dollars," E. E. said. As owner of the supply store, he didn't deal in skins himself, but he knew someone who did.

"Thirty-five dollars? For an old fox?" Colby asked.

"Yessir," E. E. continued. "I believe that price depends on the condition of the pelt, you understand, no bullet holes or anything, but thirty-five dollars is the last price I heard and that was just last month. The skins need to be stretched and dried, you understand. But if you and Tim bring me one, what I'll do is ship it to an outfit I know of in St. Louis, Missouri. Generally within about a week or two, they'll send me the check. I can give you the check or apply it to your account. Ever how you want to work it."

"You know I saw a fox this morning?" Russ said. "If I'd have known he was worth thirty-five dollars, I believe I would have taken a shot at him, Sunday or no."

"Well Russ, if you're aiming to get that fox, I'd say you'd better hurry, because once I tell Tim about him, I promise you he's as good as gone," Colby said.

"I reckon I'd give up the thirty-five dollars just to be rid of the fox. They sometimes carry the rabies you know," he said.

"I'll sure mention it to Tim and I'll surely send him and David out to see y'all, whoever wants some rabbit. It'll please them mightily, I'll tell you that," Colby said.

# SUMMER

# CHAPTER 1

Twelve days later, Timothy Grayson sat with his back against the curly paper bark of a creek side sycamore tree. He was, he judged, about three miles from home. He'd followed the creek from behind the Traylors' place until arriving here. He wasn't sure whose property he was on or even if it properly even belonged to anyone. The area was wooded and rocky, rendering it unsuitable for farming.

The sun was hot at midday but a fine and steady breeze blew cool and welcome, drying the sweat on his forehead and neck. In it he could smell the white, clean scent of the tumbling water.

The twenty-two rifle lay across his lap. As always, it was cleaned and oiled; ready, deadly. His knife—he no longer thought of it as Daddy's knife—rested in his pocket, sharper now than it had ever been. Timothy found that he had a knack for sharpening and he now honed Colby's knife as well as his own.

Regularly, he left the house just after breakfast, except Saturdays, when Colby and David went to town, and Sundays, when they all went to church.

It was Friday, the first day of July, and his father had been in the ground for thirty-nine days.

The sycamore stood about seventy-five feet from a sharp bend in the creek. The rabbits weren't normally out at this time of day, but Tim hunted nonetheless.

There was other game to be had: squirrels, groundhogs, a dove here or there. There weren't many deer around, but Tim believed that, if there were, they would come to this still and untroubled place to drink, this place of leaf and stone. He was also serene in his certainty that he could, and if one appeared, would bring it down with one swift, accurate shot to its head.

*Thirty-nine days.*

The huge and sometimes frightening man who had so dominated the life of the family since Tim's earliest thoughts had been weak when he died and, Tim knew, ashamed and horrified by his weakness.

Thirty-nine days Daddy had been in the ground and Tim wondered with a frank and innocent curiosity if Daddy's skin had rotted off yet.

Tim was not bothered by death. The blood that he had spilled in hunting was the same blood that he bore in his veins. Blood was just blood. Sometimes it got all over his hands, sometimes it didn't. When it did, he washed it off without thought or concern.

He didn't turn his head away from the smell of death and decay. It was simply how they would all smell after they had been dead awhile. If they didn't eat the rabbits and squirrels that he shot, they would begin to stink, too. It was all easily understood. Everything that ever lived also died. It wasn't a mystery and, therefore, not to be feared.

The breeze quickened and Tim raised his chin high to let the air blow down the front of his neck and onto his chest.

Tim simply wanted things to make sense, like the rifle and the knife. He knew exactly what they could do when used properly. He understood them and trusted them.

In the first days after his daddy's death, he had been unashamedly afraid, afraid and unsettled. More immediate, however, was the knowledge that his family's life would be different, different but probably not better. For Tim, there was no worse feeling than not knowing, of having no clear path, no road to take, no task to complete.

He thought back to the night almost two weeks ago when he first tried to sell rabbits to the Traylors. It should have been simple. Either they wanted the rabbits, or they didn't. They'd either buy them or they wouldn't. It shouldn't have been complicated but to him it was. Tim had been lost and confused after speaking one or two sentences, nearly sick with nerves.

David had easily taken over, as sure of himself as Tim was when he was hunting. How could it have been so easy for David? He even seemed to enjoy the bargaining. David had made the trade and the money as easily as Tim had bagged the rabbits.

Tim never had the agility with words that David had and so couldn't clearly express his fears about the uncertainty of the future and how he could help the family. But Annetta always knew the words that Tim couldn't find. She spoke to him with a strange, knowing serenity. Tim recognized her confidence mainly by his own lack of it. She had told him to wait until things settled down, wait for Colby.

He had waited and, thankfully, he hadn't had to wait long.

He couldn't express how relieved he had been to hear Colby getting up and going to work the day after Daddy's funeral. He hadn't mentioned it but later that morning Annetta had smiled at Tim. She wasn't smart the way David was smart, but she knew how to put things quietly together in her mind and knew many things that were and beyond, to Tim's occasional astonishment, what would be.

One of the quiet games that he and Annetta used to play revolved around her predictions of things that would happen that day. They were most-

136

ly small, inconsequential things, like who wouldn't be at church or who would get into trouble at school. She was rarely wrong and when Tim asked her how she knew, she would smile at him, seemingly amused that he didn't know such things. Tim figured that she didn't understand it either, but she was untroubled by her secret awareness.

Tim couldn't figure things out like David and didn't know the things Annetta knew but, sitting here, alone with his rifle and his knife, he was untroubled by the knowledge. Here he didn't have to think or figure. Here he had the calm certainty of his task—the provision of food—and the easy confidence of his eventual success.

At first, Tim had been surprised at how well he did hunting, but he soon understood that David failed because he was burdened by the gravity of taking life. Tim, on the other hand, knew it was neither right nor wrong; it was just what he could do to help his family. This knowledge had lifted him, that first night and had sustained him since.

This. This he could do. This he understood. The knife and the rifle were now as much a part of him as his feet or his hair.

Here, alone, waiting for prey, Tim had found his place among his family.

Colby had his tobacco to raise. David's place was beside Colby, helping with the hoeing and the Saturday trips to town. Tim thought about Colby. With no one waiting for an answer, he could think clearly at his own pace.

How relieved Tim had been when he knew Colby was to take over for Daddy. And how impressed he remained, every day more in awe of his eldest brother. Tim still had trouble believing that Colby had traded for a hired hand. Even Daddy had never had a hand.

One-Eyed Zach had been coming to help a day and a half every week since the beginning of June and they had accomplished much. The hoeing was caught up, the fence rows cleaned out, the chicken house cleaned and even the barn roof was repaired.

The previous Tuesday after breakfast, Colby and Zach were already on the roof, pulling out old nails and sliding rusty sheeting over the side, where David stacked them in a pile. Setting out on his daily hunt, Tim looked up at Colby, marveling at just how high the roof was.

Tim knew that Colby couldn't have grown much in just thirty-nine days, but he somehow seemed larger. Maybe not taller and maybe not broader but he was just somehow bigger, more.

Colby didn't gnaw on his fingernails nearly as much and he laughed a bit more now.

Tim also saw how Colby had started carrying Beech-nut chewing tobacco in his back pocket and would, in the afternoons, take a small chew. Never in the house, though. Always in the barn or in the back field. Tim didn't know if Colby was exactly hiding it from Mama or if Mama would even notice, but this was one of the things Tim had been able to figure out, here, alone, with no one waiting for his answer.

Colby now stood among the men after church and all the men chewed. That's why Colby was teaching himself to chew, Tim thought. He wanted to try it himself. Probably.

Tim heard a noise just at the point of the bend in the creek and sat up, alert. He was hoping it might be a big snapping turtle. One-Eyed Zach had told him that they made real good eating but were the devil to clean properly. Tim wanted to bag one so that he could get Zach to show him how to clean it. This was Zach's half-day, and if Tim could get one in the next little bit, he could get back before Zach left.

Zach was full of knowledge like that. He knew at least a little about almost everything.

At first, he had been showing Colby how to care for the vegetable garden but after the first time or two, he started to show Annetta.

Tim's twin sister—quiet and knowing, odd and dutiful—had taken over the vegetable garden and it had since thrived so greatly that even One-Eyed Zach had been surprised. With only a small hand spade and without seeming to work very hard, she kept the weeds out and the dirt turned. She carried water from the well in a bucket. She seemed not to control the garden but to understand it in a way that Tim couldn't fathom. She worked with it rather than on it, forcing it to do nothing and guiding it until it did what she asked.

The cucumber plants were spreading nicely, their rough green leaves flat and wide. The onions were shooting up as were the green beans. But it was the tomatoes that had really taken off. Under her gentle care, every tomato plant had numerous yellow blossoms and most had green hard fruit, some of which was ripening.

Zach was amazed at her progress and her natural skill. He had told her just yesterday that the Traylors were only just starting to see green tomatoes.

He heard the noise once more in the creek but saw that it wasn't a turtle. It was a good-sized fish flopping around in the mud at the water's edge, the type Daddy had called a creek chub and not fit to eat.

He sat back against the tree once more, his mind settled. There would be a turtle soon enough. Maybe not today but soon enough.

The tobacco would grow, Colby would see to that.

David would be by Colby's side, helping.

Mama would keep right on with the cooking and the wash and her singing.

Annetta would tend her garden and spend her other time as Mama's companion.

And Tim would be here, here or somewhere just the same, doing his bit, helping things along.

He had his rifle, his knife, the warm sun, the summer breeze, the creek, the fields, the game and also, he had peace, purpose and, above all, clarity.

It was enough.

## CHAPTER 2

That next Sunday, the preaching done, the men filed slowly out of their side of the church, wandering into Colby's circle. Although Colby had only been in the circle six or seven times, the men had started thinking of it in those terms. They had been gathering this way for years but for the first time, the circle had an actual purpose. Each of them thought all week of how they might be able to help: how they might offer advice without preaching, how they could teach without seeming superior, how they could help Colby without injuring his young pride.

It had naturally fallen to Russ to be the organizer, a job he was glad to do.

Surprising their wives with their eagerness and punctuality, the men showed up for church early nowadays to offer suggestions to Russ. He assured them that it was enough to talk about working their crops. Russ was mostly interested in getting Colby used to the idea of belonging, being one of them.

Russ had noticed quite a few tobacco worms on his plants in the past week and was sure that Colby had them too. He decided he might bring it up today. But before Russ reached the circle, he felt a hand on his shoulder and turned to find Lawrence Norvell leaning in close to him.

"A word real quick, Russ?" he asked.

"Surely, Lawrence. What's on your mind?"

"Well-sir, I reckon I forgot to mention something to you that happened a couple weeks ago, then again yesterday."

"Which would be what?" Russ asked.

Lawrence started grinning before speaking. "Cole bought some chew. Remember a couple of weeks back when we all talked about him having credit? It was that Saturday he first bought some. Then yesterday him and David came in and he bought two more."

Russ nodded. "You reckon he might try some today?" he asked.

"I'd say he's fixing to do more than try it. Look over at him, in his back pocket."

Russ looked at Colby and plainly saw a new pack of Beech-nut in each of his back pockets.

"Who else bought some yesterday?"

"Big Tom bought one and E. E. bought two. I 'spect one of them was gonna spring for it today."

"I'd say that is so." Russ thought for a moment. "You slip over to Big Tom. Tell him not to offer any chew. Tell him no questions, just keep his chew in his pocket. I'll talk to E. E."

Russ nodded and walked over to E. E. Robinson. As he whispered into his ear, he watched Lawrence speaking with Big Tom. The circle was nearly formed.

"…I'll just shake my head yes or no. Got it?" Russ said to E. E.

"I get you, Russ," E. E. said agreeably. "I'll be watching you."

Russ glanced over at Big Tom, who winked and smiled in what he considered a subtle, conspiratorial way. Russ groaned inwardly, dropped his head and checked Colby to see if he had noticed. He hadn't.

"Well, sir, that was some good preaching, sure enough," E. E. said. "Anybody remember what it was about?"

Russ laughed. "Better not let Reverend Tannehill hear you say that. He might tell God on you," he said.

"I don't reckon he's in earshot, so don't you worry none, E. E.," Spencer Kirk said, tossing his head towards the far side of the magnolia tree where Reverend Tannehill was speaking with David. "And don't even bother pretending you didn't already know he was way over there."

E. E. looked over at David and Tannehill, then at Colby.

"I must admit, I knew he was over there. Talking to young David again. I believe he's taken a shine to him. He's sharp, ain't he Colby? David, I mean."

"Yessir, he surely is. About as sharp as he can be. Fact is, Mr. Norvell, he's been wanting to try you at checkers," Colby said.

"I would enjoy, that Cole," Mr. Norvell replied. "A man does get tired of whipping up on the same victims day after day. Y'all coming in this Saturday?" he said.

"I imagine so. Can't see why we wouldn't," Colby said.

"Good. What I'll do is warm up on ole Spencer here and then give David a go," Lawrence said.

There was a lull in the banter. Russ broke it by announcing, "Well-sir, if I'm in there next Saturday, I'm going to buy me an extra pouch of chew. I got none on me and I reckon none of you fellas do, either," he said, looking around with eyebrows raised.

"Yessir," Old Man Tom said, "A chew would be just right along about now."

Russ looked over at Big Tom, who was staring, unconcerned, at the sky. Out of the corner of his eye, he saw Colby's hand moving toward his back pocket.

"Yes," he said to himself.

"Well-sir," Colburn Grayson said, pulling out the Beech-Nut, "it looks like I got me some extra here. I'd be glad to share it out with you fellas." Colby opened the packet, smelled it and handed it to Elijah Settles on his left. "Help yourself, Mr. Settles."

"And then pass it on, you old coot," Old Man Tom said, mockingly angry. Elijah held the packet in his left hand, reached in with his thumb and first two fingers, extracted a small amount and showed it to Old Man Tom.

"One old coot to another, you old coot," he said, putting the chaw in his mouth and passing it on.

Russ saw Colby laughing but he was momentarily concerned. The circle was unusually large today, more than a dozen, and though the men were taking modest chaws, there was no way that the pouch would make it all the way around. He was wondering if he should silently indicate to Big Tom to get his tobacco out when he noticed Colby pulling the second pouch from his pocket, opening it and handing it off in the opposite direction.

As this second pouch reached Russ, he grabbed it, extracted a chaw, looked over at Colby and tilted his head in gratitude. Colby nodded back.

Both pouches returned to Colby at about the same time. He took what was left of the first and added it to the second, folded the empty pouch and placed it in his back pocket, then extracted a large wad of tobacco from the remaining pouch. He looked up at the men in the circle and saw that every one of them were watching him, not chewing, silent. Colby held the chaw out towards them in acknowledgement.

"Fellas," he said and put the tobacco in his mouth, worked it into a ball with his tongue and parked it in his right cheek.

All the men laughed. They couldn't help it. Big Tom nearly cheered.

Colby laughed right along with them.

Later, Russ could not say what they had discussed that day but his memory of it was good and pure. There was the usual cheerful, teasing banter and the friendly needling, but on this day there was also accomplishment and joy. Colburn Grayson had been invited in, and on this bright and breezy day of rest, Colby had finally accepted.

Cole Grayson was one of them.

## CHAPTER 3

That afternoon, Colby sat in his father's rocking chair, rocking lazily, listening to the pre-game interviews. The Reds were playing Pittsburgh in a double-header starting at two o'clock. For the first time in weeks, Colby felt completely content and unworried. With David's help, he was on top of the weeds and hoeing was no longer an hour-by-hour concern. Thanks to Zach's help, the barn was in workable shape. They could go back to hoeing tomorrow.

And the tobacco grew.

It sometimes amazed Colby that, for all the worrying he did about weeds, the barn and the livestock, he sometimes forgot to worry about the tobacco. When he did remember, he would check it and find it a couple of inches higher. Every day, every week, whether it rained or not, the tobacco steadily grew, it grew and would soon be cut, housed and sold, and the bank note would be met.

A couple of times Colby had found himself staring at some insignificant detail of one of the plants: a new bud or how thick the veins were in a leaf.

Maybe things in general weren't going great, maybe not even real good but they were getting along. They had food in their pantry. They had the kitchen garden. They had meat from Old Man Tom's slaughter to look forward to. And they had the promise of the tobacco crop to carry them through one more year.

Colby sat and rocked. Mama had gone to her room. David was off exploring, and Colby could hear Tim and Annetta playing in the yard. His eyes closed by themselves, then opened again slowly. The windows in the front room were open and a mild breeze hassled the thin curtains.

Colby heard a dog bark at the same time that he heard a car pass on U.S. 60. He thought it might be time to examine the road shoulder again.

His eyes closed again. Opened, then closed again. He thought he heard Mama singing, found it curious that the singing didn't scare him, then sat up with a start to hear that the Reds were leading the Pirates three to nothing in the fifth inning. Colby had been asleep for almost an hour. He didn't know it, but Mama had walked in forty minutes ago and turned down the radio.

In his memory, he had never taken a nap. Vernon had never taken a nap. There was no statement of philosophy involved, it simply hadn't been Vernon's way to nap and so it hadn't been the Grayson way, and yet...

Colby rubbed his eyes and thought that he should probably feel guilty about sleeping during the day, even though it was Sunday, but the guilt wouldn't come. Instead, he wondered why he had woken up.

Colby heard a car door slam and briefly wondered if the bankers had returned to speak with him. He stood and looked out through the screen door. Annetta was walking back to the house while Tim walked towards their visitor, who was standing by the driver's side door of a dusty but still new-looking red pick-up truck.

Colby recognized their Uncle Jason but wasn't sure if Tim would. It had been at least two years since they had seen him last. Colby saw David walking up from the barn with a smile on his face and he knew that David had recognized their uncle also.

Tim, stiff but still respectful, stopped a few feet from Jason.

"You're my Uncle Jason, aren't you?" he asked.

"I guess I am. You're not Colby, so you must be either David or Tim. I'm going to guess David."

David, reaching the pair, shook his head.

"You'd be guessing wrong then. I'm David," he grinned.

Jason regarded David, and then looked back at the unsmiling Tim. Jason nodded seriously.

"I'd have guessed you as Tim, but I didn't figure there was any way you could be the youngest, being as tall as you are and all."

Colby saw Tim's shoulders relax and knew that Jason had said just the right thing. Colby opened the door to let Annetta in and stepped out to greet his uncle.

"You really work on a farm where there ain't nothing but horses?" Colby heard Tim ask as he approached.

"I surely do. Nothing but horses and if I told you how many, you'd probably think I was telling you a tall one. Good Lord A'mighty, Colby, I about didn't recognize you. You've surely put some distance between your hat and the ground."

Colby stopped in front of his uncle and stuck out his hand.

"Howdy, Jason. I reckon you got that letter Mama sent?"

Jason nodded slowly and shook his nephew's hand. He was surprised by the strength in the hand and the way Colby looked him steadily in the eyes, unlike the quiet, shy child he remembered.

"I did. I want to tell y'all how sorry I was to hear about your daddy's passing. I was truly fond of him."

They stood a moment in silence and then Colby spoke.

"Yessir, he was a well-respected man. He was spoken real highly of at the services."

"I imagine he was, Colby. I was sure sorry to hear about his passing. If I'd have known about it before, I would surely have made it down for the funeral. First word I had of it was that letter from your mama. It surely was a shock to me."

"Got any Pepsi's?" David asked suddenly, still grinning. It wasn't Jason that David remembered so much as the fact that, the last time Jason had visited, he had brought a box full of bottles of Pepsi.

Jason started smiling. "Well, now, if you would have asked that right off, I would have been able to recognize you as David without having to ask. As I remember it, you drank down most of a bottle, then burped so hard you had Pepsi foam coming out of your nose," he chuckled.

Colby remembered the scene and laughed out loud. "I remember you was afraid it was your brains rolling out."

"Heck, I thought sure that it was," David said, laughing along at the memory. "Does Pepsi still do like that?"

Jason's smile changed but didn't leave his face. He knew they hadn't had Pepsi since his visit three years ago.

"Find out for yourself," he said pointing his thumb at the truck. "On the seat, around the other side. Why don't y'all grab that box and take it on into the kitchen. If you was to put them in the ice-box right now, they'd be nice and cool for suppertime."

Jason and Colby watched an excited David and an unimpressed Tim take the box out of the truck and into the house. Tim didn't remember drinking Pepsi and wasn't too happy about the idea of anything, brains or not, leaking out of his nose.

"Well, Colby, I got to say that the place here is looking pretty good. Your tobacco looks as good as any I saw driving here."

"Not doing too bad, I reckon. We've been hard at it for a while now."

"I can see that." Jason gazed slowly around the farm, shading his eyes and resting them a while on the big barn. He said with genuine appreciation, "I mean it Colby. You sure enough got this old place looking good. Not just the crop either. That's new roofing on that barn, isn't it?"

"It is," Colby answered with pride. "We worked on it last Tuesday and part of the day on Friday. It wasn't near as big a job as I was afraid it was going to be."

"And all that fencing out back looks fairly new."

"Well, sir, not all of it is exactly new. We done some repair work on the worst of it and just cleaned out some of the rows."

"Who's we? You and David?"

"Us and an old fella named Zach. He works for Russ Traylor full-time, but he's been helping me out a day and a half a week. In the fall, me and

145

David are going to work a bunch for Russ, Colby said. "I reckon it's an even swap," he added quickly.

"Sounds like a good even swap to me," Jason said. He looked slowly around the farm again, stopping his gaze on the lush vegetable garden. He shook his head slowly.

"I'll be durned," he said.

"Why's that?" Colby asked.

"Well-sir, I don't mean nothing ill by it, but I must admit that I had it in my mind that y'all might be in pretty bad shape. This farm here is something to be proud of but making any kind of living off this land was as much as your daddy could do and he was…well…I mean, he was Vernon Grayson. What I mean to say is, I reckon I'm impressed."

Colby nodded. "Daddy taught me how to work."

Jason let out a laugh. "I can see that he did."

"David has been a big help to me, too." Looking toward the house, Colby said, "We're going to have an early supper. You're more than welcome to join us."

"I'll thank you for it, Colby. Fact is, if it wouldn't be too imposing, I had it in my mind to spend the night here. That is, if y'all got some extra room on the couch."

"Sure we do, Jason. You could sleep on the couch or you could sleep in Baby-Anne's bed. She sleeps with Mama most nights now." Colby began walking toward the house.

"Colby?" Jason called after him. Colby stopped and looked back at his uncle.

"How is your mama doing, Colby?" he asked.

Colby started to answer when they heard a loud hooting, followed by laughter from inside the house. They both knew that David and the twins had already gotten into the Pepsi. They looked at each other, smiling at the happy sound.

"How about we enjoy supper and talk after?" Jason suggested. Colby nodded as they walked into the house.

They stopped just inside the front door and Colby watched Jason look around the room. When his eyes reached the radio, Colby said, "I was listening to the Reds when you pulled up."

"They win?"

"They were when I shut it off. We'll check here in a minute. Mama?" Colby stood still and listened. "Mama?" he called again. "Jason's here—"

Before he finished, Anne walked silently into the room. She smiled weakly.

"Jason," she said.

"Hello, Anne," he said and held out his arms to her. She allowed herself to be enfolded.

"Vernon…" she said with a hitching breath.

"I know, honey. I know. I'm so sorry. I wish I had been here."

She remained in her brother's arms, whispering, "He died. Vernon died. Vernon's dead."

"I know honey. I know," Jason said and smoothed Anne's hair. A bit embarrassed, Colby wondered if he should go outside but he was grateful that Mama could get some comfort after all these weeks.

Finally, Anne sniffed, pulled away from Jason and wiped her nose on the dishtowel she was holding. She looked directly at Colby, then smiled at Jason.

"I'll bet you about didn't recognize Colby," she said.

"I just about didn't. He's grown more than I would have thought possible. He's looking more like his daddy."

"Jason's going to stay to supper, Mama, and then spend the night here, too." Colby said.

"That's nice. The tomatoes are finally coming on. Annetta brought me three really nice ones from the garden and I'll make some extra biscuits and gravy."

"That sounds great, Anne. It really does," her brother said.

"Then you and Colby can talk," Anne said.

"And you too, Anne. Don't you think?"

Colby watched his mama's face, saw her eyes begin to float and her features disappear into her soft, poignant song. But she collected herself with what he knew was a huge effort. Her eyes refocused on Colby, then Jason.

"I don't know, Jason. I just don't know. Colby's been running things. He's doing real good, too. Everybody says so. I listen to everybody and to what they say, even if I don't always speak back."

"Still, Anne, don't you think you ought to join us?" Jason asked.

Colby saw her eyes begin to glaze, although he wasn't sure if he was seeing fresh tears or the onset of her song. Jason saw it too and put a hand on her back.

"Okay, honey. It's okay. Me and Colby will talk after supper and if you feel up to it, you'll talk too. Okay?"

Anne nodded weakly with relief and returned to the kitchen. Colby listened for Mama's song. After a few moments, Colby realized with surprise that Jason, too, was listening for same thing. Jason finally looked at Colby, sharing a moment of keen understanding. Jason nodded.

"Let's go drink a Pepsi before supper," Jason said.

## Chapter 4

Supper that night was a mirthful and happy meal. Anne fried two of Tim's rabbits, served with a big pot of brown beans and a double batch of biscuits with rich, creamy gravy. She diced up the tomatoes with an early cucumber and a few green onions, all drizzled with vinegar.

"Lord Almighty, Anne!" Jason exclaimed. "You dang sure ain't forgot how to cook. I'll swear to that. I honestly can't remember the last time I ate fried rabbit. I'd forgotten just how good it is." Speaking to Tim, he said, "And you're the one that bagged them?"

Tim smiled broadly. "Every one of them. The ones in the icebox, too. I also skin 'em and clean 'em. Colby give me Daddy's knife. I go out most every night now between supper and sundown. Truth is, I've been getting so many, me and David's been selling to some of the other farms around here."

"Well Tim, if you're selling them, then I'd like to buy a few to take back with me. They don't allow no hunting on the farm where I work, on account of the horses. Heck, even if I was allowed, I can promise you that I couldn't never bag that many. Even when I did hunt regular, I couldn't have got this many in a whole season of hunting."

"He head-shoots them, too," David piped up. "I figure that makes them a little more valuable when we're selling them."

"And these tomatoes!" Jason marveled. "We have a pretty good size garden that we all help out on at the farm, but I don't think we've gotten the first one out of it yet. That your work too, Tim?"

"No, sir," Tim answered. "After Daddy died, Colby and One-eyed Zach was working it, but now I reckon Annetta does most all of it. She waters and weeds it anyway, don't she, Colby?"

Colby swallowed his mouthful of biscuits and gravy, and smiled at Baby-Anne. "Yes, she does. I think maybe she's as good with the garden as Tim is with the hunting. Leastways since she took it over, it sure has come around. I meant to ask at church today if anyone else had tomatoes yet."

"Well, I know we sure don't in Lexington. They sure have hit the spot." He looked at Anne. "Everything has, Anne. This is about the best I've eaten in a while and I sure thank you. It was wonderful."

148

"I'm so glad you liked it, Jason. I really am," Anne replied, rising and clearing the table.

Tim rose next. "Think I might go on out for a while," he said. "I haven't been down to the creek behind the Traylors' place in a week or so."

Colby nodded. "That'll be fine, Tim." He looked at David. "And I believe you got some milking to do."

David stood in agreement. "I sure do."

As Annetta began helping Mama clear the table, Jason looked at Colby and raised his eyebrows. Colby shot a quick glance at his mother.

"Why don't we just go on outside, Jason," he said. Jason stood behind his chair, waiting for Colby to lead the way.

"Mama?" Colby said. Anne smiled softly and shook her head once.

Colby understood. "Me and Jason are gonna go on outside now."

"That's fine, Colby. That's fine," she said.

Once outside the house, Colby paused, not sure where to go, then headed for the walnut tree where he and Russ had talked on the day of the funeral. Although it had been only a matter of weeks since that day, it seemed to Colby as if it had happened in another life. The walnuts growing on the tree were small, small but hard, bright green, rough-skinned, tough and full of promise.

He squatted down and looked up at his uncle. Jason sat in the grass, his back to the tree trunk.

"I said it before, Colby. This is some piece of work you've done here. It couldn't have been easy."

Colby smiled. "Easy ain't exactly the word I'd use. Most of the work ain't been complicated, though there's been a whole lot of it. Just a matter of getting it done."

Jason looked up at the sky. "I've been gone a bunch of years but that is one thing I do remember. Tobacco farming isn't real complicated, but a man has to stay at it."

Jason reached into his shirt pocket and brought out a pack of Lucky Strikes. He pulled one out, tapped the end on his Zippo lighter and lit up. Colby pulled his Beech-nut out of his back pocket and put a small plug in his mouth. Jason watched, then grinned.

"That'll put hair on your chest," he said.

"Did you start chewing when you were my age?"

"Never did take up the chewing. Started smoking when I was about fifteen. Course by then, I'd done moved away."

"To Lexington?"

"Well, no, not Lexington at first. First I lived here with your mama and Vernon."

"You lived here?"

"Sure did. For about a year after Anne married your daddy."

149

Colby spit to the side. "Why?" he asked.

Jason looked back at the sky and smoked so long in silence that Colby thought he had said something wrong. Finally he stubbed out his cigarette and with one finger, dug a small hole and buried the butt.

"You knew your daddy's daddy, didn't you?"

"I did. He didn't die till I was about four. His name was Denton. I called him granddad. His wife died before I was born."

Jason smiled at his own memories. "Denton was a good man. Honest as a man could be. That's what I remember most about him. Straight up honest. That and his barn."

"Still the biggest barn around," Colby said.

"Colby, I'm going to bet that you don't know anything about your other grandparents, do you?"

"I know that your and Mama's mother died about a month or two after you was born. She don't really talk about her father. He dead, too?" Colby asked.

Jason shook his head slowly. "I don't really know. His name was Green P. Wagner. What's more, although it may be hard for you to hear, I don't really care. I don't know if he's alive or dead. Somewhere in between I 'spect."

"I don't think I quite follow you Jason," Colby said in confusion.

"He was a drunkard, Colby. And I don't mean just a fella who drinks too much every now and then. I'm talking about a bad, awful drunkard; mean and hateful. We had a farm, our family, not too much different from this place. My father had it from his father, but I'll tell you one thing. It didn't ever in my memory look anywhere near as good as you got this place looking. I reckon my father drank instead of farmed."

"I did know that y'all was poor."

Jason looked away and shook his head again. "We was worse than poor Colby. Poor is one thing, but the house I grew up in...I reckon it wouldn't be Anne's way to tell y'all about that house and about me and her and Lily when we were kids. If she hasn't told you about it, then I'll not either. The details don't much matter now, anyway, but I will say this to you, it was worse than just about anything you could imagine. Daddy was a mean drunk, abusive and not just with his fists. I got many a taste of the old man's fists, as did your mama and Lily but there was worse than the beatings, a lot worse."

Colby felt his head beginning to buzz and casually spit his chaw into his hand and threw it into the yard.

"Worse than beatings? How?" he asked.

"Well, beatings is all I ever got but for your mama...especially for your mama..." He lit another cigarette. "I ain't going to go all into it now, Colby, I just ain't. But I will say this, your mama took the worst of it, the worst of it by far. Fact is, by taking the worst of it, she kept it from being as bad on me and Lily. The way she sings like she does? I remember when she didn't sing like that. It didn't really start until after…until after the…" Jason's words trailed off and he took another drag from his cigarette, then wiped the sweat from his throat. "The things she done to get between us and the old man, that's what started her singing. It started then and I guess I might have been hoping that by now, she wouldn't need it anymore. She sings when she's worried, worried or hurting bad, Colby, she sings so she can keep on going. She been singing more since Vernon died?"

"Yessir, she has. More here lately, but I reckon she's been singing like that 'bout long as I can remember."

"Well, I guess that's what she paid. What she done, it would have been hard for any person, old or young but she was young. Seeing her now makes clear to me just how young."

"Does Lily sing?" Colby asked.

"I wish I could say, Colby. She left about a year or two before Anne and Vernon got married. In Florida, last I heard. She wasn't singing before she left. She was smart to leave. It was the smartest thing she could have done. I do hope she's happy."

"And you sure enough don't know if your daddy's alive or dead?"

"Sure don't, Colby, but I expect dead. When Anne and Vernon married, they brought me along with them to live here. That summer, the old man managed to burn the old house down. Nobody knew if it was on purpose or not and truth is, no one much cared. He disappeared and the bank got the land. Wasn't even a crop planted on it."

Colby picked blades of grass, rolling them into balls and tossed them. He thought there were questions he should ask but didn't know what they were.

"So how long was you here, living here?" he finally asked.

"Oh, not more than a couple of years, I suppose. I know I could have stayed on. I wasn't a bad hand. 'Course I couldn't keep up with Vernon but then again, no one could."

"So how'd you end up in Lexington?"

"E. E. Robinson. He owned the farm supply. He still does, I suppose."

Colby nodded.

Jason continued. "He was right friendly with the fella that used to deliver the fencing nails and other hardware. It all come out of a supplier in Lexington. Me and Vernon was in there one day when he was making a delivery. This driver was telling E. E. about this farm, Alladon, that was growing real fast on account of them having the stallion who sired a horse that ran second in the Derby and then third in the Belmont. Said they was hiring able-bodied men who had even a lick of sense. I walked over and asked if he wasn't just telling tales. He said it was every word true. E. E. wrote down the name of the farm and the directions for me and when that driver made his next delivery, I helped him unload his truck, then rode back to Lexington with him. I remember I had two dollars and ten cents in my pocket. I offered the driver fifty cents to pay for my ride. He was a cheerful fella, can't remember his name though. He refused the money. Said he was going that way, anyway."

"And you've been there ever since?"

"Ever since that very day. I started out on the maintenance crew, fixing fences and such. We also did all the mowing of the paddocks. At that time, they had four gasoline-powered tractors, now they must have a dozen or more."

"And they pay you wages to do nothing else but mow?"

"Naw, Colby," Jason answered. "I don't mow at all now. I've been there thirteen years. Fact is, I've done real good. I'm what they call the broodmare manager. I take care of over forty mares."

"By yourself?" Colby asked in amazement.

Jason smiled and shook his head. "Not by myself. I got twelve men that work for me. Mostly my job is just making sure all those men are doing what they're supposed to be doing."

"They call you boss?"

"No," Jason said with a laugh. "They call me Jason."

"You ain't married. You got your own house there in Lexington?"

"No, I ain't married. Might be soon enough, though. I have a pretty steady girl. And yes, I do have a house. I reckon that's the main thing I wanted to talk to you about, too. It ain't my house exactly. It belongs to the farm. They let me live in it, though, rent free. I just pay the electric bill and the telephone bill."

Colby's eyes widened. "You got a telephone? All to yourself?"

"I do, Colby. Another thing I got is plenty of room. This house has a kitchen, a living room and three good sized bedrooms. It's also got a bathroom with a tub and shower and a flushing toilet."

"Dang. That must be something to see…" Colby let his words drift off. He looked at the walnuts, then directly at Jason. He had finally seen where Jason was heading.

Jason silently lit his third cigarette, letting Colby adjust to the idea, then nodded and said, "I owe your mama more than I could ever repay Colby. Fact is, I'm a bit shamed that I didn't come to see her more often. Just figured if enough distance was between me and this place, I wouldn't never have to think about it much. It was wrong of me but I'm trying to do right by Anne now. If you wanted to, Colby, you and your mama and David and the twins could come up and live with me. Wouldn't be no rent due from you and I've already asked the farm manager. He said it'd be just fine with him. And I wasn't sure until I saw what good shape this place is in, but I know you could earn a wage working there. None of the men I got could have kept this place together like you have." Jason watched Colby, who continued to roll balls of grass. He had lived with Vernon long enough to know what was going through Colby's mind.

"We're family, Colby. I know we haven't seen a whole lot of each other, but we are family. Wouldn't be nothing like charity. It's family. And I owe Anne." Jason took one more drag off the cigarette, then crushed it out. "I owe her."

Colby didn't look at his uncle but instead stared out over his front field and on to the road. He thought wildly for a moment of how it would feel to ride in Jason's truck, going not just to town or church but well beyond, away from here and all the worry, the work, the house and Denton's big old barn.

Did the trees and the fields look the same there? Were there more cars? And horses. Giant fields with horses grazing idly, horses that never had and never would pull a wagon or plow; horses, sleek, well muscled horses, just for racing.

A house, bigger than this, with running water and a flushing toilet. Rent-free, no bills to worry about and food never a concern.

He looked then at his hand, at the calluses, the thick dirty nails, the embedded dirt and the embedded strength. Over his left shoulder he saw Denton's barn, his barn, with the new roofing that he and Zach and David had installed.

*His* fields, *his* fences, *his* barn and with it all the implicit toil in long, endless, hot days, hotter now than only six weeks ago. Six weeks ago, when he had stood under this very tree, speaking with Russ.

How different he felt now, how completely ready to consider any and all options, for himself and his family. Six weeks. Under this very tree. He looked steadily back at Jason.

"Surely you remember Russ Traylor, don't you?" he asked.

Jason nodded. "I do."

"Well-sir, on the day of Daddy's funeral, he asked me to step out here and speak with him a minute. We was standing but we was just about where you and me are now. He offered to help me. Offered to answer questions, give advice if I needed it, like that."

"I'd a-been surprised if he didn't offer. He was ever a decent sort. Smart, too." Jason said.

"He is that," Colby agreed. "Ain't a bit of doubt about it. I hadn't really thought none about it until just now, but the fact is, I reckon I was a might rude to him. I don't reckon, I know I was. Told him flat out we didn't need no charity, didn't need it and wouldn't have it. I shouldn't have said that."

"Well, you had a lot to think about just then, Colby."

Colby smiled and nodded his assent. "I did, sure enough. I think maybe I just didn't know of nothing else to say. I just said what I thought Daddy would want me to say. Still don't make it right."

"I'd just bet you a five-dollar bill he don't hold it against you none," Jason said.

"Oh, I know he don't. That ain't his way. When he walked away, he told me I had to start being a man now. I didn't quite get him then but maybe now I do. It ain't just me saying what Daddy would have said. The words ain't the thing. This hoeing we've been doing, the fences and barn and all? They ain't the thing either."

Colby paused a moment, choosing his words. "All the things I say, all the work I do, it's because of this land here. It's what we got. It's what we've always had. Me, my daddy, granddaddy, his daddy named Jordan and his daddy named Andrew. I reckon it's all become fairly clear to me in the last few weeks. Everything they ever done, everything I done, whatever happened then or now or later, this land is still going to be here. I couldn't leave it, Jason. I just couldn't. I'd be letting ever one of them down. Ever one of them. All the sweating and work they all done? They did it to pass this land down, keep it with the family, leave it for me. Ain't no way I could turn my back on that. Just ain't no way."

Jason looked steadily at his nephew, not overly surprised by what had been said, but in awe of the quiet and sure way it was said: the calm, respectful certainty.

Young Colby—young, shy Colby, now and from now on, invisibly draped in the ponderous chains of Southern manhood; composed, thoughtful and with frightening serenity—calmly informing Jason that he would continue at an arduous task that Jason knew that he, himself, would never, or could ever, take on.

"Well," was all Jason could manage.

"Don't think I ain't grateful for the offer, Jason, 'cause I am. I just can't leave."

## CHAPTER 5

Jason lay on the couch in the front room. It didn't take the Grayson family long to fall asleep after calling it a day. It had been only fifteen minutes since they had said goodnight and already Jason could hear soft snores from their rooms.

Sleep, for Jason, never came easily, sometimes not at all. Even after a long, hard day, upon lying down, the silence of the night could never conquer the disquiet of Jason's mind.

In all the years since his move to Lexington, it was the memories that burned him as he lay, trying to sleep. Plain, straight memories, oily black memories, hot brutal memories that needed no context or trigger.

Every night, no exceptions, invading him as he lay down, and he knew why, why they ground their way into his mind and blossomed cruelly only when he lay in his bed, at night, when it was dark, quiet, because it was as he lay in his bed as a child when the worst of it happened.

Jason could not remember a single night when the old man was there when Anne got him and Lily in bed for the night. She always put them to bed, though she was only a couple of years older.

It was always quiet as she put them to bed, but it was a false silence, they had known to mistrust it, this tense fakery of calm.

More nights than not, far more nights than not, the old man would stumble in, not intentionally loud or quiet, simply unaware or uncaring of the time, unaware of the need or even the existence of propriety, of respect for a sleeping household.

As Jason lay on the very couch where he slept for over a year, he felt his heart beat faster, faster still, and he knew it would be far into the night before he slept, if at all.

No matter how far the distance, in miles or years, the helpless rage and unbearable humiliation made him small again, small, weak; weak and helpless, emptily enraged and feeble.

So horribly helpless.

Jason didn't know how old he was when it first started. He knew that he couldn't have been more than eight or nine making Anne twelve or thirteen.

At the beginning of it, the old man would walk into their bedroom, sitting on the right side of the bed that Anne and Lily shared.

The side Anne slept on.

And the old man, speaking with drunken, syrupy sweetness, with a false tenderness that even Jason, at his young age, mistrusted.

And Anne, the first time, trusting the old man, so grateful to have a soft word from him, so grateful, going with him.

Into the bedroom of their mother.

And Anne, screaming.

And the old man, slapping her into silence.

The second time, much the same as the first, one month later.

The third time, just three weeks later.

Then weekly.

Then two or three times a week. Every week.

And Jason, laying then as he lay now, shamed and weak, horrified, shaking and sweating.

A bayonet, supposedly from the Civil War, hung on a nail above the Wagner fireplace and every night Jason fantasized about taking it down, taking it down and running to Anne's rescue, stabbing his monstrous father in the throat, in the chest, in the face.

Knowing that he would not, that he dare not.

Every time, he lay there silently, tears of outrage rolling down his face to be lost in the sweat covering his throat and neck, mutely outraged and pitifully, shamefully, glad that it wasn't him. Quietly he lay, he must be quiet, anything to keep the old man from noticing him, anything, anything, anything at all to keep from being noticed. Silent tears, silent tears while gritting his teeth, not even daring to dream of interceding lest the old man could hear his thoughts.

Crying silently, horrified, dizzy with relief that it wasn't him.

Crying within the depths of the horrible void, the empty and worthless rage of a child.

He would lie quietly, so quietly, swollen eyed and sweaty as his father raped his sister.

He never inured himself to it, never got his young mind around the idea, every time as burning and awful as the last.

And Anne.

Anne started going to him when called, knowing how useless and damaging her refusal would be.

And Jason.

Jason beginning to understand that she did it for him, for him and for Lily. Understanding with great clarity only after he left for Lexington the unimaginable price Anne paid for him and Lily. For him and Lily.

And the song.

He couldn't tell Colby that his mama's song started there, in that terrible bedroom, its genesis in her sponsorship of his and Lily's innocence, born from the depths of her strength, her immeasurable strength, one child spending the totality of her childhood in the preservation of two others.

A child.

A child did that.

A child did that.

So many years later, Jason still couldn't reconcile what Anne had done for them, couldn't fathom the capacity this young girl possessed to protect those that needed her protection, saving as much of his and Lily's innocence as she could.

The sacrifice.

The unthinkable sacrifice.

The unimaginable sacrifice.

A child did that.

A child did that and it used her up.

Her pitiful, gentle song was one of might, of placid potency. Singing to hold herself together, not for her own sake, but for his and for Lily's.

And he knew, he knew then as now that she would never stop singing, the song a permanent piece of her, of Anne, his tough, irreversibly damaged sister.

And Jason, the man Jason, all these years later, still so tangled and shattered by his meaningless, pathetic regret, so weak, so weak and emptied by shame and disgrace that he could not feel even anger.

## Chapter 6

Jason awakened, surprised to have slept. He wasn't sure what time it was. The last time he had looked at his watch, it had been 4:25 a.m. He rubbed his eyes and swung his legs over the side of the couch.

It was still dark outside. He heard Colby scuffling about in the kitchen. He didn't smell coffee but could use a cup. Operating on fewer than two hours of sleep was not unusual for Jason. At times, he didn't even mind not sleeping, knowing that exhaustion would allow him to sleep the following night.

He pulled on his denim pants and stood, running his fingers through his hair. He walked into the kitchen and saw Colby drinking a glass of milk.

"Reckon a fella could get a cup of coffee?" Jason asked.

"Yes, sir, we got coffee. It's in the pantry there. Let me get the coffee pot." Colby found the pot and handed it to Jason. He didn't want to admit that he didn't know how to make coffee.

"This'll do," said Jason, filling the pot with water and coffee and putting it on the front right burner. He lit the gas burner with a wooden match, then lit a cigarette with the same match.

Colby rubbed his eyes and finished his milk. The smell of the coffee put him in a state of happiness. He didn't recognize it for what it was, just knew he was suddenly in a good mood.

"Haven't taken to the coffee yet?" Jason asked with a sleepy grin.

"Not yet. Smells good but the taste just don't agree with me."

"Well, sir, I got to tell you that I can't drink the stuff without cream and sugar. Straight black coffee, well, sir, I'd just as soon not drink any coffee."

"Guy that helps me, fella named One-Eyed Zach, puts buttermilk in his coffee. Says it makes it drinkable. I gotta say I wouldn't drink neither one of them by themselves and surely not combined."

"Never could stomach the buttermilk myself," Jason agreed. "As far as I'm concerned, the field rats can have it."

"We ain't got no rats that I've seen," Colby said.

"Good thing. Once they start, ain't no getting rid of them."

As the coffee brewed, Jason looked hard at Colby.

158

"I was serious about what I said yesterday, Colby. I know you got your family's best interest in mind but the offer stands. I won't pester you about it none, but the offer stands."

"Don't think I don't appreciate it, Jason, but my thoughts are still the same. I just couldn't give up on this land. I just couldn't."

"Well, sir, that's about as plain as you could put it. I will tell you this though, if anybody could do it, I'd surely put my money on you. I want you to know, as sure as I'm sitting here, that Vernon would be proud of you. He was a man unlike other men and Colby, I'm about sure that you're the same."

Colby felt chills running up his back and across his neck and on up, over his scalp. Hearing this out loud meant more to him than he could, or ever would, verbalize.

Daddy would be proud. The hoeing, the weeding, the barn repairs, the fence rows, all of it, Daddy would be proud.

"Wish he was here," Colby whispered.

"So do I, Colby. So do I."

They sat awhile in companionable silence until the coffee was ready. Jason got up and poured himself a cup.

"Ain't nothing that can't be done through hard work," Jason said and grinned.

"Ain't a thing," Colby agreed, grinning along.

"I guess you know that your daddy cut more than two thousand sticks in one day, don't you?"

"Yessir. I heard it told many a time. I don't think I could have done it."

"Probably ain't too many men that could have. I was there the day he did it. I never seen nothing like it. He was like a gas-powered machine. Cut and stab, cut and stab, fourteen hours and never slowed up. Not for a minute. Durndest thing I ever seen."

"And still got up to work the next day?" Colby asked. He knew the answer but wanted to hear it from someone who had been there.

"What are you talking about? Of course, he did. As I recall, we helped Russ Traylor the next day and he still cut over fifteen hundred sticks. I guess it was kind of legendary. A legendary feat from a legendary man. I've never heard a tale to equal it."

"I guess I've heard more than one tale about Daddy. All good, mind you. I kindly wonder why I didn't never hear those tales when Daddy was still alive."

"I know the answer to that, Colby," Jason said. "The reason is that it didn't never surprise anyone. Vernon was pure horse, with arms like a mule's legs and everybody just kinda understood that he would work like that. Wasn't no flattery or nothing in it. It was just understood."

Colby thought of the circle of men at church. Did they speak about Daddy? Did they brag on him then as they did now?

Colby didn't think so. It wouldn't be the circle's way and certainly not Daddy's way, to single out one man.

"What was understood?" David yawned, entering the kitchen.

"That your daddy was the workingest man there ever was," Jason said.

"You ever work along side of him?" David asked.

"Well, sir, I reckon I tried to work along side of him but couldn't come even close to keeping up. He didn't never say nothing about it, though. He knew I was going 'bout as fast as I could. It just wasn't nowhere close to as fast as he could go. Never said a reproachful word, though. He just kept right on being Vernon Grayson."

David walked to the ice box for a glass of milk. Joining Jason and Colby at the table, he asked, "How good a shot was he with the twenty-two?"

"With the twenty-two? Well, sir, I guess 'bout as good as anybody, though I don't remember nothing special. Why do you ask?"

"Because Tim-Bug shoots it like nothing you ever seen. He can hit a dove on the wing and head-shoot a running rabbit from a hundred feet. I never seen him miss."

Colby looked at his brother, surprised by what sounded like a challenge, daring Jason to dispute him.

"That sounds like some fine shooting," Jason said.

"It is that," David agreed and Colby saw him relax. He wondered what had put David in this challenging mood so early in the morning. After an uncomfortable silence, David said, "Well, ole Doris ain't gonna milk herself." He put his glass in the sink and headed for the front room for the lantern.

Jason tilted his head towards the front door. "That's a good hand you got yourself there," he said.

"Yes, sir," Colby answered, "he sure is a good hand. I'm proud to have him."

"He big enough to help you come cutting time?"

"I ain't real sure. Just to tell you the truth, I never done no whole lot of it myself. I did some last year but mostly I just stayed out ahead of everybody spreading the tobacco sticks. I know for sure that David and Tim-Bug can do that much this year. I reckon I'll be cutting along about as best I can." Colby finished his milk.

"That's about all anybody does. It's about like anything else really, go as best you can until you get the swing of it, then it's just another job, a hard job, but just another job."

"Just another job?" Colby asked.

"Just another job," Jason repeated.

"Well, then, that's what I'll do."

"I'd just bet you will, Colby. Then the housing it isn't near as bad, then the stripping it and tying it isn't bad at all. That stove Vernon had in the stripping room really used to put out the heat. I remember we'd be stripping the tobacco in our shirtsleeves and it wasn't more than fifteen or twenty degrees outside sometimes."

160

"Yessir," Colby confirmed, "that old stove is still going good. I did strip quite a bit last winter and wasn't never cold even once."

"You tie any last year?"

"Sure did. Tied 'bout as much as anybody except Daddy."

"Good. That's good. Everybody around here still contract with that same trucking company for the hauling?" Jason inquired.

Colby felt his heart begin its familiar gallop. He didn't want his uncle to know that he had no idea about the trucking or warehouses and auctions or how he would get paid for his crop. Would Colby have to go to the warehouses himself? Did Daddy? He couldn't remember and was stunned by how much he didn't know about the process. How could he not remember?

And what would Jason think? Colby stared blankly at the floor, shaking his head almost imperceptibly when he realized that Jason was waiting for an answer. Colby didn't know how to approach the problem. Mama probably didn't know. Maybe Zach would—Russ! Russ would know. At church on Sunday, Colby could casually bring it up.

Colby returned to the conversation. "Not too sure really, Jason. I'm going to look into it real soon here, though, figure it all out."

Jason gazed steadily at his nephew for a few seconds. "I expect you to, Colby. I know you will," he said.

"I will." Colby indicated the empty coffee cup. "You want another cup?" he asked.

"Yes, sir I'd like that. I know you're most likely itching to get busy and all but what time does your mama generally get up?"

"Oh, 'bout any time now. What I'm going to do, seeing as how you're here visiting and all, is go on out to the barn and sharpen my hoes. I gotta get started back on the hoeing today. Between me and David and Zach helping tomorrow and Friday, too, if it's needed, we should be done by the end of the week. That'll leave Saturday for me to go the store and do some other things and David's going to be helping out Reverend Tannehill at the church for a few Saturdays. The Reverend asked me about it last Sunday. Reverend's going to pay him a dollar and twenty-five cents for a day's work."

Jason whistled, "Not bad. Not bad at all. And I'm just sure that the Reverend will be getting a bargain at that price."

"He will at that." Colby said. He heard Mama rising. "Here comes Mama now. What I'm gonna do is go on out to the barn while Mama cooks breakfast. Maybe y'all can talk a little."

"That'll be just fine, Colby. I gotta be leaving right after breakfast, anyway. I'm supposed to be back by lunchtime," Jason said.

"Allright then." Colby put his glass in the sink and left.

Jason poured himself another cup of coffee and lit another Lucky Strike, then stood at the kitchen sink awaiting Anne. She came in before the cigarette was half-gone. Avoiding Jason's eyes, she went directly to the cup-

161

board for her cast iron skillet and set it on the burner next to the coffee pot. Jason backed up to give her room.

"We generally have eggs and biscuits for breakfast," Anne said.

"That sounds good, Anne. Did you sleep all right?"

"About as good as ever. I like it when Annetta sleeps with me. I like to hear her breathe."

"Yeah, I know. A lot of times I don't much care for sleeping all by myself. It's too quiet," Jason said.

Anne pulled the flour out of the pantry and the milk out of the ice-box. She cracked an egg into a mixing bowl, started to add milk, then stopped.

"Jason?"

"Yes, Anne?"

"Did you and Colby talk and all?"

"We sure did. We talked last night and some more this morning."

Anne stood frozen, utterly silent, milk in hand. Jason watched her, wanting not to direct the conversation, to allow her to ask what she needed to know, whatever that was. He was looking first at her hands, then up to her face, her eyes. He was surprised, greatly surprised, stunned.

There were tears starting there. Anne didn't cry. She never cried. Ever.

He waited, uncomfortable, useless. Finally she spoke.

"Are we staying here?" she asked weakly, nearly inaudibly.

"Yes Anne, you are. Colby's got things going. He'll raise this tobacco, cut it, strip it and sell it and then before you know it, spring will be here again." Jason said. He watched Anne as she closed her eyes, kept them closed for a moment. When she opened them again the tears were gone. They had never fallen. She went straight back to making biscuits.

And she started singing. Quietly, so quietly and Jason knew that was it. There would be no more conversation with Anne, his injured sister. He stubbed out his cigarette in the ashtray on the table.

"I'll go on out to the hen house and see if there's any more eggs this morning." he said.

## CHAPTER 7

Annetta Grayson woke to the sounds of Mama cooking breakfast. She smelled coffee and knew that it was for Jason. Neither Colby nor Mama drank it.

Sometimes she felt disoriented when she woke up in Mama's bed. The walls and ceiling were not immediately identifiable. This morning, however, she knew right where she was. She missed waking up when Colby did, seeing him get up and smiling at him. Just the two of them, the morning theirs alone.

She rolled onto her back, pulled the covers up to her chin and listened to the day's music. First, the music that everybody heard if they listened even a little: the birds waking up and starting their day, looking for food and friends; the old rooster crowing and carrying on; the slightest of winds scratching the trees outside the window; Mama rattling pans and bowls and the icebox door opening and closing.

She took a deep, satisfying breath and started listening to the other music, the music that she was fairly sure that only she could hear: the music of the world, the music of the way things are.

She listened first for Mama's music. Not her quiet song but her music. They were two different things. The music that Mama made as she went about her day wasn't melodious or pleasant. It disturbed Annetta and made her sad. Mama's music at times reached a harsh frenzy that was difficult to hear but then Mama would start singing her song and the frenzy would crest and fall away, receding, again at bay. It made Mama's music less, but it still unnerved Annetta.

It was so different from Daddy's music. Daddy's had never been frenzied, never tangled or feverish. It had been plain, loud but steady, harsh but not really unpleasant. She was still confused by the fact that Daddy's music hadn't changed, hadn't wavered, either before or during his fatal illness. There had been a few times over the past two weeks when she wished she could hear it again, even for a little while.

She listened next for Tim's music. It was plain, strong but not overpowering and fun to listen to and almost always made her happy.

163

She wanted to go into the kitchen and sit with her Uncle Jason so she could listen to more of his music. She didn't know him well, so being with him helped her hear it. What she had heard of his music yesterday wasn't particularly nice. He himself was nice. But his music almost hurt her. It wasn't loud and obvious like Mama's music, but it was somehow worse. It was muffled and ugly, capped off somehow like a lid on a barrel. She didn't like it.

Before she rose, Tim's music caught her senses again. The music rose slowly, building steadily and she sensed something new in it. Sometimes she knew what the music was telling her, sometimes not, but Tim's was growing, and she knew that soon he was in for a big day. Not today or even tomorrow but, based on the lethargic rising, maybe a week, maybe ten days. Something like that, Annetta thought. Nothing bad, she was almost sure, but something.

She had tried to explain the music to Timothy only once. He had always been delighted by how she knew things, like who would not be at church or who was coming for a visit. She had tried to tell him it was all right there in the music for whoever chose to listen. The music was almost always going somewhere, changing but occasionally predictable. That was why she was so good with the garden. She simply listened to the music of the plants. They knew what they wanted and told her. And, unlike the music in people, she could adjust the music in the plants and make it more beautiful. Her garden was her favorite place to be in the whole world.

It was all easy, really. She had tried to get Tim to remain still and open, just breathing and listening, so he could hear it, too. After thirty seconds, he had opened his eyes and said, "This is just about the dumbest thing I ever heard of," and stomped away.

She'd pay extra attention to his music for the next couple of days.

She listened next for David's music and found it easily. He was still in the barn, his milking music playing. Like all of his music, it was easy to listen to, complex yet somehow easily understandable. Like Tim's music, it nearly always made her happy.

She liked David. He was funny and nice to her. Unlike Tim, David had never once hit her. Tim had hit her often until the day a year ago when Annetta had faked crying after getting punched in the shoulder. When Tim approached her to apologize, she had punched him as hard as she could, squarely in the nose. He had held her down and bled all over her, laughing, but he had not laid a rough hand on her since.

Then, without even trying, she caught Colby's music. It was so loud and there was so much of it that Annetta couldn't believe that not everyone could hear it. At times there seemed to be an almost visible light along with it, a white light that was somehow composed of many colors.

There was so much music there that Annetta couldn't hear it all at once. Nobody else's music was like that, that big. Different melodies all playing at once, all of them strong, obvious and in conflict with one another.

She liked all the music, even if, like Mama's and Jason's, it was going somewhere hurtful. She thought it was a bit like being able to smell. There were bad smells in the world, but she still liked being able to smell. There were a whole lot more good smells in the world than bad ones.

But Colby's music overwhelmed her. There was just too much all at once for her to enjoy it. Most disturbing to her was that Colby's music was building, slowly and hugely, like a great tidal wave that she had seen in a book at school. All the strains, good and bad, pleasant and ugly, were building to a powerful, overwhelming crescendo that Annetta Grayson didn't want to hear.

## CHAPTER 8

David returned to the barn after turning Doris out in her pasture. The warm bucket of milk sat on the workbench, where Colby was finishing his work on the hoes. Colby made one last pass with the file, then set it down and released the hoe from the clamps of the vice.

"Well, David, it's been a couple of weeks or more that these hoes have been sitting here. Do you think they missed us?" he asked.

"Might be, but I don't think I've missed them none too much."

The sun was coming up slowly and assuredly. David turned the knob on the lantern, shutting out the flame. The lantern in his left hand, he reached for the milk bucket with his right when he noticed Colby studying the hoe.

"Marvin," Colby said.

"What?"

"Marvin," Colby repeated with a smile.

"No, I heard what you said. I mean, what do you mean?" David asked.

"I'm naming my hoe 'Marvin.' It's a good name, I think, and none the worse for having been used before."

"Colby, that's durn near the silliest thing I ever heard. You gonna put a name on a tool?"

Colby didn't tell David that he had recently heard on a Reds broadcast of an old baseball player who named his bat. He couldn't remember the name of the bat or even the player, though he thought it was an old New York Yankee.

"It's not just a tool, it's Marvin. Me and Marvin have spent a lot of time together. Marvin ain't never lied to me or failed to do what I asked of him. Marvin's always ready to go to work when I am and don't ever complain. What are you going to name yours?"

David beamed, warming quickly to the idea. He knew immediately what he wanted to name his. The year before, his teacher had read the class a story about King Arthur and he had a sword named Excalibur. What a great name. Excalibur, Sword of Kings.

But a hoe wasn't a sword and David knew he was no King. But still...

"I don't think I know just yet but...well-sir, maybe I do know but you might think it's dumb."

166

"I won't, either," Colby assured him.

"Alright then, Excalibur. My hoe's name is Excalibur."

"What a great name! Way better than Marvin. I like it," Colby said.

"You gonna name all the tools?" David wondered.

"Nossir, just old Marvin."

Colby laid Marvin against the work bench next to Excalibur and took the lantern from David, leaving his brother two hands to carry the milk bucket as they started up the slag path to the house.

"Is Jason gonna go on and head back to Lexington this morning?" David asked.

"He is. He's got to be back at lunchtime. He's going to eat breakfast with us before he goes."

"I like him. I remember him from before but, well, I just like him."

"I do too, David. He offered for us to—" Colby quickly closed his mouth and looked away.

"Offered what?" David asked.

"Well-sir, I reckon he just offered to, if he could, you know, help us out some way, him being family and all." Colby hoped David didn't pursue this. Colby didn't feel like talking about it.

David knew something was on Colby's mind. Colby never stumbled over his words like that. He was trying to decide whether or not to leave it alone when he saw a quick motion out of the corner of his eye.

"Colby!" he whispered urgently. "Colby, look!" he said, pointing across Colby's body.

Colby bumped into David's pointing arm, stopped and followed his brother's gaze. It took him a moment but he finally saw it. Loping, nearly bouncing, across the far field, on an early morning mission, snout low and tail high, was a very nice-sized red fox.

"I wonder if that's the same one Russ saw a while back," Colby said.

"Might could be. Didn't you tell me he said thirty-five dollars for a fox pelt?"

"I believe that's what he said. It's probably too late but let's us run up to the house and tell Tim-Bug. He probably won't get him today, but he can start going out with you of a morning. It surely won't take too long after that."

Eighty seconds later, Timothy Grayson tore out the front door, rifle held in two hands in front of his chest, dressed only in his boots and underwear.

## CHAPTER 9

Saturday morning was wet. A cool, steady rain had fallen for most of the night and it continued spitting on and off all morning. There would be no field work today but Colby didn't mind. The preceding week, he, David and Zach had caught up with the weeds and the tobacco plants themselves were healthy, thick and green. The biggest of the plants now came to Colby's chest. Almost all were growing wide white blossoms on top and Colby knew it would soon be time to top the plants. He'd ask Russ what he thought tomorrow at church.

Despite the rain, he still wanted to go to the store. David was going to ride into town with Colby and then walk on to the church for his first day helping Reverend Tannehill. David was in the barn, hooking an unhappy Leviticus to the wagon.

Colby reached into his front pocket and pulled out the money. He had searched along the road every single day but had found only three dollars and eighty cents. Still, it was enough to get what Mama needed: flour, beans, sugar, salt, some baloney—and a pouch of Beech-Nut for himself.

A few of the rails in the barn needed replacing and he thought that he might tear out all the bad ones this afternoon after he got back from the store. Zach could help him put in the new ones next week. There were plenty of nails in the barn, but Colby reminded himself to stop by E. E. Robinson's hardware store today to see if he had the rails in stock. Colby would have to buy the rails on account, as he had the new roofing for the barn. The money found along the road had been enough to feed his family so he hadn't had to use his account at the grocery but there was none left over for farm supplies.

He put the money back in his pocket as he heard David leading the mule and wagon up the slag path. He poked his head into the kitchen, where Mama and Annetta were washing the breakfast dishes. Colby winked at Baby-Anne. She smiled back.

"Mama? Me and David's going on to the store now. Okay?"

"Yes," she said. "Y'all go on ahead."

"Okay then," Colby said.

Annetta started to giggle. "Colby?" she asked.

"Yeah?"

"Y'all try and stay dry now," she said and giggled again.

"We will. I think maybe it's done let up for the day." Annetta giggled a third time, then turned back to her chores.

He headed out towards the wagon. The rain had ceased for the time, but it was still wet and gray. David's boots and the cuffs of his pants were soaked.

"We ready to go?" Colby asked.

"We sure are but I don't think Leviticus likes the rain none," David said.

"Maybe it'll hold off until we get back," Colby replied.

"Maybe," David said, then looked at the sky. "Maybe not."

They headed out the driveway. They were no more than half a mile down the road when the wind picked suddenly up, the sky turned dark again, and a steady rain began to pelt down. Colby shook his head and tried to coax Leviticus into a faster walk.

Leviticus ignored him and continued his usual steady pace. By the time they got to Mr. Norvell's grocery, they were both so soaked that they didn't even bother hurrying into the store.

Mr. Norvell sat at the checkers barrel across from Spencer Kirk. They both looked up when the boys entered, then laughed.

"Reckon it's gonna rain there Cole?" Mr. Norvell asked.

"Hard to say," Colby laughed in return.

Mr. Norvell got out of his seat. "Let me get y'all a towel to dry up with." He went behind the counter and pulled out two clean dust rags and handed them over.

"We want to get a few things, but I reckon we'll just stay in here until the rain lets up, if that's alright," Colby said, wiping his face with the rag.

"Fine by me," Mr. Norvell said and returned to his seat at the barrel. He was playing the red pieces and one glance told Colby that he was winning handily. David was also eyeing the board.

"Can Mr. Kirk win this game?" Colby asked him. David shook his head.

"No way. He's too far gone. He couldn't even get a draw in his position," he replied.

"You know, we're liable to be here a good while," Colby said. "You ought maybe to sit down and give Mr. Norvell a try."

David stood thinking a moment.

"Well, I do have to get on up to the church, but I don't reckon that Reverend Tannehill would expect me to walk in the pouring down rain. Would he?"

"Well, I don't think he would. The rain ain't gonna last too awful long."

"You wanna ask him if I could try?" David asked.

169

Colby grinned and shook his head. "Naw. You can. Go on ahead and ask him and I'll get the groceries. Go on." Colby turned and made his way down the aisles.

David meandered over to the barrel and looked down at the game, then glanced at Mr. Norvell out of the corner of his eye.

Mr. Norvell caught the glance. "Well David, I think I got him this time. What do you think?" he asked.

"You got him easy. Chase that one down and then you got his King trapped in the corner. He couldn't get a draw even if you was trying to let him," David said.

"And that's something Lawrence wouldn't never do," Spencer Kirk joked. "You win, Lawrence. What is that? Three in a row?"

"Four but who's counting?" Mr. Norvell said with a wink at David. He began setting the pieces up again. "How about you, David? Care to give me a try? I'm near falling asleep playing Spence here."

"Could I?" David asked. "I mean I played some at school and all."

"Why, surely you can. Have a seat there and we'll give it a go."

Spencer got up and gave David a squeeze on the shoulder. "Give him you-know-what, David," he said.

David sat down and adjusted his pieces so that they were all well within their designated squares.

"Why don't you go first, young fella?" Mr. Norvell said.

David moved his first piece into a center square. Mr. Norvell did likewise without hesitation. David thought a few seconds and made his second move. Mr. Norvell quickly countered.

The game progressed, David's moves still slow and thoughtful but now Mr. Norvell's moves becoming slower as well. They traded men again and again. In less than five minutes, they were both down to two men and two kings apiece. At the back of the store, Colby was picking up a sack of pinto beans when he heard Mr. Kirk whoop.

"I think you might have him, David. I think you just might have him!"

Colby hustled his beans to the front counter and laid them down next to his other goods. He saw David shaking his head.

"I don't think so, Mr. Kirk. Unless he messes up, the best I can get is a draw. I made a mistake three moves ago. I should have traded kings with him, then I could've won." David spoke without looking up from the board.

Mr. Norvell also stared at the board and agreed. "He's right. It can only be a draw. He's also right that if he had traded those kings, he most likely would've won." He looked up at David. "Should we call this one a draw and play again?" he asked.

"You sure enough just played him to a draw?" Colby asked David, who nodded.

"Well, try him again," Colby urged.

170

David and Mr. Norvell reset their pieces.

"You want to go first this time, Mr. Norvell?" David asked.

"No, no. You go on ahead and go," Mr. Norvell responded.

"You go on and get him, David. Whup him good," Mr. Kirk laughed. He suspected that Lawrence had let the boy off easy in the last game.

The game began, both players this time moving methodically, steadily. After twelve or fifteen moves, Spencer could see with certainty that Lawrence Norvell was giving David his best game and his best game wasn't good enough. Spencer watched in amazement as young David steadily carved the best checkers player around completely to pieces.

Colby hadn't played checkers too many times, but he knew, a bit after Mr. Kirk and Mr. Norvell knew, that David would win. He wanted to jump in and give David advice when David sacrificed two of his kings for two of Mr. Norvell's regular men but then saw that the sacrifice had hemmed Mr. Norvell's last man and last king into separate corners with no way out.

David had done it. He had beaten Lawrence Norvell.

There was no sound except the rain falling on the tin roof as Lawrence Norvell shook his head, then smiled. He stuck his hand across the checkerboard. David grinned and shook it.

"David, I want you to know that that's the first game I've lost since Russ beat me about four months ago. Well played, young man. Well played."

"Thanks, Mr. Norvell. I did have the advantage, going first and all."

"Yessir, you did at that. Now how about you let me go first this time. It's my pride that's at stake and all," he said, mockingly serious. David looked again up at Colby, who looked out the door.

"Still raining," Colby told him.

The rain lasted another hour and fifteen minutes and, in that time, they played six more games, each having the first move three times. David played to a draw all three times Mr. Norvell went first and won two out of the three when he went first, including the last game.

"I will be durned!" Mr. Norvell exclaimed in concession as he removed his last piece from the board. "I will just be durned. You're how old again?" he asked.

"Eleven," David said, beaming. "I'll be twelve this September."

Spencer Kirk put a hand on Lawrence's shoulder. "Don't let it worry you none, Lawrence. Won't nobody hear about it from me, except for everyone at church tomorrow and also everyone I see for the next month or two. I mean, I ain't gonna ride into Morehead or Lexington and announce it or anything, not unless someone is going that way anyway and can give me a ride back home," he said. He clapped his friend on the back. "You need some help out of your seat there or can you walk?"

"I will be durned," Mr. Norvell repeated. He got up and walked behind the sales counter and began adding up Colby's items. "I'll be dipped in molasses."

"I thought you said you'd be durned. Can you be both?" Spencer asked, laughing.

Lawrence looked up from his work. "Sure enough, y'all. I ain't never seen nothing to beat it. I've been playing checkers for forty years and winning regular for thirty-five. Truth is, I kinda thought I was 'bout as good as a fella could get. Reckon I was wrong. That'll be three dollars and twenty-five cents there Colby."

Colby counted out the money.

"You ain't mad or nothing are you Mr. Norvell?" he asked, quietly.

"What's that? Mad? Nossir, not mad, not one little bit mad. I'd say confused is closer to the mark. I really and truly don't mind taking a licking, I just didn't think there was anyone anywhere close to give me one. I'd sure like to try him again," he said, then looked over at David, who was at the barrel with Mr. Kirk. "How about a rematch David? Next Saturday sound about right to you?"

"Yessir, I'll be riding in with Colby most likely. I'd like to," David agreed happily. Spencer Kirk nodded in agreement.

"I'd like that, too. You know who else would like it? Pert near everybody I know, and I can just about guarantee there'll be an audience."

"Alright, then," Mr. Norvell said.

"Yes, sir," David said and began helping Colby with the groceries.

They put the boxes in the back of the wagon and Colby used his hand to push the rainwater off the seat.

"Daggone, David. I didn't know you was that good at checkers," he said.

"I didn't either, Colby. But it's just a kind of math, really. Figuring out what could happen, then what's probably going to happen, then how to make it happen. It's just looking out ahead of the moves. Most people just look one or two moves ahead. Mr. Norvell looks five or six ahead. That's why he wins all the time. The way you beat him is to look seven or eight moves ahead."

"Seems like an awful lot to keep straight in your head. More than I could do anyway."

"Colby?" David started, concern in his voice.

"Yeah?"

"He wasn't mad or nothing, was he?"

"Naw. He wasn't mad. Just surprised is all. I will tell you this though. You're gonna be famous at church tomorrow. They're gonna be talking about this for a while."

"You think?" David asked proudly.

"I don't think, I know." Colby looked up at the sky. "Rain's done for sure now. I guess you'd best head on to the church."

"I will. You don't think he'll work me past dark, do you? It's a long walk home."

## CHAPTER 10

At church the next day, Colby spit a quick, sure stream of tobacco juice to the ground between his feet. He was listening to Spencer Kirk's description of the checkers match.

"…and then he says, four times he says, 'I'll be durned.' Like he couldn't think of nothing else to say. And then when he does think what else to say, what he says is, 'Well I'll be dipped in molasses.' In molasses!" Spencer said, by now laughing so hard tobacco juice trickled over his bottom lip. Everyone in the circle laughed, too, including Mr. Norvell.

"It was a for certain butt-whipping," he admitted. "He just plain beat me is all. Just plain beat me. We played eight games and the best I could do was draw him five times. He's that good."

"Dang, Lawrence, you gonna retire now?" Big Tom asked.

"No sir, we're fixing to play again this Saturday. I don't 'spect none of you fellas will want to watch though."

The men in the circle all began laughing and teasing, making their plans for the coming Saturday. Colby laughed along with them, then glanced around for his family. Mama was with the other women. Tim-Bug and Baby-Anne were running and playing with the other children and David stood with Reverend Tannehill, talking quietly. Reverend Tannehill saw Colby looking in their direction and, his hand on David's shoulder, they headed towards the circle.

Colby turned around, never leaving the circle and Reverend Tannehill and David stopped before him. David took one extra step to get away from the Reverend's hand.

"Reverend," Colby greeted him.

"Ah, Colby. Young David here was just telling me about his checkers match yesterday. It would seem that he is the new champion," Reverend Tannehill said.

"I never said champion," David interjected, glancing at his brother. "I just said I beat him three times is all."

"Quite so, David. I stand corrected."

With a nod towards David, Colby said, "I'm hoping you got a good day's work out of him, Reverend."

"I certainly did, Colby. An exceptional day. The windows have greatly needed attention for some time now. The putty needs replacing and the frames and sills want painting. This project I thought would take a month at least of Saturdays but with David's eager help, we scraped out all the old putty and re-glazed them and we even got the old paint scraped off half of the windows, as you may have noticed."

"Yes, sir, I saw that. Y'all planning on painting this coming Saturday then?"

The Reverend and David nodded in unison.

"That is my plan, God willing," the Reverend answered. "I must admit that David's enthusiasm has made me a bit more ambitious in my plans. The hedgerows all around haven't been touched in years and my bit of a flower garden is somewhat sad. With David's energetic help, I am of the belief that the appearance of this church could take a very large step forward."

"Well, good," Colby said. "But if you're wanting help with the garden, Annetta over there would be the one to help. She's got a way with gardens."

"No, no. That's quite alright. Me and my new helper will handle things," the Reverend said. He turned to David. "Well, David, shall we say this Saturday at about the same time?"

"Yessir. I'll be here. And, thanks." David said.

"Thanks be unto the Lord." Reverend Tannehill turned to make his way towards the women's group.

Colby nodded at David and turned back to the circle. The conversation had moved from the checkers match to tobacco worms. It was the peak time for them in the growing cycle and this year they were more abundant than usual.

"Yes, sir," Elijah Settles said. "I've seen worse years but not too awful many. How about it, Cole? You fighting the worms pretty hard?"

"Yes, sir, Mr. Settles. I am. I can't really remember how bad they were last year but I bet I've pinched the heads off of two or three hundred so far."

"Pinch the heads off 'em, do you?" Big Tom asked.

"Well…yessir. I don't think I'd care none to just squish 'em," Colby said.

"Naw, that's not what I meant. To properly kill a 'bacca worm, you're supposed to bite the head off."

"Now Big Tom, don't you be trying to get him to do that," Russ said, then turned to Colby. "Truth is Cole, when Big Tom here was about eight or ten, his daddy told him he'd give him a penny apiece for every head he bit off. What'd you earn that day Tom? Two, three cents?"

Big Tom started laughing.

"Four cents. What kept me from earning five is that I threw up right down the front of my shirt. It was the most honest four cents I've ever earned. And the hardest."

Colby looked behind him. Timothy was standing there listening. Colby turned back to the circle and said, "I reckon I'll just stick with the pinching."

"It couldn't have been all that bad, Tom," said James Caudill.

"You ever try it for yourself?" Big Tom asked.

"No, sir. Never did fall for that one myself."

"Well, sir, let's just do this, then. I'll pay you a *nickel* apiece for every one you bite off. You'll know how bad it is then."

"I'll just stick with the way ol' Cole there does it."

"Alright, then," Big Tom began with a half-smile and a nod. "The offer stands. I'll pay anyone a nickel apiece for every 'bacca worm that they bite the head off of."

There was a lull in the conversation, some unsure if Big Tom had his feelings hurt or not. Finally Russ Traylor jumped in.

"Anybody else topping their tobacco this week?" he asked. Most of the men nodded.

"This week or next," Old Man Tom said.

"Did mine this past week," E. E. Robinson said. "You Cole?"

"I suspect so," Colby replied. "Just about every bit of it's gone to flower. I imagine I'll just pinch 'em off like I do the worms," he said with a laugh. He looked over at Russ, who was smiling but not laughing.

"I think I'll do what I usually do and use a pair of shears. I tried pinching them before," Russ said, untruthfully, "but it damaged the stalk on account of the stem being so tough and all. Couldn't really pinch them off clean. What I do now is use shears. I'm still using the same shears I bought new from you twenty-seven years ago, E. E."

"Is that right?" E. E. asked. Russ nodded.

"It is. You sold the same kind to Vernon didn't you?"

"I did. Probably ten years ago. They still around Cole?"

Colby tried to appear at ease. "I think they're up on the work bench there. I'll most likely give 'em a try."

## Chapter 11

On Monday, Colby stood in the barn carrying on a debate with himself. It was after breakfast and David hadn't joined him yet. Tim-Bug had gone out well before breakfast, hunting the fox but had had no success. When Colby looked up at the house, he saw both of his brothers approaching the barn.

He wanted to go ahead and get the tobacco topped. He had found two shears, but he wanted Zach to help him with it. It couldn't be too complicated: just cut the bloom off. But how far under the bloom should he go? Should all the blooms be snipped, even the small ones? Even the ones that were just budding? Colby knew he should have swallowed his pride and just asked Russ yesterday. Stupid.

He could wait until tomorrow, but he was planning to ask Zach to help replace the barn rails. He had had no trouble getting the old, warped ones down on Saturday but putting new ones in correctly wouldn't be easy. Colby pulled out his Beech-Nut and took a chew. He wanted to decide before the boys got to the barn. He looked at the new rails lying in a neat pile, then at the shears on the work bench. He decided he had more to lose by messing up the tobacco plants, small though the chance might be. If the rails weren't exactly right, then Zach could help fix them on Friday.

David and Timothy reached the barn.

"No luck with the fox?" Colby asked.

Tim shook his head. "Not today but I'm pretty sure I saw sign of him. That longer grass over there by the fence, where it's still a little wet, I could see pretty clear something about the size of a fox had been walking there, more than once. I also saw some poop that was about the right size."

"You see any tracks around the chicken coop?" David asked.

"You know, I did. But we ain't got no chickens dead or gone. You know, what I ought to do is sit up tonight with the rifle, looking out the window. That's just exactly what I'm gonna do. Come to think of it, I can't hardly believe we're not missing some chickens already."

"Been lucky, I guess." Colby said. "You going out hunting?"

Timothy shook his head. "Not just now. I'm going this afternoon," he replied. At the work bench, he looked in several old coffee cans until he found one that had no nails or screws in it. He picked it up and showed it to Colby.

"Could I use this?" he asked.

"Don't see why not. What for?"

Tim mumbled and looked at his feet for a moment.

"Well…nothing, really. Just something I wanted to do. I'll bring it back."

"Alright, then," Colby said, amused.

Timothy left, can in hand and headed towards the back field.

Colby turned to his remaining brother. "Well, David, I was thinking you and me might turn ourselves into carpenters today."

David looked at the new rails, then up in the rafters to where they would be installed. "How many we have to put in? Have you counted?" he asked. A glance at the neatly stacked pile of new lumber told him there were seventy-two rails there. He hoped they didn't have to put them all in.

"Well, I took out fifty-four on Saturday, but the truth is, there's still some that could be replaced, if we get these other ones done."

David looked up again and said, "Pretty high up there once you get to that top level."

"It is that. Good thing is, there's only three or four at the very top. Almost all the worst ones were lower down." They each tied on a dirty canvas nail pouch, slid a wooden handled hammer between pouch and jeans and got to work.

It took them all day, with only a short break for lunch but they finished it. Their biggest obstacle wasn't, as Colby had feared, getting the rails into place and holding them there. Their biggest problem was simply driving the nails. Neither one knew what type of wood it was but it sure wasn't pine or some other soft wood. They bent many nails and would have to pull them out and start again. It was late in the morning before they found a rhythm in driving the nails, eventually hitting them on the head most of the time. It helped to hold the hammers closer to the head, losing some power in the swing but gaining accuracy. They had started at the very top and by mid-afternoon had reached the bottom level.

Timothy walked in and, without looking at them, set the borrowed coffee can on the workbench and covered it with an old seed sack. Colby and David didn't notice him until he was standing right under them.

"Colby, I was going to go on out with the rifle for a little while, unless you need me."

Colby didn't look down from his task.

"That's alright. You go on ahead and go. We'll be done directly," he said.

A couple of hours later, the job was finished.

"Well, David, that wasn't as bad as I thought it might be," Colby said.

"Not too bad," agreed David. "But I know my right arm's gonna be sore tomorrow. Swinging that hammer all day is different from hoeing."

"One good thing, if the Reverend needs you to do any carpentry for him, you'll be ready."

"I reckon." David said flatly.

Colby watched his brother move to the work bench. "You like him alright and everything?" he asked. "Working for him and all?"

David untied his nail apron and put it with the hammer on the bench.

"He's okay, I guess. He's different than on Sundays. Friendlier, I guess."

"You don't sound too excited."

"Well, no. It's only that he kinda hovers over me, puts his hands on my back all the time. Maybe I'm just used to having room to work. I don't know." David sounded ambivalent.

"But you do want to keep working for him, don't you? I mean, you're helping him out and your pay really helps us out," Colby said.

"I aim to keep on working for him. Ain't no problem like that. It's no big deal, really. No big deal at all," David said and headed up to the house.

## CHAPTER 12

On Friday morning, Colby and David were back in the barn after breakfast. It was the middle of July and extremely hot. The summer had been mostly mild, with high temperatures in the low eighties, sometimes even in the seventies, with just the right amount of rain. But today it was already in the mid-eighties and the sun wasn't high in the sky yet.

With Zach's help, they had topped all of the tobacco on Tuesday. Zach had shown them how to cut about halfway between the bottom of the bloom and the topmost leaves. The Graysons had only two shears, so Colby and David had used those and Zach had used his pocket knife. It took them all day working at a steady pace.

On this warm, muggy morning, One-Eyed Zach appeared in the barn doorway and looked up.

"Well, sir, I reckon old Mr. Summer's here sure enough," he said.

"Gonna get right hot today, ain't it Zach?" Colby said with a grin.

"It surely is. We done dodged it up to now but it's about that time. Good tobacco growing weather, though. Hot, steamy-like. That old tobacco do love that steamy weather. We get some good rain mixed in about once a week or so, you gonna have you some great big tobacco plants."

"Radio said it's likely to rain this Sunday," Colby said.

"Yessir, I heard that, too. Russ told me."

"He getting along alright? I don't never see him except on Sundays." Colby said.

"'Bout as good as ever. You know Russ, working the fields, trying to stay out of Mrs. Traylor's way. They got a letter from their youngest yesterday."

Zach entered the barn and noticed the scythe clamped in the vice on the work bench. Colby had already sharpened the axe and the hatchet.

"Might be I know of a fella who's got a mind to work on a fence row or two," Zach said.

"Yessir. That's a fact. That row at the back of the back field and the one that runs between ours and Russ's are in pretty bad shape. I thought we'd spend the morning cleaning them out and that'll leave us free to hit the hoeing again next week," Colby explained.

179

"That suits me. I imagine it'll be time to hit the weeds again next week. Tobacco likes this weather, but so do the weeds."

As he said this, Timothy walked in, carrying his rifle. "Morning, Zach," he said.

"Morning, Tim. Off hunting? I'm just about ready for some more rabbit."

"The truth is, I'm not seeing as many rabbits as I was. I hope I haven't hunted them out."

"That ain't likely," Zach said. "A rabbit doe can throw three, four litters a year. Might be that they just scared of you," he added with a wide smile.

"Might be. I've mostly been looking to bag me a fox. Colby and David seen one and I've seen sign of him. They said a pelt's worth thirty-five dollars."

"I believe that. No luck though?" Zach said.

"Not yet. I don't hardly know where to hunt him," admitted Tim. "I know where to look for rabbits but not so much the fox."

"Well sir, that fox is hunting them rabbits, same as you, so you might just keep looking around the brush and the briars, but I might have something else you could try."

"What's that?" Tim asked eagerly.

"Mr. Fox, he got to drink water, just like everything else. If I was you, what I'd do is find me a fresh water source and hunker down there at sunset and after. What I'd do is find me a quiet hiding place and just wait but it got to be downwind of the spot. Mr. Fox, he can smell better than you and me can see. You don't want him to catch a scent of you on the wind."

"You know, Zach, I think that's a good idea. I know just exactly the spot, too. Thanks," Timothy said. "Colby?"

"Yeah, Tim."

"We still got plenty of rabbit in the icebox, you know."

Colby nodded.

"I know. You go on and bag that fox. I'll tell Mama you might not get back until after supper."

"Okay. Thanks!" he said and headed towards his spot by the creek.

## Chapter 13

The next day, Colby and David were climbing aboard the wagon for the trip to town when Timothy ran down, stopped at Leviticus' nose and put one hand on the harness.

"Colby, you said just about everyone's gonna be there to watch David?" he asked.

"I don't know for real sure, but I'd just about bet everyone'll be there. At church last Sunday, they all said they would."

"Even Big Tom, you reckon?" Tim asked.

"I expect so."

"Then can I come too?"

"Well, sure you can. Come on and go with us," Colby said.

"Alright, I will. Give me just a second, though." Timothy turned and darted into the barn. Colby and David watched to see what Tim-Bug was getting but he was lost in the shadows by the workbench. He came out with a small parcel wrapped in an old feed sack. Using his free hand, he jumped up into the back of the wagon.

"What you got there, Tim-Bug?' Colby asked.

"Aw...just something," Tim muttered.

Colby looked at David and they both shrugged their shoulders. Colby flicked the reins and gave the command to Leviticus, "Let's go!"

The old mule obediently began plodding forward. As they reached the top of the slag path and drew even with the house, Colby looked over at Annetta's vegetable garden. The corn was lush and tall, the tomato plants sagging with fruit and the green beans were running riot. Squash and cucumbers grew in abundance with onions, green peppers and potatoes. Mama and Baby-Anne would start canning this coming week. Every day that Zach came to work, he inspected it and marveled.

Turning onto the road, Colby asked David without looking at him, "You nervous at all? I mean with everybody watching?"

"Well, maybe a little," David conceded. "I ain't nervous about the checkers though. But I do hope they all know I got to be getting on up to the church. It ain't raining today and the Reverend will be expecting me."

"They know. Just tell them how many games you got time for, then stick to it. Won't be a problem."

"Alright then, how about six? That'll take about an hour or less."

"Sounds about right to me." Colby nodded.

When they arrived at Norvell's store, they had to park out in the road. Colby counted eight wagons and one car—Doctor Cardiff had apparently heard the rumors, too.

"Geez!" David exclaimed. "All these people really come just to watch me and Mr. Norvell play checkers?"

"Looks like it," Colby said and climbed down.

"Whoa!" Timothy cried, seeing the crowd. "I sure hope you give him another whoopin'. That's Big Tom's wagon over there ain't it?"

"I believe so," Colby answered and led them into the store.

When David walked in behind Colby, the gathering cheered.

"There he is! The man with the plan," James Caudill said.

"The new champion!" E. E. Robinson proclaimed.

"The Checkers King!" Big Tom agreed.

David slowed his walk, hanging behind Colby. He looked down at his feet but grinned hugely.

Colby saw Russ talking to Doctor Cardiff; Russ nodded a greeting. The men gathered around David and led him to the chair opposite Lawrence Norvell. The board was already set up.

"I hope ya'll know that I can't stay but a little while. I'm helping Reverend Tannehill on Saturdays now, I think I got time to play six games. Okay?" David said, settling into his seat.

"Well, sir, you do me like you did last Saturday and it won't take too awful long," Mr. Norvell told him.

The men gathered closer and Colby wedged his way directly in behind David. Timothy went around the other side and Old Man Tom waved him close, giving him a good spot.

"Well, David, should we flip a coin for first move?" Mr. Norvell asked.

"Alright by me," David agreed.

"How about I flip it and you call it?" Mr. Norvell suggested, pulling an old silver dollar out of his pocket. He flipped it, caught it and slapped it down on his wrist.

"Heads," David said. It was heads.

David made his first move and they were off.

The final results varied little from the previous Saturday. David won two of the three games when he had first move and played Mr. Norvell to a draw the other games. After the last game, Colby looked up at Russ, who had moved beside him.

"He ain't just a little bit better, Colby," he said, "he's a whole lot better. There ain't a man in here who could beat him. I mean not a one of us."

"I know I sure couldn't," Colby said.

Lawrence Norvell rose from his chair, shaking his head. He raised his eyebrows at the crowd.

"Boys, he's the best I've ever seen. Ain't no two ways about it." He stuck his hand out as he had the previous Saturday. "Congratulations, young fella."

"Thanks, Mr. Norvell," David said. "I've gotta be getting on up to the church now, though. I hope we can play again sometime."

"I'd like that son. I surely would."

The crowd began to disperse, talking about particular moves David had made and teasing Lawrence.

"Colby, I'll be on home along about dark," David said and left.

Colby and Timothy made their way over to E. E. Robinson, who was about to return to his own store.

"Mr. Robinson? You remember my brother Tim, don't you?" Colby asked. "He was wanting to ask you something real quick."

E. E. looked down at Timothy. "Well, alright. What can I help you with?" he said.

"I was wanting to ask you about the fox pelts," Timothy said. "Colby says they're worth thirty-five dollars. Is that right?"

"It is. I ship them to St. Louis, and they send back a check, then I give the check to the harvester."

"Harvester?"

"Of the pelt. When a fella is hunting or trapping for pelts, it's called harvesting."

"Okay then, once I bag the fox, what I need to know is about skinning him proper. Is there any special thing I should do or maybe not do?"

"Well sir," E. E. explained, "the first thing is to shoot him like you shoot your rabbits, through the head. You don't want no bullet holes in the pelt."

"Okay, then what?"

"You'll want to go real slow and careful, get as much of it as you can, as high up on the neck and head as you can get and also the legs. Make real sure your knife don't slip and slice the pelt."

"And what about the tail? They'll want that too, right?"

"They will, but you'll want to be real careful again with the tail. What you'll want to do is just kind of peel the tail, skin all around the bottom of the base then just kinda roll it off. Make sure you keep it attached to the rest as good as you can though."

"And that's it?"

E. E. shook his head. "Nossir. After that, lay it out flat, fur side down, then you'll want to scrape it real good. I've heard of fellas just using a tobacco knife. There'll be a lot of what I call viscera, just stringy old tissue that needs scraping off. It'll take you a good bit to get it all off but once you do, take you some salt and rub it all over the inside. Make sure you don't get none on the fur, though, 'cause that'll make the fur fall out. Hang her up and let her dry a day or two, then bring it on in and I'll ship her off."

"That don't sound like no whole lotta trouble," Tim said and glanced over at the door. He saw Big Tom leaving with Russ, Doctor Cardiff, James Caudill and Old Man Tom, all still talking and laughing about the checkers match.

"Thanks Mr. Robinson. Could you excuse me a second? I gotta talk to Big Tom here," Timothy said and scurried over to the departing group of men with a hand in the air. Colby watched him, puzzled.

"Hey, Big Tom! Big Tom!" Tim called.

Big Tom stopped, as did the other men. "Hey, Tim. That surely was something, wasn't it?" he said, referring to the checkers.

"Yes, sir. David's smart like that. I was wanting to show you something."

"Okay. What is it? I'm all outta rabbit, so if you got one, I'm buying."

"No, sir, don't have none today. It's something else."

"Okay. What?" Big Tom inquired curiously.

"Well, remember last Sunday after church, you was talking about the tobacco worms and all?"

"I do. I've been fighting them all week."

"Well, you was saying you'd give a nickel apiece for any that a fella bit the heads off of?"

A grin made its way across Big Tom's face. "Did you bite one off?" he asked, reaching into his pocket for a nickel.

"Well, more than one actually," Tim said and walked to the back of the wagon. He picked up the old feed sack and reached inside, pulling out the old coffee can. Big Tom's smile widened and he pulled all of his change out of his pocket. He had sixty-three cents in coins and he'd be glad to give it over.

Tim walked up and offered the can to Big Tom. All the men, including Colby, looked inside and burst out laughing. The can was over three-quarters full. James Caudill laughed so hard he held onto the side of the wagon and doubled over.

"I hope you brought some folding money there, Tom," he wheezed.

Tim looked around, unsure if he was being laughed at or not. "I bit 'em all off. I did. I didn't pinch none of 'em. I even left the heads in there so you could see how clean they come off. Couldn't do that by pinching, you know."

Big Tom looked dubiously into the can and picked out a small handful of worm bodies and heads. Smiling, he showed them around and all the men inspected them and agreed that the heads had indeed been bitten off.

"Well sir," Big Tom said admiringly, "I can tell the difference between a head that's been bitten off against one that's been pinched off and I do believe that I owe you some money."

Colby said, "You really gonna pay a nickel apiece for those?"

Big Tom nodded. "I surely am. A nickel apiece is what I said, so a nickel apiece it is. This'll be a good lesson for me about what my daddy used to call letting your alligator mouth getting out in front of your hummingbird butt. How many you got there Tim? You counted 'em?"

"Yes, sir, I did." He stammered, reluctant to give up the number. All the men looked at him, wanting to know.

"Well?" Russ said, grinning broadly. "I just got to know."

Tim looked down at the ground.

"A hundred and six," he mumbled. A roar of refreshed laughter went up as the men clapped each other on the backs.

"A hundred and six! A hundred and six at a nickel apiece!" they yelled. Timothy brought his eyes back up and began smiling a bit.

"I counted them three times just to be sure," he said.

Big Tom looked at Russ. "How much is that, Russ?" he asked.

"Five dollars and thirty cents." Russ and Doctor Cardiff answered together. Big Tom pulled out his wallet, counted out five ones and pulled three dimes from the change in his hand. He handed the cash to Timothy.

"There you go, Tim. Fair and square."

Timothy took the money and handed it to Colby.

"Thanks, Big Tom. You want any more?" he asked, and the crowd burst out laughing anew.

"No, no. I think that'll about do it for me. I will say you earned that money, though. How'd you stand it?"

"Well, the trick is to bite right where the head meets the body. I bit the first couple kinda' in the body and got all kinds of worm juice and guts in my mouth. You bite 'em right at the head and they don't hardly squish at all."

Colby took four of the dollar bills and offered them back to Timothy. "You need any more shells for the twenty-two?" he asked.

"I could use a box sure enough," Tim said, taking the money and going back into the store. The men watched him go.

"Well that was surely something," said Old Man Tom Walker. "I reckon we can score two for the Graysons this mornin'."

"Thanks, Mr. Walker." Colby said. "I'm glad you're here. Are you still planning on slaughtering next Saturday? If you are, David won't be able to help on account of him helping the Reverend and all but Tim could help."

Old Man Tom shook his head. "No, sir, I'm not and I'm glad you mentioned it. I'm gonna go ahead and put it off about a month. Some of them shoats is actin' a bit off. Ain't eatin' like they should. I'm wantin' to make sure they ain't got some kinda virus in 'em before I go to slaughterin' 'em. Probably do it a month from today. That'll still put a good bit of time between it and my big slaughter in the fall."

"What's the difference between a summer slaughter and the big one in the fall?" Colby asked.

"Well sir, in the summer, I'm just aimin' to get a good bit of lard rendered and I make whole hog sausage with the rest. The big fall slaughter is when I get the hams and all that good middlin' meat. Can't cure all that proper in the summer. Gotta be cold out else the blow flies will get to 'em."

"Best whole hog sausage you'll ever eat," said James Caudill.

"I'm just about ready for some myself," Doctor Cardiff offered. "I'll plan on stopping by next month. Well gentlemen, I've got some calls to make. Take care of yourselves," he said and walked to his car.

The other men began leaving one by one, until only Big Tom and Colby were left. Big Tom glanced at the grocery door. Timothy was still inside. He looked down at Colby, hesitant.

"So, uh, Cole. David's helping out Reverend Tannehill is he?" he asked.

"He is. Every Saturday. He's getting a dollar and twenty-five cents a day."

Big Tom looked out over the road towards his family's old blacksmith shop, thinking. He finally turned his gaze back to Colby.

"That money coming in handy, is it?" he asked.

"It surely is. I don't reckon we're near to starving, what with the garden coming on and all but we do need it. I'm already in debt to Mr. Robinson over there. Without that money, I'd probably end up owing Mr. Norvell here, too. Truth is, I don't even want to think about that happening. I don't like owing money. I owe a bunch to the bank, and it makes my nerves rattle."

Big Tom remained silent a moment, thinking some more. Finally he spoke. "You reckon David could help me on Saturdays? I'm thinking about cleaning that old place over there and slapping a For Sale sign on it." He pointed at the old blacksmith shop.

"Well, really, I don't think that'd be doing the Reverend right. David said he'd help him," Colby answered.

Big Tom nodded again, struggling.

"Not keeping him after dark or nothing, is he? I mean, David's home every Saturday night?"

"He was last week. Just working the days. I don't imagine it'll be past that," Colby said in puzzlement.

Big Tom went quiet again. Timothy was coming out of the store. Big Tom looked at Colby.

"Alright then, I'll see you tomorrow," he said and walked to his wagon, speaking under his breath. Colby couldn't catch what he was saying.

"... Mind your business, Tommy. Mind your own business," Big Tom was whispering to himself.

## Chapter 14

That evening, an hour before dark, Colby sat in the rocking chair listening to the Reds. They were playing the second game of a double-header in St. Louis. Tim-Bug had gone fox-hunting an hour earlier. David wasn't home yet, and Mama was already in bed. Hearing movement in the kitchen, he looked up to see Baby-Anne in the doorway. She seemed to be listening for something, looking out the front door, before letting her eyes rest on Colby.

He smiled at her. "You alright, Baby-Anne?" he asked. She didn't answer but instead simply climbed into his lap, put her head on his chest and snuggled down comfortably. He put his left hand over her shoulders and his right arm across her knees. They sat like that for a few minutes, Colby a bit surprised but happy. She was too big to be babied but it was nice just sitting here with her. Colby figured she just needed to feel safe for a little while. He rocked and listened to the game.

"Do you ever hear the music, Colby?" she finally asked.

"The music? What music? You mean like Mama? With her singing and all?" Colby replied. The thought popped into his head, not for the first time that maybe his daydreams about playing for the Reds weren't just a bit like Mama's song. The thought made him nervous.

"Not that song, Colby. The music. Just the music of the way of things. The music of the world."

"You mean like the wind blowing and the birds singing and all like that?" Colby tried to understand.

"No, not really like that, maybe a little but I'm talking about just the music, it's…I don't know what else to call it," she said.

"Well, then, no, I don't reckon so. I'm not sure even what you mean."

"I heard Timmy's music really loud today. It was good, happy, big. It's been building for a while now. I could just tell that he's going to get his fox to-night. I'm just sure of it. It's all right there in his music," she tried to explain.

"You are good about knowing things, but I never heard you talk about no music before."

"It's always there. It ain't scary or anything, it's just there. And David? David's not having a good day. His music's changing. Not a lot, not right now, but it's changing. I don't like the way it's starting to sound. It bothers me. I'm scared for him, but I don't know why."

"You think he don't like working for Reverend Tannehill?"

"I'm not sure really," she said.

"Well, I ain't too worried about David. He can surely handle himself. Tim-Bug told you he whipped Mr. Norvell again in checkers didn't he?"

"He did. Don't surprise me, though." she said.

Colby laughed. "No, I don't reckon it would."

They sat for a few more minutes. She stirred and asked, "Are you getting tired, Colby?"

"No, not really. I'll make it to the end of the game," he said.

"That's not what I mean. I mean wore down, tired. You've been doing a lot of work. More than anybody I ever seen, except Daddy and I know you're worried a lot. I know that you still don't sleep as much as you did before Daddy died. That might wear you down quicker than working all the time."

Colby kept rocking, trying not to react, but Baby-Anne had hit on it exactly right. He was tired. She was also right about the worrying. Even with things going their way—the tobacco and the garden doing well, good weather, David bringing in money and Tim-Bug bringing in food—it was impossible for Colby not to worry continuously. The only things that eased his mind were hard work and slipping into his baseball fantasies.

His hands, his back and his arms had gotten much stronger. He knew, without being particularly proud of it, that he could keep up with any grown man in the Sunday circle, but he wasn't sure if his mind had grown stronger. He wondered how a man made his mind strong. He wished his mind was strong enough to shut off the worrying part of it, which was more tiring than anything he ever imagined. If he could only stop worrying, he could sleep. It was the physical labor he had feared most all those weeks ago when he took on responsibility for his family, the daily toil and grind, the sweaty, aching muscles and blistered hands, but that wasn't wearing him down at all. He was so much stronger physically now that no one particular task frightened him or even made him think twice. His back was muscled and deeply tanned, his hands thickly callused, rough; powerful and capable.

But his mind remained the same. His body grew stronger with use but not so his mind. He couldn't stop the worry, no matter what. No new small victory, no barrier passed, no task completed, brought him relief—merely the next thing to worry about. He knew he should let some of it go but he simply couldn't. Crazily, his brain insisted that worrying could prevent the worst from happening.

Did Russ worry this much? Is this what farming was? Much was within the control of the man but so very much more was not.

The tobacco was growing well, late enough in the summer that all were sure there would be no kind of blight. But so much remained to do: cutting, housing, stripping and getting it sold and shipped off.

So very much yet to do.

And then winter would come, surviving it, staying warm, staying fed.

And then next year, getting the new crop out and then summer all over again, the work, the worry, the sleepless nights. And then the year after and the one after that and on and on…

"No, Baby-Anne. I'm not tired. Not tired at all."

Twenty minutes later, Annetta was asleep in his lap when Colby heard two quick shots from the twenty-two.

Tim-Bug had bagged his fox.

# FALL

# CHAPTER 1

Russ Traylor put away the last of his tools. Saturday, the first day of October was wonderfully cool. They all had survived a hot, wet late summer, that resulted in as good a crop of tobacco as he had ever raised, almost certainly his most profitable crop ever.

People could talk about spring or summer or Christmastime all they liked, but for Russ, fall was far the best. The brutal heat was gone and with it the seemingly endless work days. All around him was the result of toil and sweat, the lush green plants holding the promise of sustainability and, this year, even profit.

He was certain this would be a windfall crop. The tobacco plants were unusually large and the farm reports on the radio repeatedly predicted a substantial rise in the price per pound.

For the past month, Cole and David had been helping Russ and Zach two or three days a week. Though David seemed a bit shy, even withdrawn, sometimes even surly, together they had repaired the rails in both of Russ's barns and cleaned out all his fence rows. He wasn't surprised that both of the Graysons had proved to be good hands. In fact, they far surpassed Russ's hopeful expectations. Russ was happy, but not just happy for himself.

He, like the other farmers, was happiest of all for Cole Grayson. Their community was alive, alive more than it had ever been, aglow and quietly humming with the knowledge that Colburn Grayson had done the impossible, he had brought his family through. Just as the men had circled around Cole after church on Sundays, so had they circled around the Grayson family; this year, their first priority not their own crops but Cole's, not their own well-being but that of the Graysons. The annual post-harvest feeling of weary satisfaction would not be for themselves but for Cole, Colburn Grayson. And when they lay pleasantly exhausted in their beds at night, they thought with pride not of their own lush tobacco fields but of Cole's, and their own accomplishments of previous years maybe seemed shallow and mediocre. They were in a continual state of low key, even silent, celebration, calmly and reservedly ecstatic that Cole had pulled it off, and that they had helped.

Russ went up to the house and into the kitchen where Dot was at the sink. Zach would be up for supper and she was preparing mustard fried pork chops and mashed potatoes. Old Man Tom's hog slaughter had been delayed until the previous Saturday, and Russ had made him promise to carve out some chops for him before he made his sausage.

"Zach said he'd be up in about an hour," Russ told his wife.

"That'll be fine. I made a cobbler with those blackberries y'all picked yesterday afternoon," Dot said.

"Well, that's good, then. There's a whole lot more blackberries out there just waiting. I would say it's the best year I ever remember for blackberries. They just keep coming on."

"You keep right on bringing them in and I'll can them," she said. Russ regarded his icebox thoughtfully. About a month earlier, at Norvell's store, he had seen a deep freezer advertised in a Montgomery Ward catalogue and he had since been giving serious consideration to purchasing one. It was less than two hundred dollars and, with the money they could save by reducing canning and the capacity for more long-term food storage, it would pay for itself in no time. He hadn't told Dot yet.

Over at the Grayson farm, Colby was counting his tobacco sticks. He had four hundred and thirty of them and he was nearly certain it would be enough. Included in that number was an unused bundle of thirty-six left over from last year.

Cutting time, the climax of the tobacco season, was upon them. Colby was itching to move on and get the tobacco cut, thinking that would signal the successful completion of the growing cycle, but the tobacco and the wind and the sun were indifferent to his impatience. The difficult and deliberate toil of the summer months was wearying and seemingly unrewarding, the only payoff to each day of hard work was a good night's sleep. He would finally be able to rest and let go, even if just a little. Something would finally change— the fields would actually look and feel different.

Colby had taken David in to town that morning to save him the long walk to the church for his Saturday job, but Colby also went to town to meet with the other farmers to discuss which farm would go first in the cutting. They all pitched in and helped one another during the cutting during this most difficult phase of the growing cycle. It took many men to cut one field and they would fall on it like hungry locusts, sweeping sweatily through it and knocking the cutting out one farm at a time.

David hadn't stayed to play checkers for about a month and Colby thought it a bit odd. David hadn't been himself. He still did everything that Colby asked of him without complaint, but he lacked his usual spirit and didn't speak as much, and had seemed to be less curious. He was even surly and unpleasant at times. He didn't cut up with Zach or go out exploring. Colby had tried to get him interested in the Reds but David wouldn't sit still long enough to listen to a game. Colby assumed that his brother was merely as tired as he himself was.

It was decided at the store that morning that the Grayson farm would be the first, starting Monday morning. This wasn't only because the farmers were so invested in Cole's success, but it was the main reason. They, like Colby, wanted to hurry things along and get the Graysons closer to the tobacco sales and the bank payoff. Then Cole could rest and then they all could relax.

They were close, but they weren't there yet.

After counting the sticks, he collected his tobacco spears. These would be placed over the ends of the sticks once the sticks were jammed in the ground and the tobacco stalks impaled upon them. After four or five plants were on the stick, the spear would be removed and placed on the next stick. Colby had six spears and knew it would be enough. Each man would bring two or three of his own, as well as his own tobacco knife.

Colby never could figure out why it was called a knife when it looked more like a hatchet.

They would start in his front field the next morning and Colby didn't mind admitting he was nervous about it. He had never cut tobacco before. For the previous five years, he had stayed out in front of the cutters and spread the sticks, making sure they had one when and where they needed it. This year Tim and David would be spreading sticks and Colby would be cutting. Colby felt that he could keep up physically with the other men but it wasn't just about strength or stamina. There was an art to it, a fluidity he didn't know if he had, or how quickly he could develop it.

Daddy had had the required eloquent, economical ease of motion—plus he was a machine, stronger than the other men and grimly indifferent to toil. Surely they wouldn't expect Colby to be that good, would they?

He would just have to keep up, that's all. He took a deep breath and remembered that he hadn't yet encountered a task he hadn't conquered.

"Ain't a problem in the world that can't be solved through hard work," he reminded himself.

He arranged the knives and the spears in a line on the work bench and looked out through the barn door to see David coming down the driveway, home from another day of helping Reverend Tannehill. As he did every Saturday, David would put the money he earned on the old roll-top desk.

As Colby looked on, he saw Baby-Anne step out of her garden and wave David over to her with her left hand. In her right, she held something he couldn't discern. David saw her and walked in her direction, unsmiling and indifferent.

## CHAPTER 2

There wasn't much left in Annetta's garden, but that was as it should be. The root cellar was nearly full of canned goods: green beans, dilly beans, tomatoes, corn, beets, squash, peppers, pickled onions and even some asparagus. She and Mama had been canning for six weeks.

She had gone out to look for some late onions when she heard a stirring under a cucumber leaf. She bent down and found a frightened robin. She picked it up gently. The bird flapped its wings wildly but couldn't seem to fly. Its music wasn't loud, but frantic and she knew she couldn't change it or guide it. She simply didn't know what to do.

Looking up, she saw David coming home and decided to ask him. Earlier in the summer he had tried to explain to her how a bird's wing lets it fly—something about the curve on the top of the wing making the air move faster as the bird goes forward, making it lift. It hadn't really made sense to Annetta, but if David knew that about birds, maybe he would know what to do now. She waved him over. His music these last few weeks had been bad, sour and unpleasant. She wished she could help his music, but she couldn't guide it any more than she could the robin's.

"David. This poor little thing here, I just found it on the ground there," she said, holding the bird toward David. He stopped in front of her and looked down at it.

"What's wrong with him?" he asked.

"I don't know. It's scared as it can be. And it's not a him, it's a her."

"How do you know that?" he asked.

"I don't know, I just do. Can't we help it?"

David reached out and gently extended both of the wings. They moved freely.

"I don't know. Best thing to do might just be to let it alone," he said.

"I ain't either gonna let her alone. She'll die out here all alone. I'm gonna help her. You think I should put her in a box with some water?"

David shrugged; indifferent, weary, numb.

"You can if you want, she'll probably die anyway," he said, turned, and walked to the house.

"What an awful thing to say, David Grayson!" she yelled. She felt that she should be concerned about David and his music, it had been off and odd for a few weeks, but that was a plain horrible thing to say. Cradling the bird, she pulled a few cucumber leaves and followed him into the house and went to the pantry. Finding a small box from the grocery, she put the leaves in it. She gently laid the robin on the makeshift nest, then added a small saucer of water. She placed the box on the floor in the cool, quiet pantry. After thinking for a moment, she went to the icebox and took out an egg. She cracked it carefully over the sink and separated the yolk, then added it to the bird's water saucer. Annetta covered three-quarters of the box with a dishtowel then quietly shut the pantry door.

She poked her head into the front room. "Timothy," she began, dramatically ignoring David, "there's a robin in a box on the pantry floor. Please be careful of it. I'm trying to save it."

Timothy looked at her. "Okay," he said with a shrug.

## CHAPTER 3

Colby was up early. He knew that the other farmers wouldn't arrive until a bit after sunrise, but he wanted to make sure everything was right. He asked Mama to put on a full pot of coffee. When David came in from milking, Tim-Bug joined them in the kitchen.

"Well, you fellas ready for today?" Colby asked them.

Tim nodded while pouring himself a glass of milk.

"David, you?"

"We're ready, Colby. We done been over it a bunch of times. Me and Tim just stay out ahead of the cutters and make sure there's a stick when they need it. It ain't hard," David said.

"Allright then, I just remember having to hustle to keep up but with two of you, it should be easy," Colby said.

"I wouldn't mind trying some cutting myself Colby," Tim said.

It occurred to Colby, with some surprise, that David hadn't offered this as well.

"Well, we'll be cutting for two or three weeks before everyone is done, so I'd say you'll both get a chance before the end. That sound good, David?"

David's only response was an impassive shrug.

After breakfast, just as the sun reached the bottom of the fences, the boys made their way down the path to the barn. Tim and David each took a large bundle of tobacco sticks and walked to the front field. Colby carried four tobacco knives. There had been no dew, so the field wasn't muddy.

Tim and David began spreading the sticks as Colby had instructed, one for every four or five plants, the sticks laid next to the plants long ways. They had just finished the first two rows when Colby saw Russ and Zach walking up the slag path. He was glad that they had arrived first and he greeted them near the walnut tree.

Russ stopped and spit. "Well, sir, it looks like it's about that time," he said.

"Reckon so," Colby answered.

"Sure is," Zach agreed and added, "and a good day to cut, too. Not too hot and I suspect we'll have us a good breeze."

"I figured we'd just as well start here in the front field, might even finish it today. What do you think?" Colby asked.

198

"Don't see why not," Russ said. "Plenty of help coming."

Colby held up the knives. "I sharpened them all, but most of 'em will bring their own, I guess."

"I would say that is so," Russ said, showing Colby his own knife.

"Don't never hurt to have extra," Zach said. The three men watched as David and Tim started back to the barn for more sticks. As the boys reached the slag path, Colby turned back to the men.

"Russ, Zach, I got to say, I never really did no cutting. I mean I chopped around on it some last year but I never really cut none," he said.

Russ gazed out at the field and, after an uncomfortable moment, Zach laughed. "Well sir, we just gonna have to add this to the list of things you done learned how to do this year, ain't we?" he said.

"I 'spect," Colby said.

"Don't let it worry you none, Cole. Ain't going to be a single man here that didn't have a first time cutting," Russ added. "Also, won't be a single man here who don't think you'll pick right up on it. I promise you that."

Zach's head bobbed up and down in agreement. "Why don't we work it like this here? Why don't Russ and all the others start on the rows closest to the house? Colby, me and you'll just slip on down to the rows closest to the road and get started there. Even if the others notice, they won't care. Everybody got to learn. Russ, didn't you tell me that you the one that showed Vernon?"

"That is so. Denton asked me to. Matter of fact, it was right here in this field."

"He take right to it?" Colby asked.

"'Bout like anyone else, I suppose. I had to slow him down some because he kept stabbing his hands on the spears, trying to go too fast."

"Ain't a thing to worry about, Colby. With everybody pitching in, don't nobody care how fast anyone is going," Zach told him.

Colby nodded thankfully and looked up to see Big Tom turning his wagon into the driveway. With him were Elijah, Old Man Tom, and James Caudill. In another wagon, a hundred yards down the road, was Lawrence Norvell bringing Spencer Kirk and four others from the Sunday circle. Further down the road were five others walking together.

Colby was momentarily exhilarated, thinking that with this many men on hand, they would finish both fields today, then recalled that on Saturday they had figured on two to three days at the Grayson's. That was fine.

After everyone had arrived, they gathered in a circle, much like at church. Spencer pulled out his Mail Pouch and took a chew but didn't offer it around. Russ did the same, so Colby took his own out and took a plug.

After a moment or two, Russ tilted his head towards the field. "Don't reckon it's gonna cut itself," he said. The crew, receiving this simple summons, spread out easily and efficiently across the rows.

Zach beckoned to Colby with a nod of his head and they made for the furthest row, where Zach jammed one of the sticks into the ground at a forty-five degree angle and topped it with a spear.

"That's all there is to that part. You just want to make sure the stick is in there real good. Don't want it falling over," he explained

Colby picked up a stick and impaled the earth. It stayed firmly in place. He put the spear over the end.

"Well sir," Zach continued, "as far as cutting goes, what I always do is to spread my legs out so's I'm not having to bend over as much. I like to get right down on top of it." Colby did as Zach did.

Zach reached down and grabbed the stalk about six inches from the dirt. Colby followed suit.

"Now we just give it a whack," Zach said, chopping in a clean and sure cut. Again, Colby did the same.

Zach smiled. "Now you're a tobacco-cutting man. But this last part here is where you got to be careful. You're gonna want to spear the stalk like this," he said, confidently impaling the middle of the stalk and running it down nearly to the bottom of the stick. "That spear got to have a good point on it but if you ain't careful, you'll stab yourself like Russ said your daddy did. Fact is, I've seen more than one man stab hisself. One time seen a fella' run a spear clean through his hand so that there was two or more inches poking through the back. Took two of us to pull the thing back out."

Properly warned, Colby held the plant up, aiming the middle of the stalk at the spear and took two practice thrusts before stabbing it perfectly. He pushed it down until it matched Zach's.

"That's all there is to it," Zach said approvingly. "Four or five plants to the stick, depending on how big the plants are. Most of these are real good and big, so I'd say mostly stick with four per stick."

"Well, yeah, I reckon I can do this allright," Colby said.

"Didn't never have no doubt about that, Colby, but I was you, I'd remember not to be in no big hurry starting out."

This work, like all the other work, turned out to be manageable. For the first hour, Colby made a point of not checking the progress of the men in the other rows. He knew Zach was going more slowly than usual, both to coach Colby and to keep an eye on him but that didn't bother him. Colby had done the same for David while hoeing earlier in the year.

After an hour, however, he did look up to check because David and Tim were spreading sticks ahead of him and Zach and he wanted to make sure all the other men had sticks. Colby was not the least bit surprised that his brothers were doing their job well.

One thing did surprise him. Big Tom was clearly the fastest cutter there. He was already starting back down his second row while the others hadn't yet finished their first. Although he was tall like Vernon had been,

Big Tom was round of face and of belly, much different from Vernon's lean hardness but he had a casual, efficient gracefulness in his movements. Colby stood up straighter to get a better look and noticed that Big Tom's stance was much wider than anybody else's. He never stood all the way up between plants, staying low and always moving.

"Surprising, ain't it?" Zach asked. "A fella wouldn't know it to look at him but ol' Big Tom can flat cut."

"Sure can," Colby agreed admiringly. He bent back to the cutting, spreading his feet even further apart. It did seem to be more efficient, but Colby knew his hamstrings would be sore the next day.

## CHAPTER 4

By eleven-thirty, over half of the front field was cut. Although it wasn't hot, they had all sweated through their shirts. The younger ones, including Colby, had removed theirs. Mama and Baby-Anne had brought water to the men three times and Lawrence Norvell had brought salt tablets to help with their dehydration.

They gathered around Big Tom's wagon when they saw Anne bringing out lunch. She set down a big pot of beans. Baby-Anne brought a tray of sandwiches and cornbread. They went back to the house and returned with bowls, plates and cups and a big platter of cold fried rabbit.

The men gathered in the shade of the walnut tree to eat, joined by David and Tim. They ate in comfortable silence until Old Man Tom finally said, "Well, Cole, you're getting your first real taste of it. What do you think?"

Colby popped the last bite of his baloney sandwich into his mouth and shrugged. "About like anything else, I suppose. It ain't easy but it ain't nothing to be scared of neither. I 'spect just keeping at it until it's done is the way."

"That is sure enough the way. Back of your legs hurtin' yet?" Tom asked with a grin.

Colby smiled in return. "Not yet but I'm right sure about how they're gonna feel tomorrow." The men laughed, knowing they would all have very sore hamstrings the following day and for the duration of cutting season, those muscles getting a full workout only this time of year.

"It'll be bad the first week, then it gets better," Elijah said. "By the time you get your hamstrings trained, cutting's done with."

They finished eating and some stretched out on the ground, smoking and chewing in silence until E. E. Robinson raised his head and looked at Tim.

"Meant to tell you, Tim, I got a letter from the place in Saint Louis about that pelt. No money yet. Letter said that they are in receipt of 'one red fox pelt, condition excellent. Appraisal and payment forthcoming.'"

Tim sat up quickly.

"Really? Condition excellent?" he asked.

"That's what was in the letter. I reckon it means you'll get top price. You did a good job tanning that thing."

"And you said you thought around thirty-five dollars?"

"I think that's what it was last time. Maybe less, but could be more."

"They take all kinds of pelts, don't they" Tim asked.

"Well, I don't think they'd be looking for groundhog or anything like that. You see a beaver?" E. E. inquired.

Tim shook his head. "Well, no, not a beaver but something else. You might think I'm nuts, though."

Russ sat up, interested. "I'd just bet I know what you're about to say and I don't think you're nuts. You saw a mink, didn't you?"

Tim sat up straighter "You seen it too?" he asked. He looked over at David who would usually be interested in this sort of thing, but David lay on his back, staring silently at the sky.

"I would say that I did. At that little creek way behind my back barn. I ain't seen a mink since I was a kid. I always heard they hunted them out around 1900 or so." He looked at Elijah for confirmation. Elijah nodded assent.

"Ain't seen or heard about one in 50 years. Sure it wasn't a water rat?"

Russ nodded. "I'm sure. Tim, how about you?"

"I'm positive it wasn't no water rat, but I don't guess I really know what a mink looks like," answered Tim.

"Real dark brown, almost black, kinda like a skinny ground hog, sleek and shiny like?" E. E. asked.

"Just like that," Tim nodded.

"Well, sir, I ain't never had one to sell but it'd be worth a whole lot more than that fox, I can promise you that."

That evening, an hour before sunset, Colby was putting the tools away. They had completed the front field easily and considered starting the back but the consensus was that, since it was the first day of cutting season, they wouldn't push it. Colby was silently relieved. His legs were quivering from the unaccustomed bending and stretching. Tomorrow would be soon enough to start the back field.

David came in to do the evening milking. He walked right past Colby and to the stall.

"Well, what do you think, David? It wasn't that bad, was it? Reckon we can keep it up for three weeks?"

David shrugged. "Don't see why not."

Colby looked at him, again wondering what had been bothering David for the past few weeks. He usually liked to talk about things.

"Boy, Big Tom sure surprised me. He sure can move in the cutting." Colby said, trying to engage his brother in conversation.

"Yeah, he can. I like Big Tom," David responded.

"I seen y'all talking a while after lunch. He giving you tips on cutting?"

David shook his head. "Naw, nothing like that, we was just talking." David started into Doris' stall, then stopped. "Colby, we gonna be cutting on Saturday, too?" he asked.

"Well, I 'spect so. Reverend Tannehill expecting you?"

"I don't know. Probably," David mumbled. He looked up at Colby as if to speak, then went on into the stall.

"Big Tom was asking me questions." David said, nearly a mumble, after settling in to his task.

"Questions about what?" Colby asked.

David kept milking, his head down, focused on the job.

"About what David?"

"Well, about the Reverend, what we do, what he does while I'm there...like that."

"Well, you're working, right? The painting and the garden and the weeds and all?"

David didn't look up, but nodded.

"Yeah Colby, that's what we're doing."

"So why's Big Tom asking? He did say he wouldn't mind if you was to help him some. He told me he was thinking about cleaning out his family's lot there in town and trying to sell it." Colby said.

David shook his head, still milking.

"I don't know Colby. I don't know. He did say that he used to help the Reverend when he was a kid."

"He did? He didn't never mention it to me."

"He did to me." David said.

"And..." Colby said, realizing something was eating at David.

David shook his head again, still working. Finally, without looking up, he said, "Nothing, really. The money's good, not that hard to earn. It's nothing. Really, nothing."

## CHAPTER 5

The back field took two days to finish, thanks to a late rainstorm on Tuesday. They hit Elijah's big field next, finishing it late Saturday morning and no one was sorry to make an early day of it. At church the next day, they settled on starting Russ's fields the next day.

As they stood in the circle chewing, E. E. said to Colby, "Well, Cole, you got a week of it under your belt. You don't seem none the worse."

Colby spit, shaking his head.

"Just about like any other job, except you was durn sure right about my legs. I can't even hardly walk up the steps on my front porch." All the men laughed.

"I've noticed and I know you have too, how slow all these guys walked in today," James said. "Mine's already feeling better to tell you the truth."

"Mine, too, really." Colby agreed. "Hard on a fella's back too."

"Harder every year on mine, especially down low," continued James. "Don't reckon any of us getting any younger."

"I know I ain't, but you been old ever since I knew you, James," teased E. E.

"Well, look here who's talking. We're all getting up there, 'cept ole Cole here. It's a wonder he even has time for us old coots," said James. "But I reckon he'll be old as the rest of us before too long," he added with a laugh.

No one laughed with him.

Colby saw the children running and playing, David among them, and he was glad to see his brother laughing. Reverend Tannehill was also watching the children but noticed Colby looking in his direction.

He came up to the circle of men. "Colby, I wanted to thank you for letting me keep David working yesterday. I hope it didn't prove too great a hardship on you or the others," he said, smiling, serene.

"Not at all, Reverend. The extra money comes in real handy. How much longer you thinking you'll need him?" Colby asked. He glanced over at the children and thought he saw David, cocking an ear, trying to listen.

Reverend Tannehill put a hand on Colby's shoulder and eased him away from the circle.

"Oh, I shouldn't think more than four or five more Saturdays. As you will have probably noticed, the walls are almost completely painted. Those coal smoke stains truly were abysmal to behold. After that, I think rubbing and polishing all the pews will have our church looking truly worthy," he said. "The presence of David has truly been a gift to me, a gift that I thank the Lord my God for."

"Well, I'm glad he could help out."

"Indeed. Indeed. So I'm led to believe that the cutting is well under way."

"Yes, sir, it is. My fields are done and so are Elijah's. We're starting on Russ's tomorrow. I 'spect we'll be done with everybody's in two, two and a half more weeks."

"That is well, very well. The housing will start soon thereafter I think?" Tannehill inquired.

"Yessir, it will," Colby replied. "A month from now, I believe all my tobacco will be hanging in the barn and curing."

"Very well, very well indeed. I trust all your trucking arrangements area made?"

"Yes, Reverend. I'm using the same fella as Russ. He helped me make some arrangements last week. He hauls it to the warehouses in Morehead for a fee. I don't have to pay him until after the sales."

"Good, Colby, good. Even in times of trial, we can see the Lord's blessings, if only we look, if only we look closely enough."

## CHAPTER 6

One-Eyed Zach woke at his customary early hour on Saturday, October 29th. They were set to finish housing the Grayson tobacco today. It had taken nearly three full weeks for the men to finish cutting all the farms, having lost two full days and most of another to rain. It was rain that was on his mind as he looked out the door. He was glad they had a good start at Colby's because he was certain there would be rain this afternoon, no later than tonight. The light, insistent breeze and the clean, nearly electric scent guaranteed it.

He decided to walk on up to the house without making himself any breakfast or coffee. He wasn't really hungry and he would accept a hot cup from Mrs. Traylor. He looked around at the fields. The experimental area where they had tried the thinner mix of ammonium nitrate had yielded neither more nor less tobacco. It hadn't hurt to try but even if it hadn't worked, it wouldn't have mattered. Zach knew that this was the best crop he had ever helped Russ grow. All the plants were so big that nearly every stick had room for only four each. In previous good years, they could still get five plants on most of the sticks.

As he neared the house, he saw Russ rocking and chewing. Zach stopped at the steps, put his right foot on the lowest one and started rolling a cigarette.

"Mornin' to you, Zach," Russ said.

"Russ."

"Done had your breakfast this morning?"

Zach shook his head. "No, sir, I didn't have none this mornin'."

"Sick, are you?"

"No, sir, not at all. Just ain't hungry is all." Zach finished rolling his cigarette.

"You want some coffee, Zach?" Dot called from inside.

"Yes ma'am, I wouldn't mind havin' me a cup," Zach called back. Dot came out carrying a mug and handed it to him.

"Thank you," Zach said with a nod. He took a sip as Dot went back inside.

After half of his cigarette and a few sips of hot coffee, Zach nodded toward the Grayson farm.

"Well, sir, wrapping it up today, I reckon," he said.

"Reckon so," Russ agreed. "I'll be glad to have it done with. Tell you the truth, I ain't the only one. We'll all be glad to see it housed. Even more glad when it's sitting in the warehouse with a 'sold' tag on it."

"Well, that'll be soon enough I guess," Zach said.

"Soon enough. Hope so anyway. Soon enough." Russ said.

Zach nodded and finished his coffee, then walked to the door. He knocked and handed his mug to Dot.

"Thank you for the coffee," he said.

"Anytime, Zach. You keep him off the bottom rail today, hear?" she requested.

Zach smiled. "I'll do what I can."


By the time they got to the Grayson farm, almost all the other farmers were there. David was already gone to the church for the day, but Tim was there and excited. Colby had agreed to let him work in the barn today, running the top rail. At the top, he wouldn't have to hand any of the sticks to men above and could concentrate on just hanging the sticks off of the rails.

"Just don't be in no big hurry at all," Big Tom advised him. "Top rail, you'll have plenty of time between sticks. Just get it set down and move on forward, ready for the next one."

"And hold on all you can when you're moving," James added. "Your legs ain't as long as the rest of ours, so move slow and careful-like. Won't nobody be waiting on you, so no hurry. And hold on to the rail above you while you're walking. Hold on, ain't no reason not to."

The so-called top rail in the Grayson barn wasn't the actual top rail. The barn was so large that the true top rail was two courses higher than had ever been needed since Denton built the barn.

"And you won't be up there all day either." Colby said. "We'll swap out jobs, just like yesterday. We'll put you back on the wagon after an hour or so."

"That's fine, Colby. I'll be fine either way. It won't even take us all day anyway," Tim said.

"No, it won't. I'm thinking you'll be out hunting by two o'clock."

Zach shook his head. "Doubt that. I don't 'spect anyone gonna be doing much of anything this afternoon," he said.

"Radio said we could get some rain this evening," Colby said.

"Oh, it's coming sure enough."

Russ put in a chaw. "It going to hold off long enough for us to finish?"

"I 'spect so," said Zach.

Since he was the oldest, Elijah started out driving the wagon. Colby was on the bottom rail with Zach above him on the second, and Tim was above them. While they waited for the first wagon load to arrive from the field, Zach showed Tim some tips about how to stand and move.

The first load arrived with Big Tom on the wagon. He grabbed the first stick and handed it up to Colby, who handed it up to Zach, who handed it on up to Timothy.

Tim confidently set it down so the tobacco stick rested on the two parallel rails. He moved forward as Zach was settling his own stick and was easily ready before the next round started up. Keeping his balance with his legs spread, one to each rail was a bit of a problem, but soon found an equilibrium and was able to keep moving forward. As soon as the first load was off the wagon, Tim looked down between his knees at Colby and grinned.

"It's not that hard, really. Half of it is just keeping from falling," he said.

Colby smiled up at him. "Yessir, that's about all there is to it. A couple more loads and we'll swap out."

"Shoot, Colby, I could stay up here 'til we're finished," Tim claimed.

"I know you could, Tim-bug, but let's just go on and swap out like we been doing."

By noon, they were done. On the last wagon load, Tim ran bottom rail. He handed the last stick up to Russ and jumped out of the rails into the wagon. He wiped the tobacco dust and crumbs from the sweat on his neck and chest.

Zach, who was driving the wagon, grinned at Tim.

"You're a tobacco-hanging man now, Tim," he said.

Tim jumped out onto the barn's dirt floor. "I guess so. Not too bad. Not too bad at all. Kinda gets to itching with the shake coming down and all when a fella's on bottom rail. Don't think I'd want to run bottom all day."

"Not too many would care to. We still got a lot of tobacco to house 'fore we're done. Ain't no use at all wearing yourself out."

After handing the last stick up, Russ climbed slowly and carefully down.

"Not getting done any too soon," he said, looking out through the barn door. "Already clouding up."

"Yes, sir, it's coming in, coming in for certain." said Zach. "You fellas need some help getting Leviticus unhooked?" he asked. Colby shook his head.

"Thanks anyways, but Tim-bug will have it done in no time. Russ, where we going next? E. E.'s?"

"I 'spect so," Russ answered said as the remaining men trickled into the barn.

"Well, that's it, then," James Caudill said. "I'm heading for home before this rain kicks up too awful bad."

## CHAPTER 7

Later that afternoon, Baby-Anne lay in her bed, her left arm draped over her eyes. For the first time in her memory, the music was unbearable. It made her heart race and it hurt.

While David's music had been harsh and unhappy for weeks and Mama's wasn't much different than it ever was, it was Colby's music that frightened her most, and overwhelmed her. It had been building all summer, getting bigger and louder, and she hadn't known why. And it hadn't scared her, at all, it hadn't scared her.

Until today.

Today.

All summer, she couldn't tell where the music was taking Colby. She had felt like an expectant spectator of a great event, one member of an audience, never wondering how or if it might affect her. But now she knew it would not only affect her, but also everything she loved, everything she was, and everything that she knew.

Whatever was to happen was happening now, now, today.

She could hear Colby in the front room, listening to the radio. Timothy was with him. As the first drops of rain hit the tin roof of their house, she heard a crescendo. She knew that it wasn't the final peak, the final surge, and that scared her most of all.

She pulled her feather pillow over her face and cried silently.

Colby sat in the rocking chair and Tim was on the couch. They were listening to a comedy show but neither could get too interested in it.

The sky, which had been gray for an hour, went suddenly as dark as twilight, as midnight. The steady rain became a downpour almost instantly, and a flash of lightning, paired with booming thunder, quickly followed. The electricity went out. The room went dark and the radio was silenced.

"Whoa, that was a close one," Tim said and the room lit up four times in quick succession. The accompanying thunder of each strike was nearly simultaneous. Neither of them had ever heard thunder nearly that loud; Colby could feel vibrations in his skull from the clap.

The sky went black again, then another type of illumination took the lightning's place.

Colby's heart was hammering as he got out of the chair and walked to the front door. He opened it a crack and knew before looking what had happened. The front of the property was still dark, but the back was lit by an orange light. He knew, knew, knew before knowing, that Denton's Folly was on fire.

Burning, burning, on fire.

The four successive lightning strikes had all hit the barn. The far end of the barn was engulfed where the first two strikes had hit and, in the center, where the other two strikes had landed, flames were rising quickly, blistering and hungry, already leaping through the roof.

Colby started out the door but Tim grabbed him by his shirt collar.

"There might be more lightning!" Tim yelled. Colby ignored him, lunged forward and broke Tim's hold. He ran out as Mama and Baby-Anne entered the front room.

Colby ran down the coal slag path. He thought wildly that the heavy rain would put out the flames. As he neared the barn, he saw that the interior was utterly engulfed, the only colors orange flame and black smoke. Flames shot up as if from Hell engulfing the walls and scorching nearby trees. Then Colby heard Leviticus and Doris screeching in deathly agony and knew that it was over.

Over.

So quickly, so quickly. The heavy rain had just started ten or fifteen minutes ago and the lightning had hit one minute ago, and it was over. All of it. All of it.

Over.

He fell to his knees and clearly felt an electric shock of outrage, fear, and futility scramble across his back, neck and shoulders. Fists clenched in his lap, he knew that no sense could ever be made of this. There could be no reconciliation between the beliefs he had fostered in his short life so far and what had just occurred.

He had done everything right.

Everything.

The work. The worry. The sweat and the cramps.

Since Daddy died. Since the spring. The hours, the toil, the sleepless nights—and in just a few moments, on a Saturday afternoon in October, it was over. Over.

Just over.

He bowed his head and looked at his hands, the rain still pouring down, puddling in his hands, his clothes soaked through.

He thought he could hear some kind of music in the wind and tried to focus on it. This then, was this then the fleeting comfort of the misty realms his mother knew so well?

He could surrender to it...rest his mind there, rest, relax, forget... forever. The fire, the barn, the tobacco...it wouldn't matter anymore. None of it would matter.

Tim-Bug ran up behind him and knelt on one knee beside his brother. Colby looked over at his youngest brother, water pouring off his chin and brow.

"It ain't fair!" Colby yelled the ground. "It ain't daggone fair!"

Tim knew he couldn't feel what Colby was feeling, but knew that the word now lay with him.

"Fair don't enter into it now, Colby. And your getting killed by lightning ain't gonna help nobody!" Tim yelled.

Colby shook his head slowly. "It's...I just..." he stuttered. Tim grabbed Colby's shirt collar.

"It don't matter right now, Colby! It just don't matter. It's just an act of God, like Reverend Tannehill preached last Sunday. We can't do nothing about it."

"Like Noah," Colby said, looking at his brother, then back at the engulfed barn.

The smell, the smell of treated wood burning, of melting sheets of tin roofing, of burning tobacco, and horribly, of the cooking bodies of Doris and Leviticus.

"Yeah, I guess, whatever. It don't matter much right now!" Tim yelled. "We'll ask Reverend Tannehill about it tomorrow. But there just ain't no sense in getting struck by lightning or getting drowned out today. Let's go back in the house. Mama and Baby-Anne are probably worried," he said.

Colby raised his head and looked at the barn. Even through the rain, he could feel the immense heat of the fire. The rain was capturing the ashes and embers and slamming them back into the ground.

Colby looked at Tim.

"The Reverend," he said.

"Yeah, Reverend Tannehill. We'll talk to him tomorrow."

Colby rose to his feet and Tim rose with him. They turned to the house and saw Baby-Anne in the front doorway, Mama behind her, a hand on Annetta's shoulder. Tim walked that way and as he reached the door, he saw that Colby wasn't following.

"Let's go, Colby," he called.

Colby shook his head. "I can't wait until tomorrow. I can't. I got to know. I got to know today. I'm going to the church," he said. "I'll bring David back with me."

"At least wait 'til it quits raining," Tim said.

Colby looked to the west. Already the rain was easing and there was a sliver of blue sky on the western horizon. He shook his head wearily, blankly.

"It's already about given over. I gotta go. Stay here with Mama," he said and turned to go. He looked back to make sure Tim was doing as instructed but only Baby-Anne was there. She looked frightened and confused, afraid. He looked at her. It was very nearly like all the silent, shared mornings that they had shared before Vernon's death.

Just the two of them. Them alone.

But now Baby-Anne wasn't sharing with Colby a quiet moment, a daily conspiratorial moment. Now, it was something much, much more, more but not better, not sweet or pleasant.

As Cole looked at her, he knew, knew, that it was not something to be smiled at, or remembered with fondness.

What he saw, on her, in her face and in her posture was not something to be shared. It wasn't something that connected them, but rather separated them.

What he saw on the face of his sister, unmistakably, wasn't fear, wasn't pity or anger.

What Colburn Grayson saw on the face of his little sister was only sadness.

## CHAPTER 8

By the time Colby got to town, the sun was poking its way through the last of the storm clouds. He could still smell the smoke in his wet clothes.

At the crossroads, he looked over at E. E.'s store. There wasn't a chance that he would be able to pay off his account now. He saw Norvell's grocery and thought of food. He had two or three dollars in the roll top desk with no hope of any more money coming in. His heart began a frenzied gallop, much worse than what he was used to. His breath came only in gulps, as if there wasn't enough air.

He turned and vomited into the grass at the edge of the road. He felt sweat popping out on his scalp and neck. He vomited again, and again, until he dry heaved and the sweat dripped off of his chin and tears dripped off his nose.

Feeling no better, he collected himself, wiped the sweat from his face and the tears from his eyes and continued down the road to the church.

"There has to be a reason," he thought. "There has to be a reason, a plan. There has to be some kind of sense to it. I did everything right. Everything. I did everything right. Everybody, everybody said I did right. Everybody."

Repeating this over and over to himself, he trudged on, numb and drained. The words became a litany with no meaning, repeated, recited, serving only to keep more painful thoughts out of his head.

He reached the church and started toward the sanctuary but noticed that the door to the Reverend's living quarters was ajar. Hearing voices, he detoured by the magnolia tree, reached out his right hand and knocked on the door.

"Reverend?" he called. The door swung open at his touch.

David leapt up from the bed, struggling to pull up his pants. The Reverend, naked from his shirt down, stood up with one hand extended towards Colby.

Colby stared, trying to make sense of the scene before him. David buckled his belt and ran from the room. His shoulder brushed Colby as he fled out the door.

Colby turned and watched David flee. Silent and confused, he turned back to stare at Reverend Tannehill. The preacher held his right hand out towards Cole.

"It's love, Colby. It's all about love," the Reverend implored.

"But....but..." Colby stammered. "It's not, it's...this ain't..." He looked once more out the door and saw that David was far away, sprinting towards home.

This was beyond Colby, far beyond. More than anything he had yet faced—Vernon's death, the endless toil, the fire—this was beyond him. Completely and wholly beyond him.

This was a problem that hard work could not fix. For the first time in his life, here was a problem that hard work could not fix, could not even start to mend. There was no getting on top of this, no outworking it, no outlasting it. Stubbornness could not repair this.

Colby needed help. At last, he acknowledged it, he embraced it, and for the very first time, felt no shame. Something had happened here that was completely beyond his control, beyond his understanding, beyond his teaching and abilities.

His head swam and again he thought he could hear some kind of weird music, some kind of song, whispering at the edge of silence. It was calming, soothing. There was relief in that song: peace, comfort. He wanted to surrender, to both swallow it and to be engulfed by it. No more worry, no more planning, no more thought. Peace, peace and comfort lay within...but...but...

David.

David needed help.

This single thought called Colby back from the brink, called him back from the wonderful, painless freedom of the song that whispered, glistening and ideal, in his mind.

David needed help.

David needed help.

He looked into the Reverend's eyes, started to speak, then shook his head. He turned and fled out the door, in pursuit of his brother. He knew he would never catch up; David was fast, faster even than Tim-bug. Running out of the church lot and peering down the road, he could barely see David, far, far ahead, running in the center of the road.

Colby stopped, unsure that he wanted to catch up to David. What he would say? What could he say? He stood in the middle of the road, staring at his feet. This was too much. Way, way too much. No thoughts, no solutions, no words of his father came to him and he was astray, blank; empty and lost.

*Russ.*

*I got to talk to Russ.*

David needed help and Colby had no idea how to help him. Colby couldn't even help himself. He once again felt the repulsive electric thrill across his chest and neck, and knew that if there was anything in his stomach, he would vomit again.

>*I got to talk to Russ, tonight, now.*
>*Russ will know what to do.*
>He had to.

## CHAPTER 9

Russ Traylor had witnessed the lightning and heard the thunder claps and wondered at first if the lightning had hit his property. He went to the back porch and looked out. The rain was still coming down, and at first he couldn't tell where the lightning had struck, or if it had struck at all.

From the edge of porch, he looked around the western edge of the house. He saw nothing and went to the other end. When he poked his head around, he saw the smoke. At first he wondered how there could be so much smoke in the middle of this downpour, but then he knew what had occurred. Sickened, he knew.

The Grayson barn was on fire. Denton's huge barn was on fire, burning, engulfed, doomed, as was all of Cole's tobacco.

Dot came outside. "Russell, is everything alright? That lightning was close," she said. Russ looked at her blankly.

"Cole," he finally said desperately. "The barn...Cole...tobacco on fire," He grabbed her arm. "It's on fire!" he cried. He stepped off the porch and started toward the Grayson farm.

"Russell! Russell! Come in out of that storm, Russell Traylor!" Dot yelled. He looked back at her, then toward the Graysons'.

"Right now, Russell! What's happened?"

Russ turned back in defeat and walked up the porch steps, past Dot and into the kitchen.

He ran his hand through his soaking wet hair. "The tobacco. Cole's tobacco. Gone. It's gone. It's on fire. Gone. Burned up, gone." he said. His eyes roamed the room, settling on a dish towel beside the sink. He picked it up and mopped the rain from his head and face, then turned back to his concerned wife.

"It's gone. Just gone. All of it. Burned up. Gone, all of it. Gone. Just, just gone."

"What!? What!? No, Russell, no!" Dot burst out, tears starting in her eyes. "It can't be. It just can't!"

Russ set the towel down on the counter and rested his hands on either side of the sink. He stared down miserably, shaking his head, unfocussed, confused.

217

"No, no, no. It can't, it can't, it just can't…end like this," he said. Dot heard his voice crack. It scared her. She had never seen him this upset, this close to losing control of himself. Even when their son died, Russ had stayed strong and in control of his emotions. He had, Dot knew, been maintaining his strength for her, for her and their other son, but this, this was different—this was so very different.

Now there was nobody to be strong for, his family didn't need strength, didn't need an example. He could feel what he felt, think what he thought, and it nearly destroyed him.

And for the first time in their long marriage, Dot Traylor did not know what her husband needed. She put an arm around his old, broad, strong back, the back that had worked so unceasingly; the back that had pained him for twenty years and made him moan when he rolled over in their bed in the middle of the night; the back that she knew could keep the weight of the world off of her and the boys; the back that she had grasped in the midst of passion; the back that now felt defeated and small. She put her head on his shoulder.

"Pray with me, Russ. There's nothing left to do but to pray for them. Pray with me," she said.

Russ stayed immobile for a moment, then shook his head slowly. He looked into the blue, blue eyes of this woman, this upright and capable woman, this strong, sure woman, this woman to whom he had pledged himself, over thirty years ago; sworn himself, in front of his family, her family, and in front of God.

And he had meant it.

"I won't," he declared. He straightened up a bit and looked her in the eyes. "No, ma'am, I won't."

"It's all there is, Russell. We've all done everything else there is to do. Praying is what there is left. Nothing else is left."

"I will not," Russ repeated vehemently. "I will not pray to no God that would do that to Cole. I won't. I won't do it."

"Maybe God didn't do it," said a quiet voice from the porch. The Traylors turned around to see Zach at the screen door.

"Zach, come in, come in," Dot said, waving to him. Russell stood up straight, running a hand again through his thinning gray hair.

Zach pulled the screen door open and entered, shaking his head. "I just can't hardly believe it," he said. "I just can't hardly believe this at all."

"What'd you mean, maybe God didn't do it?" Russ asked. "If God didn't do it, who did?"

"Maybe I ain't sure what I mean, Russ. Can I sit down?" Zach replied, motioning toward the table and chairs.

"Of course. I'll put some coffee on," Dot said. Zach sat and Russ joined him.

Zach began, "I never did no whole bunch of school. But my mama, and some other ladies, they taught me how to read. I could always read just fine. The Bible there," he said, pointing towards Dot's Bible on the pie safe, "I've read that plum through two different times. Cover to cover. First time when I was fifteen"

"And?" Russ asked.

"And, I reckon I don't know. What I always wanted to figure out is if God's running things day to day or if he just made us and then turned us loose.

"Right here and now though, I don't 'spect it matters too awful much. Don't matter much at all.

"The best parts of the book just says to love one another, help one another and Russ, listen to me now Russ, that's just what we done. That's just what we all done. That's just exactly what we all done."

"For what? For what exactly?" Russ asked. "How does this work out for anybody?"

Zach shook his head. "I don't know, Russ, I just don't," he said again. "I've pondered for years, my whole life I guess, as to why there's suffering and hard times. If God's running things day to day, why don't he just fix it? If he ain't running things day to day, then what does anything matter. Why not just do whatever we want?" He shook his head and took a sip of coffee. "I can't really make sense of none of it, I just can't figure it."

Russ looked at Zach, looked at him with new eyes, and encouraged him to finish,

"The only answer I've ever come up with, and there ain't no doubt that it ain't all that great of an answer, is that suffering, bad times, pain, evil—it just got to be. It just got to be Russ. "

Zach looked hard at Russ, and Russ looked back. Did it matter? Did any of this matter? Zach stared at Russ, and continued.

"For reasons we won't never be able to understand, pain and hard times just got to be." Zack said. He looked at Dot, then back at Russ. "Maybe God's just doing like the rest of us do, just doing what he has to. Maybe it pains him more than me and you could ever understand., doing what he got to do. Maybe he just doing what got to be done." He shook his head again. "I don't know, Russ, I wish I did. Only thing I know for certain is that I don't want God's job."

Russ stared at the table before him. "Still don't make sense, it just don't." he said.

"Maybe it ain't supposed to," Zach said. "I don't know, Russ, maybe it ain't supposed to make sense. For right now, though," he said, looking out the window, "the rain's 'bout given over. Maybe we got to do only what we can do, like we always do, what we done ever since I came here. Go and help however we can. Maybe, maybe that might be all that God wants of us. I truly don't know. Maybe it ain't our job to make sense of it. It probably ain't our job, but that don't matter neither. Why don't we walk on over there and do what we can?"

## Chapter 10

The sun was setting on the far side of U.S. 60 as Colby turned into the Grayson driveway. He looked back towards the barn, where black, oily smoke was still lazily rising. He could hear the remains of the structure popping and crackling.

Leviticus and Doris. He'd have to bury their big, charred bodies.

No. No. There would be nothing to bury, except maybe some bones. Leviticus and Doris were gone, gone like the tobacco. Dead.

*Gone.*

He continued towards the house, hoping to find David there. He wanted to see him, to reassure him—to do, to do, something…

*What had David done? What had happened?*

As he neared the house, he saw Russ and Zach walking up the slag path. Colby looked at his mama and noticed that she was looking back at him. At him, her dark, brown eyes sharp, sharp and without doubt, certain…directly into his eyes, for the first time since Daddy died, directly into his eyes.

She was not singing. She was calm, unwavering; focused and solid; sure. Colby was confused, but also reassured. She was more focused than he had seen her in years—maybe ever.

"David's here," she said calmly as Colby neared. She looked directly into his eyes, focused and in no doubt. "I've talked to him, Colby. I've talked to him."

"Mama?" he asked.

"Yes, Colby. Yes. I've talked to him," she repeated as Russ and Zach stopped under the umbrella of the walnut tree.

"Cole," Russ said, holding his right hand up, "I don't hardly know what to say. I just…it ain't right. No sense. It just don't make no sense. None of it, not one thing about it. It just, it just don't make no sense."

Colby understood that he was speaking of the barn and the tobacco, but he looked back at his mama.

"Is he alright?" he asked her.

Mama nodded. "He is, or he will be, Colby. He will be," she answered.

"Mama? He told you? I ain't certain here…I don't know—"

"I am, Colburn Grayson," she interrupted. "I am certain." She looked back at the remains of the barn, at the fields, the house, as if seeing them for the first time. "I am certain. I am certain, Colburn."

"What?" Russ asked, looking at Anne. "What? Cole, what?"

"Mama, I need Russ's help," he said, and Anne Grayson nodded.

"Yes," she said. "Nothing wrong with that, Colby. I'll put some coffee on. You talk, then you come on in the house." To Russ she said, "You'll help, Russ. You'll help us. We need your help. You're a good man, and you'll help us."

She started back to the house, but turned back as she reached the porch.

"It can't be tolerated. It can't be borne, Colby. It can't," she said, then went in.

Colby watched her enter, then turned to Russ. He said nothing, gazing steadily at the tall man.

"Cole, it ain't right. It just ain't right," Russ said.

Colby could only nod in reply.

"Cole, I got some money saved up," Russ offered. "I know it ain't your way, but I could help here, I could help and you could pay me back later on. It ain't nothing but money, just paper really and…"

"I need your help, Russ," Colby said.

"I know, I know and I'm willing to," Russ began but Colby raised his right hand and shook his head.

"Not that Russ. Not that. The Reverend…David's been helping him at the Church. He's been acting funny for a couple of months, David I mean, since right after he started and today, today…"

Russ looked at Colby, over at Zach, then back to Colby. He felt cold, remote; grim and hard.

*At the top of all this, all of this, all this, today, of all days…this.*

*This.*

He knew, just knew before Colby continued, what was being brought to light.

Before his oldest son had died, the boy had helped the Reverend at the Church and Russ had had suspicions. He had thought something was wrong, amiss, not horribly wrong, but he had done nothing.

*Nothing.*

His son had gotten ill after six weeks of helping at the Church and Russ' suspicions had slept, stowed away behind the sorrow, behind the necessity of being strong for Dot, strong for his other son, strong for everybody, because that's what he was, behind his unwillingness to consider, to consider, that even more could be amiss, it had slept.

It had slept, slept, slept and then died, unneeded, unwelcome, too painful, too much, too much to deal with on top of their loss.

Russ stared down at Colby, and Zach looked away, his right hand covering his eyes.

"Cole, tell me." Russ said. Colby looked at Zach, then shook his head.

"Tell me now, Cole." Russ said.

"I went up to the Church. I wanted to talk to the Reverend. I wanted to know why, why God would do that...if there was a plan...plan or maybe punishment, or something. I walked in and David was putting his pants on, and the Reverend too. Both of them, Russ. Both of them was puttin' on their pants. Bad...it was bad. He ought not to have been doing that," he said, not sure if he meant the Reverend or David, or both.

Russ, cool, collected, staid Russ, felt his heartbeat quicken. His heart hammered. He felt cold, cold.

"I believe you, Cole," he said, and his head was clear. He had no confusion, no doubts, and it was to him a sick, twisted relief.

He now had a direction, a place to bestow his outrage. He took two steps toward Cole and put a hand onto his shoulder.

"We'll take care of this, Cole. All of us. We'll take care of it. We'll fix it. We're going to go see the Reverend here in a little bit." He turned to Zach. "Zach, I want you to go and tell Big Tom and Elijah and Lawrence too. We're all going to meet at Norvell's grocery in a half hour. You too, Cole. Be there in a half hour."

Colby nodded, indifferent, pathetically grateful that someone, finally someone, was telling him what to do. He nodded at Russ, than again at Zach.

"Alright, then. And Cole?" Russ added. Colby turned around and looked at him.

"Bring that rifle of yours."

Colby nodded again, glad again that finally someone was telling him what to do. He walked into the house.

When he opened the door, Colby saw that Mama was alone in the front room, in the Grayson rocking chair. He was relieved. He didn't want to have to talk to David just yet. He didn't know what he would say.

"Mama, you know? You talked to David?" he asked his mother.

"I do, Colby," she answered. "He told me. He don't know what's happened exactly but he's scared, scared. He thought he was helping...the Reverend told him lies...lies, and he thought he was helping, but now he's just scared, Colby—scared most of all what you'll think."

Colby strode quickly to the rocking chair and put his hand on his mama's shoulder.

"Tell him I ain't mad, Mama. I ain't mad. Not even a little bit. Tell him, please tell him."

"I will, Colby. I'll tell him. He'll get past it. We'll all get past it. It's what we do. It's all there is left to do." Anne stood up and the rocking chair kept rocking. She put her hand on Colby's neck and looked into his eyes.

"Colby, my Colby, you've done so much. How proud Vernon would be," she said softly and her eyes glistened. "Hear what I'm saying, Colby. Hear me now. He would be so proud, Vernon would be so very proud of you, so proud, though he would never have said it to you. So proud."

"I tried, Mama. I really tried. I promise you I done my best." Colby felt unwanted tears starting in his eyes.

"Of course you did Colby. I know you did and I should have done more. I should have done more Colby, more. More.

"I know you done your best, Colby, but now more is asked of you. More is asked. Listen to me. Listen to me now. You're strong like Vernon was, Colby. Strong. Strong and smart. Not smart in the same way as David is maybe, but smart like Lily, or maybe like Timothy. Smart like all of them but rolled into one. But times come," she went on, "when smart don't matter. When strong don't matter. When all that really matters is doing what's got to be done. Necessary, needed, what's got to be done.

"That was all I could ever do, the only thing I could do, but I did it, Colby. I did it. More is asked of you now. Like it was of me, more is asked. Demanded, Colby. Demanded." She glanced at the front door. "What did Russ say?"

"He said to meet him at Norvell's in a half hour."

Anne nodded in approval. "Yes. Yes, Russ is a good man. And you know that you must go. You must go and meet him, him and the others." Tears spilled again from her eyes. "It must be, Colby. It simply must be. The right or the wrong just don't matter now. What's happened, this man, the Reverend, it can't be abided, his actions can't be abided. It ain't fair that it falls on you, son, my son, but we all just do what must be done. What just must be done. Your daddy did it and I did it, and now you will do it, my son, my strong, strong son. This can't be borne. It won't be borne," she finished.

Colby leaned forward and kissed her on the forehead.

"I know, Mama. I know," he said.

Anne Grayson walked to the gun rack, reached up and took down the twenty-two. She handed it to Colby.

"I heard Timothy say that it's shooting a little to the left," she said.

## Chapter 11

Cole Grayson held the rifle in his left hand, its barrel over his shoulder. Out of habit, he thought he should check the ground for money. But no, the money that he suspected Zach had been leaving there all summer was no longer important.

None of that mattered. Everything that had consumed him for so long had become meaningless, inconsequential. He turned left and started walking up the road. He looked up at the stars. They were the same as they had ever been.

He was numb. He no longer had the energy for thought, for consideration. He was done, done thinking for a while. Mama seemed to know, Russ seemed to know, and that was enough for him.

Mama. His mama. He felt her here with him and it somehow made him complete. It wasn't just up to him. Finally, finally someone had given him a direction.

*It couldn't be borne.* That was what Mama said and Colby knew she was correct. Whatever else had happened—Daddy, the barn, the tobacco—this couldn't be borne.

Without warning, Colby found himself standing at home plate at Crosley Field. The fans in the stands were completely, unnaturally quiet. They were pensive and awed.

Colby stepped to the edge of the batter's box and stopped. He spit a stream of tobacco juice into the dirt next to home plate, knocked the dirt off his cleats with his bat and gazed out at the pitcher, who was faceless, tall; broad and unweary.

It was Game Seven. The Reds were behind, 6-4. There were men on second and third. Colby couldn't remember the scenario, if he had been injured or if he had been the star of the game so far. It was confused, refusing to clarify itself in his mind. The familiar chills did not scoot across his arms and the back of his neck.

The pitcher delivered a high fastball on his first pitch and Colby lined it over the left field fence for a home run. The crowd started to roar, but Colby just kept walking, unmoved, walking along U.S. 60 in the clear velvet inkiness of another Kentucky evening.

He turned his face up at the stars again and realized he was sweating. As he wiped off his face, he stopped, listening. He was very close to Norvell's and he heard some kind of music. Not radio music. Not someone playing, but some kind of music.

Some kind of music.

He could keep plodding on to Norvell's and then on, but why? He didn't know why he was going, or even what he was doing.

The music was nice, soothing.

He thought briefly of Mama and something, he didn't know what— he saw Big Tom approaching him from Norvell's.

"Cole," he said. "Cole….I maybe should have said. I knew…when I was young, after my Dad died…He, he…I maybe knew…"

Cole saw that Big Tom had his own rifle. "Tom. Tom," he said. He looked up and saw Russ and Lawrence and Elijah and James Caudill. He nodded again.

"I 'spect we gotta go and see the Reverend," Cole said.

The men were silent, almost frozen, waiting, awed.

Finally, Big Tom spoke. "I 'spect so." he said.

Cole started down the road to the church, silently, blank.

The other men followed.

Cole Grayson stopped in the church gravel lot. He heard the men behind him stop. He had forgotten they were there at all. The rifle in his right hand felt greasy, greasy but ready, capable; capable and eager.

He glanced first at the Reverend's living quarters. No light or sound came from within.

He checked the Sanctuary. It was lit up and the men heard a lash, a strike and then a yelp. Cole headed straight toward the door on the left and turned the brass knob. Without pausing, he entered and walked three-quarters of the way down the aisle to the altar. The men followed, silent.

Reverend Lucas Tannehill knelt in front of the altar, naked. His back bled openly and wetly where he had been flogging himself with what looked like a harness strap, punishing his sinful flesh. Tears wet his face and he was covered in sweat.

As the stunned men watched, Tannehill looked to the heavens, swung the leather strap again over his head, and connected wetly with his back. Sweat and blood sprayed from the strike.

Cole walked steadily the rest of the way to the altar, shifting the rifle from his left hand to his right, trailed by the still silent group of men.

Tannehill looked first at Cole, then at the others. He was breathing heavily, gulping air, wheezing. He looked back at Cole.

"Love Colby. It was love. All of it, all of it, love, it was all about love." he said, weeping anew.

Cole Grayson stood unmoved, silent, and the men stood behind him.

"Colby! Colby, please hear me, I am a sinner. I know it! I know that I am, a sinner, as were all of Jesus the Nazarene's apostles. All of them, every one, to a man, imperfect, flawed. As we all are, Colby! Colburn Grayson! All of us imperfect sinners! All of us," Tannehill cried and hung his head, staring down at his bloody, sweaty hands.

Cole Grayson knew that the Reverend was right. Absolutely, completely right. The music stopped in his head and he knew then that only he heard it, flat, blank, the music empty and false, meaningless and even useless, and he would do now what he simply had to do, like Mama said.

Like Mama said.

The music just didn't matter. Nothing mattered except what must be done.

What must be done.

"All of us, Reverend. All of us sinners. I know," he said.

The Reverend then looked up at Colburn Grayson and he saw it. For the first time he saw it.

It wasn't David. It had never been David. The light had never been David.

It was Colby.

The light, the unbearable light, the perfect, pure light, the enormity, the perfection; Colby; it had always been Colby.

How could he possibly have missed it before? What veil had been before his imperfect eyes?

In this moment, this final moment, he felt only gratitude, absurdly, horribly, gratitude.

How grateful, how grateful he was to bear witness to the great Colburn Grayson, God's chosen, the Great Colburn Grayson in this, the moment of his ascension. The Light was about Colburn Grayson, of him, through him. How great was his God, that he would create for this world a perfect creature like Colburn Grayson.

What he had thought was David's great beauty and light was merely the reflection of the magnificent radiance of Colburn Grayson.

"Cole," Russ said. "You don't have to do this, Cole."

Cole nodded. "I know I don't," he said and the Reverend saw Colby's light dim, die, extinguish; he saw the radiance leak away and knew only then the magnitude of his horrible sin.

He, Lucas Tannehill, had stripped the God-given light from Colburn Grayson, had ruined it, befouled it, belittled it, and that, that was his greatest sin. By far, by far, his most unforgivable sin.

His utterly unforgivable sin.

"The Lord my God and his Son Jesus Christ have forgiven me, Colburn Grayson," he said.

"So have I, Reverend," Cole Grayson quietly replied and Tannehill knew, knew without consideration or thought, in that moment, that moment, that his time on this beautiful world was over, his life, his mission, his life, was over. But his life, his mission, his purpose: there was still so much to do. He must live. He must foster love, spread it, invest in it.

"If you do this deed, you will burn in Hell forever, Colburn Grayson," Tannehill said.

"I know," Cole said. He took two steps forward while extending the barrel of the rifle. He placed the tip on Tannehill's head, just above his forehead over his left ear and pulled the trigger. Tannehill slumped forward, face down, and Cole saw blood gouting from the wound and so knew the heart was still beating. He thought of the rabbit from so long ago, his first attempt at killing.

He worked the slide and racked another shell. He placed the barrel an inch to the left of the weeping wound and pulled the trigger again. The bullet entered with a slapping click and now neither wound bled. Cole racked the slide again but didn't chamber another shell. He stood immobile, wondering what they would do now.

Russ Traylor stared at him, mouth open and utterly lost. Elijah gaped at the body and dropped his hands to his sides. James Caudill covered his face with his left hand, gasping and choking. Big Tom wept openly.

"It shoulda been me," he sobbed. "I shoulda…no, Cole, no! It shoulda been me…not you…not you…"

Russ walked to the front pew and sat, his head in his hand, then turned to the young man with the rifle.

"Russ," Cole said, "I reckon we'd best call the law."

Russ stood quickly.

"No, Cole, no. No law. Not this night," he said, shaking his head. "Nossir, not this night."

Big Tom hurried to Cole's side. "No, Cole," he repeated Russ's words, wiping his face dry. "No. We done took care of things here. No law needed. No law. Not this night. Not tonight. This is us Cole, only us." He motioned to the others. "Come on y'all. We're gonna take care of this body here and Cole's going home." He looked at Cole. "I mean it now, you go on home. This here is the end of all this. There won't be no questions, we'll just say he up and left. You don't never got to think on it no more. Me and these fellas here are gonna make this body disappear. I know a sink hole, a sink hole no one else knows about. He's gone Cole, he's gone. It's all over, over and done with now. We're gonna take care of it from here. Russ, you go on and walk home with him. Russ, you hear?"

"I do, Tommy. I hear."

## Chapter 12

Russ and Cole stopped at the Grayson driveway. The crickets were still chirring, not recognizing that summer was over. Neither had spoken on the walk back. Cole hadn't needed to and Russ didn't know what to say.

They stood at the mailbox. Russ gazed upon the Grayson house, back at the smolders of the barn and then at Cole.

"None of it, Cole, none of it is right. Ain't none of it fair either," he said.

Cole shook his head. "Fair don't enter into it, Russ."

"'I would say that is so," Russ agreed. Cole nodded, once.

"I best be getting on in, Russ."

"I know, Cole. Me, too. I'm just going to cut across your back field there, if that's okay."

"That's fine."

Russ nodded at Cole and started walking. He stopped, his rifle held low. "Cole?" he called. Cole stopped and Russ cleared his throat. "Don't matter much maybe, but I want you to know something. What you done here this year, what you done…the tobacco, the farm, all the work…"

Cole waited, mute and indifferent.

"I believe it to be the single greatest deed I have ever witnessed, maybe ever even heard of," he said, then nodded one last time to Cole and then walked home.

All was quiet in the house and that was good. Cole checked the rifle to make sure there was no shell in the chamber and hung it back on the wall. He threw himself into the rocking chair, staring absently at the wall. The radio was off and that was fine. Silence was fine.

He didn't rock, he didn't move, just sat still and silent; grim and sure. He felt hollowed out and that was fine, too: empty, empty like the rifle's chamber, as if there was a hole in his chest. There was no music, no baseball, no hope, nothing left and all that was fine.

Empty, done.

He eyed the rifle on the gun rack and tried to remember if the barrel was longer than his arm. If he turned it around, would he still be able to reach the trigger? He gazed down at his hands, not really caring if it would reach or not. It just didn't matter. Nothing mattered.

He stayed like this for over an hour and would have remained thus all night except for a shuffling noise in the kitchen. Annetta was there, looking sleepy but aware. She walked to the rocking chair and, without asking, crawled into Colby's lap.

Colby, thinking that she needed comfort after the day's traumatic events, put his arms around her. He would comfort her, then send her back to bed. He rocked and shushed her, but in another moment, his head was on her shoulder. Her arms ended up around Colby. It wasn't Baby-Anne who received comfort but Colby.

She was on his lap, small, thin, wispy but strong, substantial, and she held him, cradled him, rocked with him and hushed him as he wept. Heaving, shaking, he wept.

The tears that poured from him were pure, shameless, without implication or meaning…shameless tears of quiet necessity.

For the first time since that awful day on the lumber pile, so seemingly long ago, so very long ago, Colburn Grayson wept, but this time he wept without dishonor, without feeling that he shouldn't weep.

In this moment, this moment, he knew, completely and entirely knew, for the first time, he knew, discovered, realized…

He had not been at all spending his strength over the summer, not spending, not using, but rather storing, saving, amassing it, storing it here, here in his tough little sister, in David, in Tim-Bug.

In Mama.

These people, these simple and perfect people were the repository of his strength. It was there, always there, simply in escrow, like a savings account, an inexhaustible account. He had seen and done more in six months than most would experience in a lifetime and not only was his family together, they had comfort and hope to offer to Colby.

The thought staggered him and he wept all the harder.

What he had given, what he had done, now Baby-Anne gave it all back, ten times over, a hundred times over and in that moment, that perfect, silent moment, Colby knew that he had done right.

It wasn't this land, this farm, that immense barn. None of that had really mattered. All of that had never been it.

Daddy had been wrong, misguided, wrong and that was all right. He had no blame to fling at his daddy. Daddy just hadn't known, maybe hadn't ever needed to know.

What mattered was his family, here, together. In that single, crystalline instant, he felt himself change, harden, consolidate. He felt like a mountain, a mountain of bull horn and harness leather, his arms made of seasoned oak, his mind as clear and sharp and shiny as the freshly sharpened business end of Marvin.

He had failed, yes, maybe he had failed with the tobacco crop but he had not failed in the attaining of his goal, but rather in the setting of his goal.

His family was together, here…together, one.

He had triumphed, above all considerations, all toil, all conditions or concepts.

His family was together, together and here, here for him.

Here for him.

Cole took a deep breath and wiped his eyes and nose on his sleeve. He looked at his sister, his eyes red and his face wet.

"You think you'll like living in Lexington?" he asked.

"Lexington don't matter, Colby. You know that now. Where don't matter, but yes, yes, I will like it. I'll have a bit of a garden and David will have books to read. Timothy will be good with the horses. He'll understand them and they'll understand him. Mama will sing when she needs to and we'll get along. We'll all get along just fine."

"And me?" Cole asked.

Annetta looked at him, wiped his face with the sleeve of her dress.

"Why, whatever you want, Colby. Anything. I don't know if it's a gift or not, but you have the power of will. You can make things be by wanting them to be," she said. Colby nodded. Annetta buried her face in his chest. She could hear his music, could hear it, feel it and it was pure, so pure, so clear, so beautiful and so very, very bright. She wanted to breathe it, drink it…so beautiful…so clear.

Colby nodded again.

"I know what I want," he said.

# CHAPTER 13

Colburn Grayson stood for the final time beneath the walnut tree in front of the Grayson house. He turned his head and spit a stream of tobacco juice onto the ground. The splatter landed next to a freshly fallen walnut. The walnut hull was green, green and strong, fleshy, substantial, ripe and full, guarding the life that lay within, the seed, the nut, the promise within.

He looked back at Denton's huge barn, the remains still in a blackened, messy heap, then saw his Uncle Jason carrying the last box out of the house. It was Friday, November 19th. Cole and his brothers had been housing tobacco at the other farms since the fire, doing their part as the others had done for them, helping. Everyone's tobacco was now hanging in barns, curing and waiting for the sales.

This was the second time in the past week that Jason had been here. The previous Saturday he had come with his truck and a borrowed trailer to haul most of the furniture that the Graysons were taking to Lexington. All that was left were the beds, the radio and some boxes of clothes and kitchen things.

Yesterday, Cole had met with Maurice White from the Bank of Morehead and signed papers giving the bank power-of-attorney to sell the property. White assured Cole that the bank would take what was owed and forward all "remaining monies" to the Grayson family at Alladon Farm in Lexington. Cole trusted that this was would take care of any debts he had accrued in his one season as a tobacco farmer. He had avoided using his account at Norvell's and the check from St. Louis for the fox pelt had more than covered the money he owed to E. E. Robinson. Cole had insisted that Tim-Bug take the difference, so Tim now had two dollars and ten cents in his pocket.

Cole turned to the two men next to him. One-Eyed Zach and Russ had come to see them off. Zach finished rolling a cigarette, lit it and said, "'Bout all set, it looks like."

"Yessir. That's just about the last of it," Cole replied and spoke to Russ. "I hope you get a friendly neighbor, Russ. Mr. White said the place might not sell until spring."

Russ nodded and spit into the grass. "I 'spect they'll be fine, Cole. I ain't worried none."

Cole looked again at the truck and trailer. Both were full, the loads tied down and secure. David, Tim-Bug and Baby-Anne were already jumping into the bed of the pick-up, where they would make the trip. Mama was climbing into the cab, scooting toward the middle and making room for Cole.
Jason came over and extended his hand to Russ. "Russ, it sure was good seeing you again," he said. "And Zach, thank y'all for your help loading things here. I appreciate it." He shook Zach's hand in turn.

"Why shoot, it's just only my pleasure there, Mr. Jason. Glad to help," Zach said.

Jason started toward the truck and Cole started to follow but took only half a step before stopping to look back at his friends.

"Russ, Zach, I know what y'all done. I know what y'all done, all summer and I know you didn't do it just so's I'd say thank you. But thank you," he said extending his right hand to Russ, who shook it, then to Zach, who did the same. He walked to the truck, climbed in beside Mama and closed the door. Jason started the engine, put it in gear and they started their trip to Lexington.

Cole would always remember that trip, the first time he had ever ridden in a truck and the first time he had ever been out of the county. He would remember his brothers' laughter as they stood in the bed of the truck and threw rocks at the passing road signs. He would remember Annetta smiling at her brothers, laughing and enjoying their competition.

He would remember seeing his right hand hanging loosely before him as his elbow rested on the open window sill and knowing, knowing, that his hand was rougher and stronger than his Uncle Jason's, rougher, broader, stronger, but also knowing that it wasn't important—it was just the way things were.

He would remember the breeze coming through the windows and Jason telling him about the farm, the people of Alladon, the horses, the work.

He would remember the sun, shining on their backs, lighting the way before them as they traveled west to Lexington.

He would remember seeing things as they traveled the road that he had never seen before, the lands, the barns, the houses.

But above all, he would remember, he would remember always until he grew into a man, a strong, tall, capable man and so into old age, he would remember...remember...

The whole trip to Lexington, that entire trip, that trip that was sad but was without bitterness, that whole sad but hopeful journey, above all, the whole way there...

His mama did not sing.

## The End

## About the Author

P. Shaun Neal is a lifelong resident of central Kentucky. He is a 1987 graduate of the University of Kentucky with a Bachelor of Arts Degree in English where he studied under authors Gurney Norman and Ed McClanahan. He also won the Dantzler Award for Fiction.

At age fifteen he began working in the construction industry and made a career in concrete construction; the majority of that time self-employed and building truck stops, State Highways, bridges and airport runways. The love of, and need to, write fiction stayed with him throughout his life, and he worked on and off on this first novel for over twenty years.

In 1991, he and his wife, Lisa, built a house on five acres in Jessamine County, Kentucky, where they still live with their sons, Stormy and Conley, along with two dogs, three cats, three horses.

In addition to writing, his other artistic endeavors include woodworking and drawing portraits. His drawings have been shown in numerous art galleries in and around central Kentucky.

*Mama's Song* is his first novel, and he is currently busy writing the sequel, tentatively entitled *The Man in the Wind*.

BOOKS BY BOTTOM DOG PRESS
HARMONY SERIES

*The Pears: Poems*, by Larry Smith, 66 pgs, $15
*Without a Plea*, by Jeff Gundy, 96 pgs, $16
*Taking a Walk in My Animal Hat*, by Charlene Fix, 90 pgs, $16
*Earnest Occupations*, by Richard Hague, 200 pgs, $18
*Pieces: A Composite Novel*, by Mary Ann McGuigan, 250 pgs, $18
*Crows in the Jukebox: Poems*, by Mike James, 106 pgs, $16
*Portrait of the Artist as a Bingo Worker: A Memoir*,
by Lori Jakiela, 216 pgs, $18
*The Thick of Thin: A Memoir*, by Larry Smith, 238 pgs, $18
*Cold Air Return: A Novel*, by Patrick Lawrence O'Keeffe, 390 pgs, $20
*Flesh and Stones: A Memoir*, by Jan Shoemaker, 176 pgs, $18
*Waiting to Begin: A Memoir*, by Patricia O'Donnell, 166 pgs, $18
*And Waking: Poems*, by Kevin Casey, 80 pgs, $16
*Both Shoes Off: Poems*, by Jeanne Bryner, 112 pgs, $16
*Abandoned Homeland: Poems*, by Jeff Gundy, 96 pgs, $16
*Stolen Child: A Novel*, by Suzanne Kelly, 338 pgs, $18
*The Canary: A Novel*, by Michael Loyd Gray, 196 pgs, $18
*On the Flyleaf: Poems*, by Herbert Woodward Martin, 106 pgs, $16
*The Harmonist at Nightfall: Poems of Indiana*, by Shari Wagner, 114 pgs, $16
*Painting Bridges: A Novel*, by Patricia Averbach, 234 pgs, $18
*Ariadne & Other Poems*, by Ingrid Swanberg, 120 pgs, $16
*The Search for the Reason Why: New and Selected Poems*, by Tom Kryss, 192 pgs, $16
*Kenneth Patchen: Rebel Poet in America*, by Larry Smith,
Revised 2nd Edition, 326 pgs, Cloth $28
*Selected Correspondence of Kenneth Patchen*,
Edited with introduction by Allen Frost, Paper $18/ Cloth $28
*Awash with Roses: Collected Love Poems of Kenneth Patchen*,
Eds. Laura Smith and Larry Smith with introduction by Larry Smith, 200 pgs, $16
*Breathing the West: Great Basin Poems*, by Liane Ellison Norman, 96 pgs, $16
*Maggot: A Novel*, by Robert Flanagan, 262 pgs, $18
*American Poet: A Novel*, by Jeff Vande Zande, 200 pgs, $18
*The Way-Back Room: Memoir of a Detroit Childhood*,
by Mary Minock, 216 pgs, $18


BOTTOM DOG PRESS, INC.

P.O. BOX 425 /HURON, OHIO 44839
HTTP://SMITHDOCS.NET